"I don't make promises,"

Sully said. He'd ceased believing in promises or much else when he was six. And he'd never uttered one. The thought of doing so now, to this woman, had panic licking up his spine.

"I'm not leaving until you promise you'll come back to me." Ellie's voice was resolute.

There had to be a way out of this mess. Instincts honed by a lifetime of training told him that things with his job were about to turn deadly. Everything he'd been waiting for was about to break, and he had to get her out of here. He had to get her to safety.

Ellie moved closer. Her palm glided up his back to stop at his shoulder. He squeezed his eyes tightly shut for a moment, as the familiar wanting, guilt and desperation warred within him. The waiting stretched between them. The words shouldn't have been so difficult, so terrifying to speak.

"I promise."

Dear Reader,

The kids are on their way back to school, and that means more time for this month's fabulous Intimate Moments novels. Leading the way is Beverly Barton, with *Lone Wolf's Lady,* sporting our WAY OUT WEST flash. This is a steamy story about Luke McClendon's desire to seduce Deanna Atchley and then abandon her, as he believes she abandoned him years ago. But you know what they say about best-laid plans....

You also won't want to miss Merline Lovelace's *If a Man Answers.* A handsome neighbor, a misdialed phone call...an unlikely path to romance, but you'll love going along for the ride. Then check out Linda Randall Wisdom's *A Stranger Is Watching,* before welcoming Elizabeth August to the line. *Girls' Night Out* is also one of our MEN IN BLUE titles, with an irresistible cop as the hero. Our WHOSE CHILD? flash adorns Terese Ramin's wonderful *Mary's Child.* Then finish up the month with Kylie Brant's *Undercover Lover,* about best friends becoming something more.

And when you've finished, mark your calendar for next month, when we'll be offering you six more examples of the most exciting romances around—only in Silhouette Intimate Moments.

Yours,

Leslie Wainger

Leslie J. Wainger
Executive Senior Editor

Please address questions and book requests to:
Silhouette Reader Service
U.S.: 3010 Walden Ave., P.O. Box 1325, Buffalo, NY 14269
Canadian: P.O. Box 609, Fort Erie, Ont. L2A 5X3

UNDERCOVER LOVER

KYLIE BRANT

Published by Silhouette Books

America's Publisher of Contemporary Romance

SILHOUETTE BOOKS

ISBN 0-373-07882-X

UNDERCOVER LOVER

Printed in U.S.A.

Books by Kylie Brant

Silhouette Intimate Moments

McLain's Law #528
Rancher's Choice #552
An Irresistible Man #622
Guarding Raine #693
Bringing Benjy Home #735
Friday's Child #862
Undercover Lover #882

*The Sullivan Brothers

KYLIE BRANT

married her high school sweetheart sixteen years ago, and they are raising their five children in Iowa. She spends her days teaching learning-disabled students, and many nights find her attending her sons' sporting events.

Always an avid reader, Kylie enjoys stories of love, mystery and suspense—and insists on happy endings! When her youngest children, a set of twins, turned four, she decided to try her hand at writing. Now most weekends and all summer she can be found at her computer, spinning her own tales of romance and happily ever afters.

Kylie invites readers to write to her at P.O. Box 231, Charles City, IA 50616.

For Brian, Vicki, Dick, Barb, Gary, Karen, John, Carla, Mike, Glennis, Paul and Aleta. Here's to many more years of laughter, craziness and memories. (Can't wait for our retirement home!)

Prologue

"**Y**ou screwed up big time, Bobby."

It wasn't the words that had the cold snake of dread twisting through Bobby Ames; it was the flat, emotionless voice delivering them. Sweat trickled down his narrow shoulder blades, and he rubbed a grimy hand over his stubbled chin, trying to still its trembling. His own rank odor drifted around them, a souvenir of the long minutes he'd spent hiding in the Dumpster. He'd congratulated himself for evading the man, but he hadn't crawled out of the stinking filth five minutes before he'd caught sight of his stalker again.

The cool air blasting through the Miami shopping mall was only partly to blame for Bobby's shivering. His eyes darted about frantically, thoughts of escape colliding with the dull certainty that to move was to die. The slim ceramic knife wasn't visible right now, but he knew it was there, slipped inside its casing in the man's boot. He was never without it, and his skill was legendary.

"I swear to God, Roarke, I din't rip ya off. I mean—" he tried for a laugh that came out a nervous titter "—do I look crazy to you?"

Those cold gray eyes turned on him then, and Bobby began to shake in earnest. "To me? No, you don't look crazy. You look like a dead man."

Fear clawed its way through Bobby's skinny body, icing his heart, sending freight trains through his pulse. "C'mon man, don't say that. I'm the best runner ya got."

"You've been using." Roarke drew a cigarette from the package in his shirt pocket and put it between his lips. Then he bent forward, and Bobby's breathing stopped until he saw the tip of the cigarette glow.

If Roarke had gone for his knife just then, his movements would have been little more than a blur. The cold bastard was capable of doin' him right here, he thought bitterly, with no more thought than he'd given to lighting his smoke. Roarke was capable of anything.

"No, I ain't. I swear I ain't."

The man's eyes were without mercy. "You're a liar. I knew that. But you're a thief, too. I can't let that go, Bobby. You understand. I've got a reputation."

Rivers of sweat streaked down his body, and it got harder to breathe. "Roarke, I swear to God it was just a taste. Really. And you can count on me from now on, I swear ya can. Man, I'm beggin' ya. Give me another chance."

The acrid smell of smoke swirled up around him, and the next words sounded his death knell.

"I don't give second chances."

Pride, if he'd ever had any, was long forgotten. "God, no, Roarke, don't. I'll work for free a month, how's that?"

The bright Florida sun poured through the overhead skylights, gilding the dark gold in Roarke's hair, clubbed back in a short ponytail. His hard, expressionless face never changed, just as it never changed after drinking a beer or slicing a man to pieces. Bobby had seen Roarke do both; he'd heard of him doing more. Much more. Rumors grew fast on the street, but there were few he didn't believe about this man. The thin, pale scar under his chin was supposedly a legacy from a dealer who'd crossed him years ago. The dealer, the story went, had died a particularly hideous death. Bobby had no way of knowing the truth of the story, but he did know that people who crossed Roarke disappeared. That was fact. Right now every deadly thing he'd ever heard was racing through his brain, and he knew he'd never been closer to death.

His nose seemed to run continuously these days, and he wiped it with the back of his hand. Resignation flowed through him, his fate certain. He raised his red-rimmed eyes to the man beside him, ready to make one last plea, knowing it was as useless as a prayer.

But those empty eyes weren't trained on him anymore; they were directed over Bobby's shoulder. Not being the focus of that ruthless gaze relieved the tight knot of nausea in his belly a fraction. And then the other man moved, and Bobby recoiled, face averted. The expectation of that narrow, deadly blade was so real he could feel the first slice, the burning agony soon to be followed by a blessed numbness. He was sobbing in earnest now, pleas and promises tumbling incoherently from his lips.

Moments ticked by before reality crept in. Bobby looked up, and then around. He was alone on the bench in the mall, still surrounded by crowds hurrying along. He was invisible in the way street people sometimes were, his bizarre behavior repelling, rather than attracting attention. It took a few more moments for his heart to remember to beat again, for his lungs to begin drawing air.

He didn't see Roarke, and the opportunity to escape beckoned. He looked from side to side wildly, unable to believe that the threat, so certain only moments ago, was gone. More likely it was a trick, one designed to get him out of the mall into a place where his death would go unnoticed a while longer.

But then his fearful gaze focused on that familiar form again, standing across the crowded mall. In morbid fascination he remained where he was, staring as the tall man spoke to a woman with long dark hair. As Bobby watched, Roarke put his arms around the woman, and she buried her face against his chest.

Shock held him frozen in place. Not that it was strange to see Roarke with a woman. He had plenty of women, plural, as many as he wanted. They'd always meant as little to him as a man's life, easy to pluck, easy to discard. But Bobby had never heard of one that was capable of stirring any real feeling in the bastard. A flicker of curiosity lit inside him as he watched Roarke pat the woman's narrow back.

Reality crept in, and the ice in his veins thawed a little. As odd as the scene was, he'd just been handed a reprieve, and he felt like a cat on its ninth life. Furtively he looked around and rose from the bench on legs still inclined to tremble. He sidled into the throngs of people, which parted automatically for his rank form. He swiped at his nose again as his pace quickened. He was getting a chance that most never had, and he was going to make good on it. A few minutes' hot-wiring a car, and he could be on his way out of Miami, away from Roarke, away from the knife that had so many lives dripping from its lethal blade.

He thought longingly of his one-room apartment. He didn't own much; he preferred to put his money up his nose, but thanks to the last delivery he'd made, he had a nice little stash there that would have lasted him another day or two. He could feel the beginnings of the craving poke its head out of the dark caverns of his soul.

With rare, clear thought he shook off the beginning of

the temptation as he scurried through the crowds. The nose candy that had begun to rule his life was like a god to him, but life itself was dearer. He needed to be sure that he was well away from Miami, from the state, before he stopped running. Even then he knew he'd never be able to stop looking over his shoulder. The look in Roarke's eyes, the moment his own death had seemed certain, would linger in his nightmares for the rest of his life.

Chapter 1

Six months later

Elizabeth fished around in her purse, fingers scrambling for her keys. Her job at the Miami Gallery of Art was satisfying and interesting, and filled her with a quiet sense of accomplishment. But she'd been anxious to get home that day. The design for a new piece had been dancing in her head all afternoon, and her hands itched with the need to sink into the damp clay.

Absently she pushed back her sheaf of heavy, dark hair, tucking one side behind her ear for a better view into the jumbled contents of her purse. Spying her keys, she snatched them up and fit one into the front door of the old apartment building. Inside she used another key to open her mailbox and extracted the contents.

She avoided the temperamental elevator and walked up the four flights of stairs. The walls of the stairwell were cracked, but they sported fresh paint and glowed from the day's scrubbing. The steps were well swept and free of debris. Mr. Abrahamson, the odd little landlord, was a demon about dirt. Unfortunately he wasn't as conscientious about needed repairs around the building.

She flipped through the three items she'd received that day, two bills and a letter from her mother. A pleased smile crossed her lips, and she hurried even faster up the next three flights. She forced herself to wait until she was inside her apartment to open the letter. It was a small pleasure to be savored, and anticipation made it sweeter.

She walked down the quiet hallway toward her small one-bedroom apartment and unlocked her door. Automatically she glanced at the answering machine. Its message light wasn't blinking, so she continued by it. Shrugging out of her blazer and stepping out of her pumps, she dropped cross-legged on the love seat to read her mom's three-page letter. It was chatty, full of news about the win at bingo Wednesday night, and the wonderful restaurant she'd visited with friends. Smiling tenderly, she imagined her mother writing it, sitting at the small table in her tidy kitchen, penning the words in her neat, careful hand.

A shadow loomed over her then, blocking her light. Her gaze flew up in alarm, her heart jolting straight to her throat. It took a moment for recognition to filter through the panic, and another for relief to follow.

"Sully! My God, you scared me to death!"

The splinters of late-afternoon sun turned the man's hair a brighter shade of gold, while leaving his face partly in shadow. For an instant she had the fanciful notion that he looked like an avenging archangel, a broad-shouldered rescuer of the downtrodden. And then he shifted into the light, and the image shattered. Although it sometimes seemed as though Sully had appointed himself her personal guardian angel, there was nothing saintly about his hard face. She hadn't realized until that instant just how much she'd missed seeing it.

She dropped the letter and bounced up to hug him, brushing a kiss against the faded scar beneath his chin. "Welcome back! How was your trip?"

"Okay."

He was stiff and still in her embrace, as always, his arms motionless at his sides. Not for the first time she was reminded of a wary animal that had been kicked once too often and now mistrusted human contact even as he needed a friendly hand. At least *she* thought he needed it, though he would be the last to admit it. He was a man who seemed to exist on the outskirts of society, always looking on but rarely joining in. She'd made it her mission long ago to coax him back inside.

She tilted her head back and surveyed him, her arms still linked around his waist. The hug was an affectionate gesture between friends, and one she'd repeated dozens of times. His skin was warm beneath her touch, his body heat radiating through his clothes and warming her in a curiously sensual transfer. Her fingers flexed involuntarily at the unexpected sensation, and she felt her cheeks flush. Hastily she dropped her arms and stepped back. That flash of awareness was unfamiliar, and somehow seemed a violation of their friendship.

He swept her with a considering gaze. "You look a little shorter. Did I scare a couple inches off you?"

Her hand went to her heart in a gesture of shock that was only partially feigned. "That sounded amazingly like a joke, Sullivan. Is it possible you picked up a sense of humor in the last few days?"

He shook his head, and held up the small packet of tools he'd taken from a drawer in her kitchen. "What I picked up was a new lock for your bathroom window. I used my key to let myself in so I could install it before you got home. Didn't look like Abrahamson was ever going to get to it.''

She nodded in mock seriousness. ''I owe you a big thank-you for that. I can't tell you how worried I've been that some enterprising bad guy will scale the outside wall, squeeze through that foot-wide window and force me to defend my virtue using only the deadly bathroom plunger.''

Not surprisingly there was no hint of humor on his face. If there was one thing Sully took seriously, it was protection. ''Your problem is you don't worry enough. I've told you before—''

She held up a hand to stem the certain lecture, having heard it often enough to recite it for him. She did so, in singsong. ''I know, I know. I shouldn't take my safety for granted. I have to be on guard at all times. I can't predict the lengths others might go to get what they want.'' A mischievous smile played across her face, and she peeked up through her lashes at him. ''How am I doing?''

It didn't draw an answering smile from his chiseled lips—smiles were much too hard to come by—but one corner of his mouth twitched. ''If you could just follow those instructions as well as you can repeat them, I'd die a happy man.''

She grinned and moved toward the compact kitchen. ''Well, I don't want to start measuring you for a toe tag just yet, but believe it or not, I am careful. I'm just not paranoid. And before we get into a discussion of that particular topic, why don't I get you something to drink. Are you thirsty?''

''What are you offering?''

''I don't suppose you took up tea drinking while you were gone?''

He snorted, and she heard rather than saw him relax into the recliner that was placed next to the love seat. It was a mismatched piece, but it suited his large frame much better than her other furniture. She'd passed it in the window of a used-furniture shop on her way to work one day, and she'd had a sudden vision of him in it. Without a second thought she'd gone inside the shop and bought it, bullying two of the men who'd worked there to deliver it for her after work.

She reentered the room and handed him a beer, one he'd stocked her refrigerator with himself. She waited as he twisted off the top and dropped it in her outstretched hand. Then he brought the bottle to his mouth and tipped it, his eyes sliding shut in appreciation for the icy taste. Her lips curved, and she lingered, watching him. She liked to see him like this, comfortable and relaxed, or as relaxed as he ever seemed to get. It was little enough to do for him, after all he'd done for her.

"When did you get home? This afternoon?"

He took another healthy swallow before answering. "Early this morning. Drove all night."

"And…" she prompted. Sometimes it was as if words were as precious as nuggets of gold to him, he used them so sparingly. He had always been more open with her than with anyone else, but that wasn't saying much. Whenever he went away for a few days, it was like he closed up again, and she had to start over, coaxing him to talk to her.

He reached up to tug on a strand of her long dark hair. *"And,"* he mocked, "it was a routine run to Dallas. Complete with endless summer road crews, detours and a blown tire outside of Georgia."

"Yikes." She grimaced and then laughed. "Sounds like every trucker's nightmare. Bet you're glad you're not assigned to drive the long runs for the company very often."

"Yeah." He released her hair, and his expression blanked again. "Real glad." He changed the subject, watching her through hooded lids. "So. What have you been up to lately?"

"I finished that piece I was working on when you left. Do you want to see it?"

"Of course."

She fetched it from her bedroom and handed it to him. The seconds he spent studying the intricately worked pottery seemed to stretch interminably. She shifted her weight from one foot to the other, feeling like a schoolgirl waiting while her teacher read her English assignment. Finally his pale gray gaze lifted to hers.

"It's good, Ellie. *You're* good."

His simple, sincere words filled her with a quick burst of pleasure, the use of his name for her warming her as much as his praise. He was the only one who called her "Ellie," the name growing out of a joke when they'd first met. "I'm glad you like it. It's yours."

His face went still. "You don't have to do that."

"I want to. C'mon, Sullivan, what's the matter? Afraid it won't go with the rest of that bachelor decor of yours?" she teased, crossing to the love seat and sitting down.

"You shouldn't be giving these pieces away. They're worth money. I keep telling you, these would sell."

She leaned back on the love seat comfortably. They'd had this discussion before and knowing Sully, would again. He believed in the dripping water-on-a-stone methodology; for a man of few words, it was amazing how often he repeated some of them. She valued his opinion for what it was, an expression of faith of one friend in another. And they were friends, had been for years. She knew without asking that he had few others.

"I was thinking of you when I threw it," she replied honestly, referring to the term used for shaping the wet clay. "I made it for you."

His eyes slowly left the piece in his hands and lifted to hers. She held his gaze, feeling a flush crawl up her cheeks. She wondered if anyone besides the artist would see the similarity in the piece of pottery and the man before her. She'd carried an image of him in her mind for weeks, so as to best design something that reflected him. Narrow at the bottom, the piece gradually broadened to the top in sleek, masculine lines. It embodied strength rather than beauty, solidity and endurance. It had seemed strangely intimate while she'd worked on it, as if she'd invaded his very personal boundaries with the constant thought of him.

"I'm honored. Thank you."

Her smile bloomed in response to his gruff words. He refused to listen to her gratitude, so she'd thanked him with the only talent she had, and the knowledge lay unspoken between them. She didn't know what she would have done without him six months ago when the world had tilted on its axis, and thrown her life a-kilter.

"What's wrong?"

His eyes were sharp, she thought ruefully, at least when it came to her. Her voice was easy when she answered. "I was just thinking of my long road to freedom."

"Regretting that you didn't try to get Carter back?" The casual tone, the expressionless face, couldn't mask the sharpness in his gaze as he waited for her answer.

She shook her head, smiling slightly. "Not ever. There's something about walking into his office and finding him with his pants unzipped and his pretty associate's head in his lap that tends to void the unto-death-do-us-part stuff."

He studied her carefully, but she knew there would be no trace of shadows in her eyes. If there were, he'd have seen them. She'd never learned to mask her emotions well, and her efforts would be pitiful when confronted with Sully's piercing gray regard. He had a way of stripping away pretenses to discern the true feelings beneath. Although it was Carter who worked as a county prosecutor, she'd often thought Sully would have made a formidable one himself. Faced with that stoic presence, criminals would be likely to blubber out their crimes.

"I don't know what I would have done if you hadn't suggested this apartment."

He shrugged. "It was next to mine, it was empty and cheap. No big deal."

"No big deal," she echoed softly. But it had been. For a woman who had gone right from her mother's tiny house to a college dorm room, then to being the wife of a man like Carter Robinson, it had been a very big deal. She'd had nowhere to go when she'd left her husband. Even now the memory of that helplessness, that utter sense of despair, was enough to make her chest go tight. She'd had no money, because Carter had controlled that. She had no friends, because they had been carefully selected by her husband, as well.

All except Sully. Ever since they'd met on the college campus, she and Sully had formed a bond, one that she'd refused to break even when she'd fallen in love with Carter and he'd demanded it. The two men had despised each other from the first, and her efforts to bring them together had failed miserably. She'd learned that it was better to see Sully by herself, occasionally meeting him for coffee or lunch. Refusing to drop her friend had been the only thing she'd ever denied Carter, and each time she'd seen Sully her husband had sulked like a child for days.

Not that she and Sully had always stayed in close contact. Months would go by without a word from him, and then he'd appear on her doorstep again. She'd tried to phone occasionally, but as he'd told her, he spent little time at home. His appearance at the shopping mall had seemed like one more oddity in that curiously fragmented day. She'd left Carter's office blindly, not even realizing where she was going. Her world had shattered, and she'd had no idea how to go about repairing it.

Her chin rose. She'd never be that helpless again. The years of being Carter Robinson's wife, with no life of her own, had slowly sapped her of her confidence. She'd grown to doubt every decision she'd made on her own, to second-guess every idea.

She'd accept part of the blame for allowing her self-confidence to erode, minuscule increments at a time. But she'd never forgive Carter for using her trust to deceive her in every way a man could. There were few absolutes in this world, but she thought honesty should be one of them. How peculiar that Carter, with his bright smile and disarming manner, had turned out to be so untrustworthy. Yet Sully, who was more guarded than anyone she'd ever known, more full of secrets, should be so dependable.

She slid a look at the man frowning at her from the recliner. He'd babied her, cosseted her, bullied her. It was he who had brought her to his building, he who had arranged for her to rent the small apartment next to his. He'd loaned her the money, taken care of the paperwork and even called her attention to the gallery's Help Wanted ad in the newspaper. Two and a half years toward a degree in art history hadn't been much in the way of marketable skills, but the job, if not high paying, was at least in her field. She was supporting herself, without taking a thing from Carter. She hadn't wanted anything from their house except some clothes, her potter's wheel and her kiln.

As if he had read her mind, an uncanny habit of his, he said soberly, "The divorce is going to be final soon."

She nodded, her eyes steady on his. She knew he worried that she was still hurt by Carter's actions, maybe even still had feelings for him, but he was wrong, as she'd told him many times before. The sense of betrayal hadn't faded, however, and the final scene with her husband still rankled. Those two things had been enough to kill any lingering love she'd felt for him.

She'd been a naive nineteen-year-old when she'd met Carter at the University of Miami. She'd been charmed by him immediately, and a little awed—the tall, good-looking president of the law review actually paying attention to her, Elizabeth Bennett, a shy little mouse on a needs scholarship. He'd seemed like a god to her then, she remembered uncomfortably, as if the heavens had showered all their gifts and most had landed at this man's feet. They'd dated for a year and a half, continuing after he'd graduated law school and gone on to land a job with the Miami prosecutor's office.

It hadn't taken much convincing for him to coax her to drop out of college and marry him. She'd been young, in love for the first time, and their life together had seemed tinged with gold. She could always go back to school later, he'd assured her, to finish her degree. But in the eight years they'd been married, "later" had never come. There had been the fancy house to buy, to decorate and then to keep running smoothly. There were his associates to entertain, his clubs to join, luncheons to host. Despite her pleas, there had not been children, either, a fact she was now grateful for. It had taken all the strength she'd had to leave when there was only herself to consider. She didn't know where she would have found the courage if there had been a child to fight over.

She liked her life now, though by Carter's standards it would seem meager. Not having things had never bothered her, but she supposed it would have troubled her more if she'd had to ask a child to exchange their opulent life for her current one.

"With the divorce final—" Sully raised the bottle again, his voice mild "—you'll get your settlement."

His words nettled her. "I never wanted that money, and you know it. You browbeat me into agreeing to it."

"He owes you."

"I won't spend it."

"You could use some of the money to get yourself a decent place to live."

She cocked her head. She'd learned to read between the lines with Sully, because the lines were so infrequent. Did he want her to find a different place, or was he afraid that she would? She couldn't tell. Although they'd been friends for over ten years, she was very aware that in some ways she didn't know him at all. "This is a decent place."

"You'll be able to afford a bigger apartment, in a better part of town."

"I don't want to leave you." The words didn't come out exactly as she'd planned. Their gazes met, and for once the habitual cool remoteness was absent from his. Instead, it was pierced with a hot, unidentifiable emotion, one that sent an answering arrow of heat straight to the pit of her stomach.

"I mean, I'm happy where I'm at," she added hastily, and watched, fascinated, as his eyes shuttered once again, leaving her to wonder if she'd imagined his reaction. Although the words that had first tumbled off her tongue had dismayed her, there was more than an element of truth in them. The bond between Sully and her had been immediate ten years ago, and had strengthened in the six months they'd been neighbors. She took comfort from their relationship, and she wasn't anxious to have it change. If this was a topic Sully returned to, it would do him no good. He may have been instrumental in helping her regain confidence and her self-respect. A natural consequence was that she wouldn't always agree with him, either.

"I may have a few regrets in my life," she said, a note of finality in her voice, "but they don't include ending my marriage or living here." She tilted her head, and studied the man before her with real curiosity. "How about you, Sully? What are *your* regrets?"

Her question hit him with the force of a fastball to the midsection. The bottle in his hand paused imperceptibly, then continued its journey to his lips. He drank deeply, as if he could wash the taste of the lies from his mouth. But the lies that were a part of his relationship with Ellie were too firmly rooted in the past. And honesty seemed to have no place in their future.

Regrets. In the darkest hours of the night, they seemed to make up the greater part of his life. It was only with the coming of daylight that they could be successfully pushed back into a dark corner of his mind, where they would lie in wait to renew their stranglehold the next time his guard was down.

He lowered the bottle and contemplated the label. "What makes you think I have any?"

She lifted a shoulder, a careless, graceful movement. "We all do, don't we? I know I often find myself wishing I'd gotten a degree before I got married. Do you ever wish that?"

"That I'd finished college? No." It was a relief each time he was able to offer her a small slice of truth. It hadn't been a degree he'd been after, at any rate, when he'd posed as a student on the campus where they'd met. "College life wasn't for me."

She was watching him with that serious quizzical expression he knew too well. She wasn't going to leave the subject alone. She had a philosophical side to her, one that could carve just a little deeper than he was comfortable with.

"But sometimes one choice we make can affect the rest of our lives." She grimaced. "Like meeting Carter did for me. If you'd gotten a degree, your life might be different, too. You wouldn't be driving a truck, for example."

The condensation on the bottle had dampened the label. Sully sent his thumbnail under the edge and carefully loosened it. His tone was bored. "What's wrong with driving a truck?"

Her eyes narrowed in annoyance. She was aware that he was being deliberately obtuse. The trouble with their ten-year friendship was that she knew him better than anyone else. And yet not at all.

"Nothing is wrong with driving a truck. As long as you're happy doing it. I'm just saying that one of our choices can limit or expand all our future ones. That's what causes regrets."

Another movement of his thumb, and he had half of the label free. He didn't need the lecture on regrets. He could have filled volumes with his personal knowledge of the subject. He slowly raised his gaze and studied the woman before him. The one who symbolized one of the biggest regrets in his life.

Her long dark hair framed her face, inviting a man's hand to push it back over her shoulder, to linger and stroke. His fingers clenched more tightly around the bottle.

"We make choices and then we live with the results," he said flatly. "What good is looking back?"

She made a face. He knew she rarely agreed with his terse, often cynical views. How could she? Sometimes he marveled that a person as trusting as she had managed to survive this life with that aura of innocence intact. It gave him all the more reason to want to protect her. All the more reason to keep their two worlds from colliding. Because that would be a regret he could never live with; if somehow she was threatened by the ugliness he immersed himself in daily.

Tact was a quality that he lacked, but one she had in abundance. As if aware of the dark turn his thoughts had taken, she seamlessly shifted subjects. "You didn't by any chance bring me a souvenir from Dallas, did you?"

"What'd you want, one of those little hats and a set of six-shooters?"

"You didn't even think of me, did you?" she accused good-naturedly. "Lucky for you, I'm going to let you make it up to me."

"I'm scared to ask."

"You can order takeout for us tonight."

He didn't smile, but his mood lightened a fraction. When he was with her, it was easy to forget and far too easy to pretend. She was a brilliant splash of color in his dreary, sepia-toned world. He was man enough to appreciate her, but not a good enough man to leave her be. So he continued his balancing act, one that allowed him to get so close and no closer.

"Pretty slick the way you worked that in."

She attempted to look modest. "Thank you. I thought so."

"What are you hungry for?"

"Pizza?"

"And just how many times have you eaten pizza this week? Or other carryout?" Her silence was all the answer he needed. "Forget it. You have to eat decently once in a while. We'll prepare a real meal." He rose from the recliner to make his way to her kitchen.

"'We'll'?" she repeated dubiously. "I've seen your skills in the kitchen, Sullivan. You don't have any."

"I can help." His affronted tone wasn't totally feigned. He inspected the contents of her freezer, and withdrew some chicken. Then he unloaded her refrigerator of its meager contents of milk, ketchup and lettuce, and started rooting around in her cupboards. He'd leave the ingenuity of the combination of those ingredients to her. That was safest. He'd be the first to admit that he was no kind of cook.

She trailed out to the kitchen without enthusiasm, put the chicken in the microwave to thaw and then jumped when he opened her cupboard and all the pans clattered to the floor.

"Exactly what kind of help did you have in mind?"

He looked up from his position on the worn linoleum, where he was stacking the pans. "Well, every production needs a director. That's what I'll do. Direct. And of course, I'll take care of everything you don't feel like eating."

"Thanks," she said wryly. "Like the saying goes, with friends like you…"

His voice was devoid of amusement as he finished the quote.

"…you don't need enemies."

Chapter 2

The chair across from Thomas Conrad's desk wasn't designed for comfort. Underlings, if they were invited to sit at all, were expected to remember their place, their inferiority compared to the man before them. The straight-backed chair would ensure that the spine in it would remain rigid, all the better for the nerves to stay alert, on edge. It served as a subtle reminder of how much more uncomfortable Conrad could make things if he so chose.

Sully's large frame was really too big for the chair. Slouched down in it, his large shoulders dwarfed its narrow back. With one booted foot hooked over the opposite knee, he gave an appearance of ease where there should have been none.

The other man watched him over steepled fingers, and Sully waited, in the effortlessly patient style that had been honed by years on the street. Conrad had recently paid a visit to his high-priced stylist, he noted cynically. His wavy dark hair was smoothed back from a wide, wrinkle-free

forehead. The threads of gray were appearing a little too
rapidly to be attributed to aging, and were artfully displayed
at the temples. His smooth skin bore the glow of his twice-
weekly facials, and his blunt-tipped fingers sported a fresh
manicure. Conrad believed in availing himself of the good
things that life had to offer.

"So, Roarke, your trip was successful?"

Sully's eyelids slid to half-mast. "You know it was."

Perfectly capped white teeth gleamed at him. "Of course
I know. Just as I knew, when I sent you to Colombia, that
you would not disappoint me."

The pause after his words was meant as an invitation,
one Sully chose to ignore. Conrad was used to being the
puppet master of his little empire; he enjoyed pulling
strings and watching his employees dance to the scene of
his making. Sully might be part of the empire, but he'd
never be considered a puppet. Not by anybody.

Silence stretched, long enough to be considered uncomfortable by someone who hadn't grown to cherish it. Conrad dropped his hands, and one went to the eighteen-carat
gold pen on his desk. He wove it between his fingers, admired its gilt against his tanned skin. "I understand that
you had a little trouble in Bogotá."

The muscles in Sully's shoulder bunched and released as
he shrugged. "Nothing I couldn't handle."

The other man laughed, and a tinge of admiration crept
into his tone. "And handle it you did, my friend. I'm told
you managed quite capably."

His ribs were still a mass of bruises from the small group
of men who'd jumped him outside his hotel room in Bogotá
three days ago. A small, dark alley nearby had been the
scene of the near silent, deadly fight that had ensued. Two
men had escaped, but the other two had been left in a heap
on the ground, their blood mingling with his. The knife
wound along his left shoulder joined a faded map of scars

on his body, and soon would be one more forgotten sign-post of his life. His own knife had served him well that day, but pain tended to tick him off, and he had reason to believe that the man seated across from him was the cause of that pain.

"Were they yours?"

Conrad didn't pretend to misunderstand the cold, flat question. He manipulated the pen in and out of his fingers, his movements nimble. "No, I didn't send those men," he replied softly, his pale blue eyes raising to meet Sully's. "I have no reason to test you that way. You've proven your loyalty to me. Over and over again."

"Difficult to understand then, why I was sent out of the country on a task a mule could have taken care of. After the last two years, I thought we were beyond that."

"And so we are," Conrad said soothingly. "You've become invaluable to me." When there was no reply, he added, "I hope you will agree that our…relationship…has been mutually beneficial?"

There was no hint of emotion in Sully's voice when he replied. "I've got no complaints."

"No, you never do." Conrad's eyes searched those of the man before him. He allowed the pen to drop from his fingers, and it rolled slowly across his desk. "You never complain. Your tastes are simple to the point of poverty. Are you still living in that charmingly quaint little apart-ment?"

Sully leaned forward and reached a hand toward him, his movement so sudden and swift that Conrad blinked. When he focused again, Sully's hand was holding the pen, which had started to fall from the edge of his desk. Conrad reached out slowly and took it from him.

In the next instant Sully had relaxed back into his chair, and it was as if his movement had never taken place. "As you say, my tastes are simple."

Conrad regarded the pen in his hand for a moment before lifting his gaze back to Sully's. "That's difficult for me to understand," he said, with a nod toward his opulent surroundings. "I have a fondness for beautiful things. Furniture, jewelry, cars...women," he added as an afterthought, clearly placing them in the same category as the objects he'd listed. "So you'll forgive my nosiness this once. I pay you very handsomely, yet you do not share my lavish tastes."

It wasn't posed as a question, but it demanded an answer, nonetheless. Sully was only surprised it hadn't been asked sooner. "The Cayman Islands," he said laconically. Conrad stared blankly.

"The money you pay me. It's in a bank in the Cayman Islands."

"The Cayman Islands," he echoed, then threw back his head and chuckled richly. "Ah, Roarke," he managed to say after several moments, "you never disappoint me. Never." The admiration in his voice was genuine. "Let me guess. No taxes, no records, no trail. Am I right?"

Sully inclined his head.

"A patient man," Conrad noted softly, "and a careful one. It's no wonder that my operation in this country has expanded due to your help. And my success has not gone unnoticed or unrewarded by my superior." He leaned back in the chair of polished cherry that matched his desk, visibly savoring Sully's reaction.

"Yes, I, too, have a boss. That surprises you?"

Sully chose his words carefully. "I never gave it much thought."

Conrad smiled, unfooled. "When I've reported to my superior, I've given you the credit you deserve. He's been quite impressed." He threaded his fingers together on the top of his desk. "Your handling of that incident with the thugs was nicely done, but especially impressive was the way you were able to get the delivery through customs and bring it to me with the contents undisturbed.'' His gaze was flat, fathomless, reflecting none of the humor in his smile. "A resourceful man is very valuable, indeed."

Sully returned Conrad's gaze unblinkingly. They both knew that if he had failed to deliver those bundles of cocaine from Colombia, he would have been hunted down and sent on a more permanent trip. He somehow doubted that destination would have included harps and angels. It had been another test, and every nerve in his body prickled with readiness. He was going to be given a chance to move up in the organization. He allowed anticipation to show on his face. Conrad would expect to see it there, and sometimes it was best to show people what they expected.

"You were sent to Bogotá because my superior wanted to get a look at you. He was pleased. You can expect to hear more from him." Opening his desk drawer, he reached inside. Not by a flicker of an eyelid did Sully reveal his awareness that Conrad kept an unlicensed, loaded Magnum .357 in the drawer. He withdrew an envelope filled with money, which he extended to Sully as he rose.

Sully stood, too, in deference to the man who employed him. Taking the envelope, he tucked it into the back pocket of his jeans.

"I trust it was no problem to get away from the freight company for a few days?"

"I took vacation time."

"And your parole officer?" Conrad probed. "He gave you no difficulty about leaving the country?"

Sully gave him a level look. "He would have if he'd known." He played the game with Conrad, as he'd always had. The man knew Sully always covered his tracks, had, in fact, several sets of identification that allowed him to move freely in and out of the country as needed. It was just Conrad's way of reminding him that despite his current favorable status, he was still just an ex-con with a record and dead-end job. Anything more depended on how well he continued to please the man.

And now he must please Conrad's superior, as well.

Conrad nodded. "Excellent."

Sully turned without another word, aware that the meeting was at an end. He walked swiftly to the door, nodding silently to Toby, the huge bald man who acted as Conrad's bodyguard.

Outside, the air seemed fresh, despite the clogging Miami smog that lingered in the dusk. Sully hadn't driven to the swanky downtown office building, choosing instead to take a bus. He caught one now, and dropped into a seat midway back, his eyes sliding immediately closed. He didn't open them again until he heard his stop called, and disembarked a block from his apartment building.

On the street corner he hesitated, fighting the now familiar temptation to go home. Ellie would be there; at least she'd be next door, her proximity a persuasive lure that would act on his willpower all evening. Even if he went to his own apartment, she might come to him, pounding on his door and laughingly demanding that he join her for popcorn. Ice cream. TV.

Sweat beaded on his forehead, and resolutely he turned away from his building, walking down the block and around the corner. He ignored the barefoot kids on the ramshackle stoops, the groups of young gangbangers posturing by the curb, trying to impress the girls and each other. Ducking into a dimly lit tavern, he wound through the tables half-filled with occupants, and found a stool at the chipped Formica bar.

The bartender put down his rag and the glass he was drying, and shuffled in Sully's direction. He stopped midjourney when Sully held up two fingers, turning away to find a bottle of blended whiskey and pour a double shot.

He slid it in front of Sully and palmed the bill on the bar in one smooth motion that belied his earlier gracelessness.

Sully picked up the glass and swirled the contents, studying the amber eddies fixedly. The bartender wouldn't be back until the glass was empty, trained to give customers their space, as well as to remember what they drank. Sully was a frequent enough visitor in recent weeks to keep the bartender's memory fresh.

He felt the surreptitious glances from the men on either side of him, but he kept his head down and the men next to him left him alone. The regulars in the place knew each other's moods as well as a spouse's, and what they knew of Sully's moods was enough to warn them away. He brought the glass to his lips and took a swallow, letting the liquid scorch a path down his throat. It was a mistake. He knew it immediately. The last thing he needed was something to get him warmer. These days he always felt on the verge of combustion.

It hadn't always been this way. His apartment had never represented a haven until he found himself having to stay away from it, to avoid the temptation of the woman next door.

A movement in the corner of his eye caught his attention, and his gaze rose before his brain had a chance to process. But the long dark hair on the occupant crouched on the floor beside a nearby table didn't belong to the woman on his mind. Instead of being the color of sleek, shiny mink, it was a more ordinary shade of brown. Her laugh, when it sounded, was low and suggestive, not light and lilting. It didn't make his gut clutch and release in mingled pain and pleasure at its sound.

The stranger retrieved the change she'd dropped and re-seated herself, and Sully's attention drifted back to his glass. He took another long swallow, anticipating the liquor's warm explosion in the pit of his belly. It hadn't been only the dark hair that had triggered some dim memory. It had been her position on the floor, crouched down as Ellie had been the first time he'd seen her.

He'd nearly tripped over her outside a classroom on campus, where he'd been posing as a student. Any other time, any other woman, and he would have muttered an apology and continued after the contact he'd been following. But something about that glossy mass of hair curtaining her features, her refusal to look up even when he'd very nearly toppled over her in his haste had caused him to pause. And then she'd reached up an impatient hand to push her hair behind her ear, and he'd seen the lone tear trickling down a cheek that could have been carved from the rarest ivory, the small full mouth that was fighting a tremble, and he couldn't have left if he'd tried.

He might have forgotten the quick surge of lust that had knotted in his gut at the sight of all that long, shiny hair, its graceful swing at odds with her awkward, jerky movements. It had never been difficult for him to dismiss tears, but when she'd turned those eyes on him, liquid with unshed dampness, for once his instincts had failed him. Her eyes were clear, guileless, and mirrored her every unspoken feeling. He'd watched, transfixed, as they'd reflected panic, shame and curiosity all flitting across the misery. He'd never been the same.

He'd squatted down beside her, and helped her stack the mountain of books she'd dropped, retaining the last of them in his hand as she'd struggled to rise under her load.

"Just put those on top, please." Her voice had curled around him, musical and light, igniting a desire to hear more. He'd shaken his head, causing her to look at him, finally, and it had been like taking a fist to the solar plexus. Her chocolate-colored eyes had been wide and thickly lashed, and only a shade lighter than her hair.

"You'll just drop them again," he'd reasoned logically.

Jerking his head in the direction of the classroom she'd exited, he continued, "Let me guess. You had a run-in with Professor Jacobsen."

Since her hands hadn't been free, she'd bent her head, attempting to wipe the telltale tear on her shoulder. He'd been shocked at the powerful urge to reach over and wipe the wetness away with the tip of his finger.

"He's very...gruff, isn't he?" She'd tried for a laugh, but the sound had quavered a bit.

"He's a condescending jerk," Sully had said flatly. He may not have been a real student at the university, but he'd spent enough time on the campus trailing some who were. He'd always found that if he listened long enough, he'd hear all kinds of information, some useful, some not. What he'd heard about Jacobsen had fallen into the latter category. The man got his kicks asking questions no one could answer, and then humiliating the students he called on. A special target of his had seemed to be freshmen girls, and Sully had felt an unexpected flare of anger for what he'd imagined had just happened.

"It's not just him," she'd confided. "It's everything. The campus is so huge, there's so many people...I keep getting lost and being late for classes...." She'd bitten her lip, as if to keep the words from tumbling out.

"Something tells me you could use coffee," he'd said. Even now he didn't know which of them had been more surprised when she'd cocked her head and looked up at him, before softly uttering, "Okay."

Once they'd been at the student union with two freshly brewed coffees before them, Sully hadn't known quite what to do with her. He'd never met anyone like her before. She'd been too damn open for her own good, and given to a forthrightness that had been unwise, even ten years ago. His emotions had warred between wanting, illogically, to chide her for her trusting nature, and an unwilling fascination for every bit of information she'd confided to him.

The battered Formica of the bar looked less harsh through the amber-colored liquid in the bottom of his glass. He tipped the glass to his lips again, his throat closing around the scalding slide of the whiskey.

Her name was Elizabeth Bennett, and she was from a small town in northern Florida. She'd been having trouble getting used to the amount of reading she needed to do, she'd told him. Juggling her part-time job with homework required more organization than she was used to. Because he'd been afraid of the suspicious sheen that had returned to her eyes, he'd reached far down into his rusty well of humor. "Poor Cinder Ellie." As a joke, it hadn't been much, but it had been enough to startle the worry from her eyes, and she'd released a giggle that had lit a slow burn inside him that had never completely faded away.

Ellie. It had become his name for her, a guilty indulgence he'd allowed himself to take secret pleasure in. It had been a long time before he'd figured out why she'd immediately given him her trust. His wasn't a face to inspire such faith, and he'd had no practice with friendship. Over the years he'd come to realize that Ellie collected misfits, stray animals and people alike, and he knew he fit in that category. He'd never cared. While he'd been uncharacteristically drawn to wiping the anxiety from those beautiful, dark eyes, she'd been extending him the first hand in his life that he hadn't been tempted to bite off.

His lips curved slightly. He was unaware that the bartender saw the difference on his features and watched him more warily. His first impression of Ellie hadn't prepared him for the sheer guts and determination she possessed. After that meeting he'd been intent on making sure he never saw her again. He hadn't understood the immediate bond that had leaped between them, and hadn't wanted the complication it presented. But neither had he reckoned on the depth of his fascination with her, his uneasy appreciation of her sweetness, her offer of friendship.

He drank again, to ease the pain of remembering. It hadn't been mere physical attraction. If it had been, he could have simply found another woman to slake that need; they'd always come too easily, and could be forgotten just as quickly. But Ellie was different. There would be none other who could match her shy, responsive smile, that slow, self-mocking kind of humor, which could be extended to him, as well, if she thought he was taking himself too seriously. He'd never seen enough evidence in this life to convince him of the existence of a higher power. But if he'd believed in any kind of god, he'd have spent many long hours on his knees praying that he could be a different sort of man, one living a much different sort of life. One he dared to share with Ellie.

He drained the liquor from his glass, raising his fingers in a silent signal to the bartender. The jukebox blared out something with a Latin beat, and a pair of entwined couples began dancing between the tables to the low bass throb.

He hadn't been able to stay completely away from her, although he should have been kept busy enough with his drug contacts on the campus. He'd made deals with himself, granting himself permission for a visit every month, a phone call every week or two. It had been his ultimate indulgence, and he'd been careful not to go beyond the rigid limits he'd imposed on their friendship.

His eyes burned, feeling like they were filled with sand. He'd gotten damn little rest in Colombia, and not much more since returning to the States. He needed to go home, needed sleep. The hammering his body had taken had subsided to a constant all-over ache. He'd rise before dawn to get to his job at the freight company, and it wouldn't be long before he was contacted again by Conrad. But he clung to the glass of whiskey in a futile attempt to defuse the pull that really drew him back to his apartment building.

Sometimes he'd lie awake for hours, damning his own stupidity for ever placing Ellie in his building. He'd learned to live with only occasional glimpses of her, carefully infrequent visits and calls. He'd wait sometimes until the need to see her was an unquenchable thirst, and when the craving got too great, he'd treat himself to the sight of her, give himself the gift of an hour or two in her company.

The whiskey's heat was spreading through his veins now, welcoming each additional taste. The men beside him departed, their stools filled by other strangers, each as interested in solitude as he. There had been times, he remembered, squinting at the inch of liquor still left in the glass, when he'd felt quite honorable about the distance he'd maintained with Ellie. Times when he'd convinced himself that their careful little friendship could continue indefinitely. But knowing that he couldn't have her hadn't prepared him for the rending pain of standing aside while she fell in love with Carter Robinson.

Just the thought of the smoothly polished lawyer made his hand tighten around his glass, his knuckles going white. He'd like to think he would have felt differently if Robinson had been another kind of man, one who would have made Ellie happy. But he had few illusions about the world, and none about himself. It wouldn't have mattered who Ellie had married; Sully would have quietly hated his guts.

But he'd loathed Robinson from the first time Ellie had introduced them. The man had represented every privilege class and breeding had to offer, as well as the ego to go along with it. He'd taken savage satisfaction from Ellie's stubborn determination to maintain contact with him throughout her marriage, because he knew their friendship had choked her husband. When he'd seen Ellie in the mall that day, shattered and weeping, he'd had to choose between the warring needs of protecting her and smashing Robinson's face. The need to protect Ellie had won out over baser emotion. It always would.

Downing the last of the fiery liquid, he set the glass on the bar, turning to survey the shabby interior of the tavern. The dim lighting did the place a small kindness, and hid the loneliness and desperation on the faces of its occupants. There was no one here who had a better place to go; no one who deserved or asked for more.

It was the kind of place that Sully felt comfortable in. A place with few airs, and no expectations. Just like him. He'd drunk enough to lure sleep, if his mind would oblige him by staying out of the apartment next to his.

He walked from the bar, unaware that the other patrons took one look at him and gave him wide berth. A more impractical man would consider the breakup of Ellie's marriage and their resulting closer friendship as something of an omen. He might be selfish enough to find pleasure in having her near for a time. But he'd never ask for more, would never accept more.

He had no experience with meaningful relationships, but even he knew you didn't build one on ten years of lies and half-truths. Telling Ellie the truth, all of it, would jeopardize more than their friendship. It might well endanger her life. And that was a risk he couldn't take.

Once outside, his watchful gaze scanned his surroundings before he turned to head back to his apartment. He was a realist, focused on the here and now. It would take a miracle for Ellie to understand and forgive a decade of deceit. He started up the street, his hands jammed in the pockets of his jeans.

He'd never been a man to believe in miracles.

Chapter 3

"So what's next, Roarke, huh?" Nushawn's grin was bright enough to light the dim interior of the shabby bar-restaurant. "The Saint," he was called on the street, because he had a countenance as angelic as a choirboy's. It disguised an almost animal-like cunning and savage ferocity when cornered. Nushawn was the charmer in the group of men at the table, but he shared a similar motivation with the others: greed.

Sully lit a cigarette and surveyed the men who worked for him. If he was a lieutenant in Conrad's drug enterprise, these were his foot soldiers. The thought filled him with harsh humor. There would be no loyalty found among this group, and certainly no patriotism. They were, however, remarkably devoted to earning money as effortlessly as possible.

"Well, it's payday, boys." He exhaled a narrow stream of smoke and cocked an eyebrow at them. "What do you usually do after I pay you for a job well done?"

Nushawn chuckled wickedly. "Mosey here spends his on hookers, don't ya, man? He won't have nothing left by next week but a couple of memories and a handful of disappointment." The other men laughed raucously, and Mosey kicked out, knocking Nushawn off his chair. The men erupted again, while Mosey glared at the younger man.

"Yeah, I like my women experienced. I ain't like you, luring little girls to empty buildings for fun and games."

Sully's stomach gave a quick, vicious twist, but he kept his face expressionless. Nothing about these men would surprise him. After all, it was their lack of morals that had drawn them to work for him in the first place. He took a deep draw on the cigarette, letting the smoke fill his lungs. More and more it was seeming as though he was spending too much of his time in the company of men just like these. Too much time in places like this one, or in far worse. Too much time dealing with nothing but drugs and death.

Was it any wonder then that Ellie seemed an oasis of sanity and sweetness in an otherwise dreary world? Any wonder that she represented the most powerful temptation he'd ever faced? Every hint of peace he'd ever found had been in her company. It should have been enough. But he was finding it increasingly difficult to be satisfied with the niche he'd carved for himself in her life.

The men were in the mood to linger over their beers, swapping insults and tales with equal fervor. Another man strode up to the table, pulled up a chair and sat down. Sully glanced at his watch pointedly.

"You're late," he said, his voice deceptively mild.

Kale Lowrey's narrow face split with a grin. "Hey, I had things to do, you know."

"He don't care 'bout getting paid," Tommy said. He was a small, melancholy man, with the furtive movements of a back-alley rodent. "Maybe you should give us his money, Roarke. Looks like he don't need it."

Kale spread out his hands. "I'm here now, aren't I? I damn well deserve my money as much as you guys do."

The conversations among the men trailed off, and all eyes went to Sully. He was known to have little tolerance for excuses, and none for mistakes. Any infraction, no matter how slight, would not go overlooked.

Sully's gaze slid to Kale, who, under the inspection of all the men, was becoming visibly uncomfortable. He took a deep, considering draw on his cigarette. When he exhaled, the smoke drifted Kale's way. His voice was soft, almost conversational. "You know, Kale, being my second-in-command is a privilege."

Annoyance flashed in the other man's eyes, but his response was respectful. "I know that. And believe me, I appreciate it."

Sully frowned consideringly, and stubbed his cigarette out in the ashtray. "Do you?"

Kale nodded, and Sully reached inside the jacket he wore and took out an envelope. Kale's fingers had almost closed around it when Sully withdrew it and removed a fifty-dollar bill from inside. Then he handed the remaining money to Kale.

"With privilege comes responsibility, friend," he said, his voice almost soundless. The bill was held up for an instant, and then disappeared into Sully's pocket. "It just cost you fifty for not living up to yours. But next time will cost you more. Much more."

The other men exchanged glances. Sully's meaning was clear, and it didn't involve money. There was silence until Kale cleared his throat. "I understand. It won't happen again." Their gazes held for a long, electrically charged instant, and then Sully looked at the other men.

"I'll be in touch soon."

"How soon?" Nushawn asked. His whole body was

bouncing to the beat of a rap song playing only in his head. "Kale says we got something big coming up."

Sully's gaze went slowly back to Kale. "Did he?" he murmured. Kale might be Sully's second-in-command, but Sully trusted him only slightly more than he did the other men.

Kale swallowed nervously.

"Yeah, man, he did, and what we wanna know is, how big's it gonna be? Do I need to make an appointment with my broker?"

The men broke up at that. "You mean your bookie, doncha, Nushawn?" one of them asked.

"I'll let you know." Sully took the fifty he'd removed from Kale's envelope and handed it to Nushawn. "Here. Pool and drinks are on Kale."

Amid hoots and jeers the men got up from the table and drifted through the bar, some stopping at pool tables and a few others going to the bar. Sully watched them disperse before focusing his attention on Kale.

"We seem to have a problem here."

Sullenly Kale looked away. "It's not like it sounded. The men have to respect me, too, you know. I didn't say much."

Reaching for another cigarette, Sully took his time lighting it. "Well," he said after the first puff, "I think you're wrong. The men don't have to respect you, because they won't be taking orders from you. I'm in charge. Don't forget that." His eyes narrowed, and his voice went low, lethally dangerous. "Don't make me sorry I let you in on this, Lowrey."

The man snorted, but tiny beads of sweat were forming on his upper lip. "Like you had any choice in it."

"We all have choices," Sully said. With an odd sense of déjà vu, he was reminded of his last conversation with

Ellie. "The difference is, in the street, making the wrong choice can buy you a bullet."

"I just thought…"

"Don't think." He reached out suddenly, and the other man flinched. Slapping him on the shoulder, Sully advised, "I'll do the thinking. All you have to do is what I tell you. Understand?"

Kale shrugged and rose from the chair. "I'm getting a drink," he muttered.

Sully nodded. "You may as well. You paid for it."

The man hesitated. "We need to talk. Plan for the next step."

"Not here. Not now."

Without another word Kale wove his way toward the front of the bar, and Sully returned to his cigarette. Idly he watched Tommy and Mosey at a nearby pool table, arguing over who had called which pocket. The noise level in the place had gradually risen, as those patrons who actually held jobs got off work and joined the regulars. They'd stay to drink, play pool and for some of them, have supper. Then they'd stumble home to their beds and start all over tomorrow.

The idea of stumbling home appealed. Not to bed—it was early, but a little relaxation didn't sound half-bad. And a shower. He stubbed his cigarette out and began to rise. Maybe he'd order something to eat before he left, since there was nothing in his apartment but some stale chips. He wound his way through the tables from the back of the bar. As he approached the front, the noise assailed him. Most of the patrons were collected here.

"Roarke, leaving already?" one of his men called. "Come on over and let us clean you out over a friendly game of pool." Sully shook his head, ignoring the ribbing from the men.

"C'mon, sweet thing, talk to me. I'm a real nice guy. Ask anybody." Nushawn's voice was heard over the melee.

"Nushawn's got a new one in his sights," one of the men said, and the others laughed.

"How's 'bout you and me go somewhere quiet? You like to dance? I'm a heckuva dancer. Watch this."

As Sully drew closer, he saw Nushawn begin to sway and do some fancy footwork, all the while sporting his trademark wide grin. But it was his eyes Sully watched. They were hard and mean. Liquor never did much for his disposition.

"I said, back off, or I'll make you sorry."

Sully paused for a moment and the floor seemed to list beneath his feet. There was no way, no possible way he could have recognized that voice. But as he turned the corner and the bar was fully in sight, he saw the stuff that nightmares were made of.

Ellie was standing at the bar, one hand tucked in her purse. Even as he watched, Nushawn danced closer to her and clamped his fingers firmly around her arm. The bartender impatiently awaited payment for the carryout food in the foam container on the bar before the couple.

Disbelief was followed by a greasy roll of nausea. In a split instant Sully sifted through the flash of possibilities, then started toward Ellie, his hand reaching for his pocket.

"Let her go. Now." He threw some bills on the bar even as Nushawn turned, surprised. But it was Ellie's reaction he was most worried about. Her eyes went wide as she turned to him, and before she could open her mouth, his hand had replaced Nushawn's on her arm, he'd snatched up the container from the bar with his free hand and propelled her toward the door.

"Not...one...word," he said through gritted teeth. Her eyes flashed, but she obeyed, walking rapidly to keep up with his long strides. They were to the corner, around it, before he slowed, his gaze scanning the street for a bus. He could see one in the distance, coming their way, and he paused, hoping like hell that it was the one that would be stopping here.

"Are you going to let me know when I can use my powers of speech again, or am I supposed to guess?" she asked tartly. She looked pointedly at the hand he still had clamped on her arm, and he released her and stepped back. He scanned the street over the top of her head and noticed nothing unusual. No one had followed them from the bar. He hadn't thought any of the men would have dared do so, but hadn't been completely sure.

The bus rumbled to a stop before them, accompanied by a hiss of air brakes, and then its doors came open. He dug in his pocket for some change and dropped in the proper amount for both of them, then led her to a seat in the back.

"Sully! What's going on? Where did you come from just now?"

Ellie was looking at him as if he were crazed, and at the moment that was close to the truth. Adrenaline was draining, leaving lingering traces of panic and guilt warring within him, layered by overwhelming relief. Two worlds colliding, he thought grimly. But nothing in his nightmares had prepared him for seeing her with Nushawn, his hand touching Ellie's creamy white skin. The memory was enough to send another chill snaking down his spine.

He ignored her question. "What the hell were you doing in that place? How many times do I have to warn you to stay in safe areas?"

She was watching him carefully. "That is a safe area. The restaurant also has decent food. It's only a half-dozen blocks from the gallery. Monica and I often order from there for lunch. I've picked up takeout there dozens of times." Monica was a woman she worked with at the gallery, Sully knew, but she didn't concern him. All that concerned him right now was Ellie.

The temper slowly faded from her eyes, to be replaced with concern. Her hand went to his arm. "Sully, are you okay? When I saw you for the first time in there, you looked…" She didn't finish the sentence; she didn't have to. He knew how he must have looked, because he knew how he'd felt. Nushawn would never know how narrow an escape he'd just had.

"How was I supposed to look?" he countered. "A scumbag had his hands on you and he wasn't just interested in dancing, sweetheart."

Her gaze searched his. "Did you know that man?"

His answer, though true, still tasted like a lie. "Nushawn works with me. He's bad news."

"Well, I've never had trouble there before. They do a good takeout business. And—" her voice grew mischievous "—believe it or not, I was all set to defend myself before you came up." She reached into her purse and withdrew a compact can of pepper spray. "I'll bet when you gave this to me you never thought I'd use it."

Something released in his chest, and he could breathe a little more easily. "Would you have?"

"I had it in my hand and ready to aim at him in another second," she said cheerfully. Pointedly she added, "I know you don't believe it, but I *am* careful. I don't take unnecessary risks. There's nothing wrong with that neighborhood or that bar. I've even seen policemen eating in there occasionally."

He turned his head, watched the scenery deteriorate as they drew closer to their apartment building. No, there hadn't been anything wrong with that bar she'd been in. It was a little run-down, but it had a decent reputation. There hadn't been anything wrong with it, at least, until he had chosen it to meet in, and brought Nushawn and his worthless friends there. *He* had been the cause for the place being unsafe; the bar had been his suggestion as a meeting place. It was because of him that she'd had a run-in with a kind of man she should never have had to even know existed.

The sweat breaking out on his forehead owed nothing to the humidity. He'd been careful to be sure he never met with the men within a mile of his apartment building. He hadn't wanted to take even the slightest chance that they would ever come into contact with Ellie. And yet by some slippery twist of fate, the filthy life he was leading had managed to touch her anyway, if only indirectly. And that was the thought that kept nipping away at his conscience, that kept his gut churning with remorse.

Her hand on his arm grew caressing. Every nerve stilled, and his gaze dropped to watch its movements.

"Sometimes I think you take your role of protector too seriously, Sully." Her words, coupled with the bittersweet sensation of that light touch, sliced into him like the keen edge of a blade. "A sense of responsibility is a good thing, unless it's taken too far. Then it can eat you alive."

Sully sat upright in bed, fighting his way out of the nightmare. The breath tore out of his lungs in huge, heaving gulps, sweat pouring off his body in heated rivers. He sat on the edge of the bed for a moment, trying to walk that tightrope between horror-filled sleep and reality. It was times like these, when nights were deepest and consciousness unwary, that the line between the two became indistinct.

He shoved off the bed, as if by putting distance between it and him he could lose the tendrils of the nightmare still curling through his subconscious. In the dark he stumbled into a chair, sending it, and the window-sized fan sitting on it, crashing to the floor.

Without pausing to pick them up, he continued out into

the apartment, heading toward the kitchen. He poured himself a glass of water and gulped it down. Then, cupping his hands under the faucet, he filled them with water and splashed it over his face and chest. He repeated the motion until the cool water was streaming over him, washing away the perspiration. Grabbing a towel, he carelessly wiped the dampness from his body, then dropped it into the sink.

Guilt had a way of haunting a man, the past and present weaving together into an inescapable trap. Most of the time he was able to keep old mistakes and regrets tucked away in a pocket of his mind, unlocked only when his guard relaxed. It wasn't difficult to understand what had elicited this rerun of the nightmare. Today his life had brushed against Ellie's in a way that was reminiscent of another time when an innocent had gotten too close.

Close enough to die.

He paced around the small apartment, driven to move. That situation had been completely different. Alberto had insisted in involving himself, even after he'd been warned of the risks. But the fact remained that there was no real way he could have realized the chance he was taking. He'd been innocent of the kind of life he'd immersed himself in, and had ended up being sacrificed to it.

Sully strode to the window, stared out into the night blindly. Ellie wouldn't be his next regret, he swore. She wasn't going to be allowed close enough to become a target. Discovering the truth about Sully and his activities could mark her for danger. Not to mention making her turn away from him completely.

The darkness seemed to press in on him from all directions. He didn't reach for a light. The shadows were too fitting for his bleak thoughts. Honesty, even if he wished to give it, couldn't be offered to Ellie. Not now.

The knock on his door was soft, but sounded through the quiet of the apartment like a gunshot. Sully whirled and stalked silently over to the boots he'd left on the floor near the kitchen. He withdrew the knife from its sheath and moved quickly, soundlessly to stand beside the door. His Glock pistol was in the bedroom, within easy reach of his bed. He thought of retrieving it, then a second later discarded the idea. It wouldn't be necessary. He was even more adept with the blade than with the gun.

He held the knife loosely in his hand, wrist cocked, and watched the knob slowly turn. The lock held and he braced himself, waiting for the door to burst in, readying himself for the bloodbath that would inevitably follow.

"Sully?" The whisper was barely discernible. If possible, his whole body drew even tenser. "Are you awake?"

He leaned his head against the wall and cursed, a silent litany of imaginative expletives. Ellie. He couldn't deal with her tonight, not with old regrets churning so close to the surface. He didn't feel capable of clinging to the careful defenses necessary with her. Didn't feel capable of remembering all the reasons for them.

The knock sounded again, more insistently. "Sully? Is everything all right?"

"Go away, Ellie." He stared into the darkness of the room, the cloak of shadows exemplifying his solitary state. He'd been alone for as long as he could remember, since childhood, really. He couldn't imagine anything different.

But that wasn't quite true. The woman on the other side of the door made him imagine a great many things, wildly impossible things. Things that made him ache and want, things he had no business even thinking.

Tonight he wasn't sure he'd be successful denying them.

"I heard the crash…then you moving around…." Her voice trailed off.

"I'm all right. Go back to bed."

His words sounded harsh, even to his own ears. But they failed to sway her.

"I'm not going anywhere until I can see for myself."

He stood there for a moment, then, muttering a curse, he found his boot in the darkness and slipped the blade back in its sheath. Then he walked to the bedroom and grabbed his jeans off the floor. Pulling them up, he zipped them but didn't bothering buttoning them. He returned to the door just as a knock sounded again.

"Sully!"

He pulled open the door as she spoke again exasperatedly. Propping an arm against the doorjamb, he contemplated her through the shadows. "What?"

"I just wanted to be sure you're all right. You're having trouble sleeping again, aren't you?"

His brain seemed sluggish. It took a moment to register her meaning. "Again?"

"Again." Her dark eyes were anxious. "I hear you sometimes, pacing around in here during the night. The walls aren't particularly thick, you know." Her words rendered him speechless, and she ducked under his arm and walked into his apartment.

By the time he'd recovered, she'd gone the few feet into the living room and turned on a lamp. He turned to face her but remained where he was, keeping the door open. She wouldn't be staying long. He couldn't let her.

He was still trying to adjust to the idea of her listening to him, not just tonight, but other nights. He was aware that her bedroom lay just on the other side of the wall from his. He was definitely aware. Many a night he'd lain awake in bed, imagining what she was wearing in hers. Imagining what she'd look like lying beneath him, wearing nothing at all.

"Sorry I woke you. It was nothing." He shrugged. "Just a dream." But she didn't appear to be listening to him. Her eyes went wide with concern.

"Oh, Sully, your poor chest! And that bandage! What happened to you?"

He blinked at her uncomprehendingly, and she crossed to him quickly and laid one soft hand against his skin. He looked down, realizing she was referring to the injuries he'd received in Bogotá. And then thought faded as sensation crashed over him.

Her fingers were moving lightly over his chest, and his heart richoceted beneath her palm. Sparks bounced in the wake of her gentle touch, sending an arrow of need straight to his loins. His eyes slid half-closed, and he watched her, letting himself imagine for an instant what it would be like if she touched him out of desire instead of concern. How she would look touching him just like that as he mounted her, before her touch grew stronger, wilder, as he slipped into her for the first time.

His need for her was as keen as a blade, threatening to whittle away at the layer of civility he'd carefully constructed, leaving his defenses in shambles. He took her wrist in his hand and stepped away.

"You shouldn't be here."

No, she shouldn't be here, in the middle of the night, wearing a silky invitation for a robe, tied hastily around her narrow waist. One quick tug would unfasten it, and it would take only a little urging from his hands to send it slithering down her arms to pool at her feet. She shouldn't be here touching him like that, looking at him like that.

He shoved his fists into his pockets. She shouldn't be here.

"Were you in some kind of accident, Sully? Heavens, no wonder you can't sleep. Have you been to a doctor? Are you in pain?"

His brain was foggy with lust and lack of sleep. It took a moment to follow her meaning, another to seize the excuse she'd given him. "It was an accident at work." The delivery of the lie filled him with weary self-disgust. "It doesn't hurt." The dull aches from the bruises and the knife wound were little competition to the jagged edge of despair that was gnawing away inside him. Her presence here only seemed to magnify his regrets.

"I hope you had a doctor check your ribs," she murmured. She'd moved closer again, closer than she should be, closer than he'd normally dare allow her. He held himself rigid as she trailed her fingers over the ribs that still protested the pounding they'd received a few days ago. He pulled his hands from his pockets, meaning to push her away, to send her back to her apartment once and for all. But his hands didn't obey the edicts of his mind. Instead, they went unerringly to her hair.

He combed his fingers through the long strands, giving in to an impulse that had burned inside for more than a decade. He pushed the heavy sheaf of hair over her shoulders, and then framed her face in his hands. Her gaze was arrested; he'd managed to divert her attention from his bruised ribs. He never touched her if he could help it; he did his best to avoid such temptations. She was looking at him as if she didn't recognize him. She wasn't alone; he didn't recognize himself.

He wasn't a careless man, nor an impulsive one. He wasn't one to ignore carefully crafted control and well-reasoned logic. He didn't willingly take falls because he could too easily imagine the sensation of slamming against the bottom. But he was very close to falling now.

Her bottom lip was trembling slightly; he watched it in fascination. Was she afraid of him? She should be. Right now he was very much afraid of himself. His thumbs caressed the delicate pulse points below her jawline, fascinated by the rapid drumming there. Then her hands came up to cover his, and his blood thundered through his system.

All he ever wanted, all he ever dreamed of, formed a hot fist of need that pummeled him with relentless urgency. He closed his eyes and fought for a control that seemed alarmingly distant.

"Sully?" Her shaky whisper pierced his longing like a bullet. He opened his eyes and looked at her. Her emotions were always easy to read. Right now was no different. There was surprise—and, God help him, desire—transparent on her face. But it was the last emotion he read there that crashed over him like a wave of Arctic water. The hints of apprehension there had him pulling away and stepping back from her. As if to remove himself from temptation, he turned away.

"Go home, Ellie." His tone was flat, expressionless.

He could hear the long release of her breath, with its tendency to shudder. Could feel the silent battle she fought to regain composure. He waited for the argument, the insistence for an explanation.

Neither came. For once in her life she did exactly as he requested. He heard her hand on the knob, the squeak of the hinges, the near-silent snick of the lock as the door closed behind her. Only then did he turn around and stare at the door.

In the still of the night it seemed to represent much more than a mere entranceway. It was an insurmountable obstacle that separated him from the only woman who would ever matter to him.

He heard the tiny sound of Ellie entering her own apartment and closing the door, and still his muscles wouldn't relax. He'd come too close to making a mistake with her. If she had given him the slightest encouragement, this night might have ended completely differently. And though his body ached with frustration, he knew it was for the best

Keeping an emotional distance from her was the most certain way to keep her safe.

The fact that it left him miserably alone, in a way he'd never before fully comprehended, was something he'd just have to learn to live with.

Chapter 4

"Did he miss me?" Elizabeth murmured as she took a deep breath and slowed to a walk beside Monica Pruett.

Her friend and co-worker slanted her a look from cool blue eyes. "Of course. He asked about you just a few minutes ago."

Elizabeth groaned. Her boss, Nathan Milway, was a stickler for punctuality, and her tardiness would not go without comment. The errand over her lunch hour had taken her longer than expected, and hurrying about in this humidity had left her feeling a little wilted. That was an additional fact Milway would chide her about, since a well-kept appearance was another of his mantras. His own tall, thin frame was always impeccably dressed in an expensive suit with a spotless white shirt and tie. He expected his employees to dress no less formally.

"What'd you tell him?" She smiled welcomingly at the small group of ladies who strolled past them, intent on examining the gallery's newest offerings.

Monica lifted one elegant shoulder. "I said you had a dire feminine emergency, and were in the rest room." She watched in cool amusement as Elizabeth colored with mortification. "I don't know who turned redder, Nathan or you. Don't be such a prude. It was the only thing I could think of that would keep him off your back. If I know our fussy boss, he won't even be able to look in your direction for the rest of the day, much less treat you to one of his famous lectures."

They parted then, each of them approaching a customer and offering assistance. Elizabeth was smiling despite herself at Monica's words. She hadn't been prepared to like the coolly elegant blonde when they'd first met at the gallery. The woman had reminded her of so many of the vain, shallow women she'd met at Carter's clubs, women whose primary interests were shopping, men and gossip. But she'd been disarmed by the almost bawdy earthiness that lurked below Monica's sophisticated demeanor. While it often embarrassed her, it was so at odds with her first impression of the woman that she couldn't help but be intrigued. She was perceptive enough to recognize the streak of vulnerability beneath the woman's polish, so she'd accepted her casual kindness, and their resulting friendship had surprised them both.

She directed her gaze back to the piece the customer was asking her about, and dutifully recited the facts about its artist. While the woman dithered over her decision, Elizabeth's attention faded again.

She was grateful to Monica for saving her from one of Nathan's reprimands, although she inwardly cringed at the method she'd used. Her friend was right; she *was* a prude. She certainly hadn't been given the opportunity to shed many inhibitions during her ill-fated marriage to Carter. Sex with him had been as carefully orchestrated as the rest of their lives, and curiously devoid of intimacy. She hadn't been encouraged to discover anything about sex that he hadn't been prepared to teach her, and his lessons had followed very stringent guidelines. She'd thought his carefulness with her had reflected his love and consideration. When she'd confided in Monica, her friend had irreverently referred to it as his Madonna complex.

She'd never had cause to regret her lack of experience before. But ever since she'd left Sully a few nights ago, she'd wished repeatedly that she had a little more knowledge to draw on. The crash in his apartment had startled her from sleep, but she'd been even more surprised once she'd seen him. He'd been abrupt, edgy. That in itself hadn't been unusual. But for once there had been a crack in his normally impregnable wall of defenses, and her heart had simply turned over.

She'd wanted to help him. The pain he'd been feeling hadn't seemed confined to the injury on his shoulder, or the awful bruises covering his chest. But then he'd touched her, and her breathing had, quite literally, stopped. Sully wasn't demonstrative, and he never, ever touched her unless it couldn't be avoided. The shock from feeling his fingers tangling in her hair, caressing her face, had driven aside her concern, and she'd been bombarded by sensation.

She answered her customer's questions about the painting automatically, her mind filled with thoughts of her best friend. She'd spent the past couple days castigating herself for leaving the way she had. Fleeing, really. But she lacked the experience to identify the startling changes in Sully's attitude. Surely his actions had been driven by nothing more than a combination of restless sleep and an aching body. But if his emotions had been indecipherable, hers had been instantly recognizable. At the first brush of his hand, a weighty ball of heat had lodged in her stomach and turned the blood in her veins molten. The intensity on his face had fired her pulse, and the throbbing had echoed in her brain.

She might not have much experience with it, but she'd recognized what she'd felt. Desire.

The admission, even to herself, sent her stomach into a slow roll. For the first time in their relationship, Sully had reached out to her in need, and she'd embarrassed herself by responding with need of a very different kind. Helping a friend had been far from her thoughts. Instead, she'd been considering how little it would take to close that distance between them, to feel his whole body against hers. To feel his mouth pressed over her own.

She bit her lip unconsciously and stepped aside as her customer squinted at the painting once more. If there was one thing she'd learned from her marriage, it was that she was a novice at reading men. She'd had no inkling that Carter was betraying the vows she'd held sacred, and she should have known her husband as well as it was possible to know a man.

So how could she trust her ability now to interpret Sully's feelings? Especially when hers had crashed around her, drowning her in intensity? She wasn't sure enough of herself as a woman to deal with the unexpected longing she'd felt. So when he'd told her to go that final time, she had gone, knowing it wasn't him she was retreating from, but her own unfamiliar emotions. Now she needed to devise a plan to return their relationship to a more familiar footing. Her unusual reaction to him couldn't be allowed to strain their friendship. She couldn't bear it if he pulled away from her because he sensed a change in her feelings for him.

Her customer was showing definite signs of interest. Elizabeth offered the woman a careful listing of the piece's advantages, chief among them, she assured her, was the price. The woman lapsed into silence again, and Elizabeth could feel the imminent sale floating in the air between them. This was where she and Monica differed in their approaches. Her friend would start closing in on the sale at this point, drawing the noose tighter with an energized pitch that either sold or terrified her customers. Elizabeth preferred to give them their space, up to a point. Nathan had been leery about her approach in the beginning, but after a probationary period, he'd had to admit that her resulting sales figures were very respectable.

"It's a very difficult decision, isn't it?" she asked her customer, turning to eye the painting critically. "Maybe it would be helpful to close your eyes and visualize the piece in the room you intend it for." The woman obediently screwed her eyes shut. "Now try to see the room as it is now, without the painting." After several moments, the woman opened her eyes, blinking at the painting slowly.

She turned to Elizabeth, beaming. "You know, it's like seeing it again for the first time. And the living room definitely needs something to liven it up. Write it up for me, will you, please?"

The woman followed Elizabeth to the gallery office, and wrote out a check for the amount quoted without batting an eye. After leaving the information needed for the delivery, she left, and Elizabeth settled in to do the paperwork for the sale.

"Congratulations," Monica purred as she came into the office. "As amazed as I always am by it, that soft-key, kid-gloves approach seems to have worked again. You should get a tidy little commission from that sale."

Elizabeth looked up and smiled. "How'd you do?"

Her friend lifted a hand. "My customer is a chronic looker. She'll be back." Her voice was wry when she added, "But she won't buy anything then, either." They both laughed.

Monica prowled around the office, taking advantage of Nathan's momentary inattentiveness. It wouldn't be long before he'd be checking on the women, manufacturing a task to busy them. "Well, don't keep me in suspense.

How'd your visit with Simon Boze go? Was it productive?''

"Oh, it was great." Elizabeth laid down her pen for an instant, renewed excitement filling her as she thought of the meeting she'd had over her lunch hour. "I owe you a very big thank-you for introducing me to your friend."

The other woman gave a careless shrug, but it was obvious the words had pleased her. "He's just an acquaintance, really. I used to do quite a bit of browsing in his gift shop. It has a nice selection of crafts, don't you think?"

"Hopefully it will soon have a bigger selection." Elizabeth crossed her fingers. "He asked me to bring some of my pottery in for him to look at. If he likes my work, he'll either buy them from me outright, or offer them for sale on consignment."

The smile Monica gave her was genuinely pleased. "That's wonderful! I knew the two of you would hit it off."

"It's not a done deal yet," Elizabeth cautioned. "He hasn't even seen my work. And I'm having a hard time deciding which of my pieces to show him."

Monica strolled by the desk and went to the coffeemaker. Pouring herself half a cup, she turned back to Elizabeth. "I like that last piece you showed me. It was different from anything else you've done." She sipped from her cup for a moment, then added thoughtfully, "It was sexy."

Heat bloomed in Elizabeth's cheeks. The piece her friend was referring to was the one she'd done for Sully. *Sexy.* It seemed a strange description of a piece of pottery, but it was so apt that embarrassment and guilt mingled within her. She'd wanted to do something special to thank the best friend she'd ever had, and it had seemed critical that the piece be right for him. But she thought now that perhaps her newly discovered feelings for him were rooted in all those hours she'd spent with his constant image in her head.

Those sleek, hard lines that had taken shape in the clay beneath her fingers had come from her mental picture of his shirtless, muscled torso, as she'd seen it when he'd worked on her ailing window air conditioner. The resulting piece was the best thing she'd ever done. But that mental picture of him hadn't gone away once the piece had been shaped. It hadn't disappeared when it had been fired, nor once she'd applied that rich, dark charcoal-colored glaze.

No, a half-naked image of Sully had lingered in her brain, refusing to be banished once its usefulness had been at an end. It had teased at her consciousness when she settled into bed for the evening, and flashed across her mind when she should have been concentrating at work. It made her uncomfortable. There had never been anything complicated about their relationship before. The boundaries he'd set were always there, invisible but effective. She'd alternately respected or ignored them, whichever she thought he needed at the time. Until a few nights ago, when those boundaries had been curiously absent, and she'd responded with an instant fire that still astonished her.

"Aha, is that a blush?" Monica asked wickedly. Sauntering over to the desk where Elizabeth sat, she set her cup on the edge and placed her palms on its surface, leaning toward her friend. "C'mon, Elizabeth, 'fess up. You got your inspiration for that piece from some pinups in *Playgirl* magazine, didn't you?" Her laugh was throaty and suggestive.

Ignoring the heat in her cheeks, Elizabeth said primly, "You have a dirty mind."

"You know it, girlfriend. But alas, *yours* isn't dirty enough. As much as it disheartens me, I have to assume that those wonderful, sleek lines in that last piece are the mere result of your genius, and not, say, from a nude model."

Elizabeth picked up the pen and bent farther over the

form she was filling out, wishing she hadn't pulled her hair up in a smooth knot today. It would have been a handy curtain to hide behind, shielding her face so her friend wouldn't know just how close to the truth she was.

"Is that how you scared away your last customer? Pointing out sexual connotations in the painting she was looking at?"

One of Monica's smooth dark brows sailed up. "Now, there's an idea. What do you think Milktoast would think of that as a selling technique?" she said, referring to their boss.

Elizabeth fixed her with a prim look, then ruined the effect by snickering. "I don't think it would be safe to find out."

"Well," the other woman said, distracted for the moment, as Elizabeth had meant her to be, "I'll be glad to come over and help you choose some pieces to take and wow Simon if you like."

"He just offered to look at my work," Elizabeth stressed. "He never guaranteed he'd buy it."

Monica dismissed her protest with a casual wave of her hand. "He'll buy your pottery. Why wouldn't he? You're terrifically talented."

Elizabeth reached out impulsively and covered Monica's hand with her own. "And you're a good friend."

Monica looked at once pleased and discomfited. "Don't be ridiculous." She drew back, picked up her cup again and drank. "I have an eye for talent, that's all." Glancing at the clock, she added, "And a nose for Milktoast. If I don't miss my guess, he'll be in here any second to check on us. I'd better get out there."

Smiling in the wake of her friend's exit, Elizabeth went back to completing the paperwork of her sale. In some ways Monica was as touchy as Sully. Both of them affected the same offhand generosity, then acted insulted if they were thanked for an act.

Her smile fading, she thought of another striking similarity between the two. Both of them were vulnerable, although in very different ways. Monica was more scarred than she'd like to let on by the messy divorce that had ended her second marriage. Sully carried inner scars, too. He'd never talked about his past, but she could smell the despair. He carried it with him, within him. She didn't know what dark and nasty events had shaped his childhood, but she sensed that they would be beyond her comprehension if he did share them. The odds of that happening were slim. She suspected that he was closer to her than to any other person in the world, and the personal information she knew about him was scanty. It had taken her months of prying to discover that his first name was John. He'd left her with no doubt that she wasn't to use it.

She finished the paperwork and left it in a file for Nathan to process. As she rose, the thought occurred to her that she also knew what Sully looked like shirtless, knew that the bruises on his torso disguised a pattern of faded scars that mirrored the wounds within him. She knew how drops of perspiration pooled in the hollow below his throat, before sliding in a sinuous dance down his chest. And most recently she'd discovered what he looked like with his constant guard relaxed a fraction.

Giving herself a mental shake, she reined in her once more wandering thoughts and headed toward the office door. Monica met her just outside the doorway with a manila envelope in her hand and avid curiosity on her face. "This just came for you, by special messenger."

Elizabeth stared at her in surprise, before dropping her gaze to the official-looking envelope. Slowly her hand came up to take it from her friend.

"Well?" Monica said, impatience edging her tone. "Open it. Aren't you dying to know what it is?"

She released the clasp of the envelope and drew the thick sheaf of papers out. Silently she perused the top sheet, then pushed the pile back into the envelope.

"You're trying to punish me, right? Trying to make me suffer for being incurably nosy. What is it, already?"

Slowly Elizabeth's gaze rose from the envelope to her friend. "It's my divorce decree. It's final now, I guess."

Shock showed in Monica's face, followed quickly by contrition. "Gosh, I could kick myself. I didn't mean to—"

A little smile crossed Elizabeth's mouth. "Don't worry about it. I've been expecting it all week."

Her friend watched her face closely. "Did that bastard of an ex-husband have it sent here just to upset you? Because if he did—"

Elizabeth interrupted Monica's dire threat. "No, I told my lawyer I wanted a copy as soon as she received one. She did as I asked, that's all."

Only partially mollified, Monica said, "Well, it sure shoots the day to hell and back, doesn't it?" Crossing quickly to her friend, she slipped her arm around her waist. "Why don't you take the rest of the afternoon off? The last thing you need is to slave away in here until five."

Shaking her head, Elizabeth asked wryly, "And since when did Nathan make you boss? Anyway, I'm fine. This decree finalizes what happened over six months ago. It doesn't change anything."

The blonde surveyed her with shrewd blue eyes. "Honey, the changes in your life are just beginning. And you may think you're fine, but you just got hit with one of those dandy little curves life likes to throw at us. You need a few hours to yourself." As she was talking, she crossed to the closet and got Elizabeth's purse. Then she put a firm hand at the base of her friend's back and guided her from the office toward the back door of the gallery.

Elizabeth dug in her heels. "Monica," she said with vague annoyance, "really, I'm fine. I prefer to stay here and work. What am I supposed to do with the rest of the afternoon, anyway?"

She knew as soon as she'd asked it that the question was a mistake. Her friend's eyes glinted. "Well, when my first divorce was final, I bought out Neiman-Marcus. After my last divorce I spent the weekend in bed with my fitness trainer." Sympathy and wickedness warred in her gaze, and with a strength belied by her slender build, she leaned forward, opened the back door and pushed Elizabeth through it. "You do whichever feels best for you, girlfriend."

Elizabeth turned around and asked frustratedly, "What in heaven's name are you going to tell Nathan?"

Monica gave her a droll look. "Elizabeth, don't you think you'll be happier not knowing?" Then she stepped back and let the door swing shut in her friend's face.

Elizabeth regarded the door with mingled resignation and amusement. There was no changing Monica's mind once she had it made up, and she doubted her ability to make her friend understand that whatever her reactions to her own divorces had been, Elizabeth didn't share them. She would have much preferred working the rest of the day than wandering around trying to fill the hours.

Aware that she no longer had a choice in the matter, she heaved a sigh and walked slowly across the small parking lot to the next street. She could always catch a bus and go home. Nothing was more soothing than thrusting her hands into wet clay, the slick glide of the material against her palms as she shaped it. But her air conditioner functioned sporadically. More likely than not, her small apartment would be sweltering. The thought occurred to her then that she might soon be able to afford a new window unit, if

Simon agreed to take some of her pieces. The prospect was cheering.

The gallery was located in a trendy neighborhood with chic shops and expensive restaurants. Her feet slowed, and she stared into a store window arrayed in the Paris designers' latest ideas of fashion. She had left racks of clothes that looked just like these behind when she'd moved out of Carter's house. She'd taken only those clothes she'd picked out herself, without her ex-husband's suggestions in mind. She'd never felt completely comfortable in the tight, glittery gowns or designer suits. They'd made her feel like a little girl dressing up in her mother's clothes, masquerading as someone else.

Masquerade. Her eyes gazed sightlessly into the next window. That was a good description of her marriage. Carter had been the master at charade, of course, as he'd used his family's money to surround himself with the props he'd thought necessary for the career ladder he was busily climbing in the Dade County D.A.'s office. Country clubs, flashy cars, an extravagant house in a snooty neighborhood and her. A dutiful, stay-at-home wife, who had made it her life's ambition to please her husband. A woman who rarely questioned him, who never disbelieved him, a woman who had been willing to be convinced that everything Carter did was for her.

She winced a little at her reflection in the glass. In short she'd been a fool, but she wouldn't be the first woman to have the stars shaken out of her eyes. Everyone seemed to think she should be mourning the loss of her marriage, but it wasn't sorrow she was experiencing.

She blinked, for the first time becoming aware that she was staring into a window advertising very sheer, very daring lingerie. She jerked her gaze away and continued walking. Her self-confidence had started to trickle back as soon as she'd moved out of Carter's house. Its store could be measured in each step forward she'd taken with her life, her job, her pottery, her new friends.

Turning the corner, she found herself face-to-face with an older woman, heavily made-up, walking three tiny, yapping dogs. The animals insisted on crossing back and forth, making a tangle of their leashes, and their owner scolded them breathlessly.

The sight elicited a giggle from Elizabeth, and a smile lingered on her lips long after she'd passed them. She could imagine how fettered the dogs felt, because she had once been just as restrained, subservient to Carter's wishes. But no longer.

The combination of Miami's heat and humidity was brutal, but she was shielded from the worst of the sun by the colored awnings on the storefronts. Despite its stickiness, the air seemed fresh to Elizabeth. It tasted like…freedom.

A smile split her face as she slowed to a stop in front of a trendy hairstyling salon. She watched for a few minutes as the stylists inside washed, wrapped and snipped hair. One hand crept to her bare neck. Tendrils had escaped the knot she'd pulled her long hair into, and clung damply to her skin. She'd never spent much time on her hair, hadn't had more than trims since she'd been in grade school. She'd worn it the same way for over two decades, long enough to hang to her waist.

Carter had preferred that she wear it up, but had begged her not to cut it. Long hair was a turn-on, he'd said, and he'd loved to watch her take it down at night. The memory had the smile fading from her lips. The act had been part of the contrived ritual he'd made of their sex life, a ritual that she couldn't help noting had been glaringly absent the time she'd walked in on him and his associate.

The doorknob turned beneath her hand, and she looked down startled, unaware of her own movement. She paused for a few seconds, then without further thought, pushed the door open.

"That sounds promising." Kale Lowrey's face was alight with interest, and he leaned forward over the table in the café booth. Tucked away in the back of the seedy diner, the two men were afforded a modicum of privacy. "How soon before Conrad contacts you again?"

Slouched comfortably against the booth cushion, Sully raised one eyebrow mockingly. "You sound eager, Kale."

"I want to play," the other man affirmed. His dark eyes burned with intent. "I'll have a bigger part this time, too."

Sully surveyed the man dispassionately. His lean body radiated the nervous excitement of a racehorse entering the track. "Your part has already been determined. Calm down. Eagerness could get you killed. Or worse, it could get *me* killed."

Kale stared at him for a moment, then leaned back reluctantly. "Nothing gets through that ice in your veins, does it?"

Sully's coffee cup was returned to his saucer with a quiet clink of stoneware. "That's how I stay alive."

Eyes glittering with resentment, Kale sipped from his cup. "Are you going to let me in on your secret? Or should I guess?" He smirked suddenly. "She sure must be something to keep you calm in this line of work."

The rest of the world slowed to a crawl as the words hung between them. Seconds ticked by before Sully lifted his gaze. "What are you talking about?" His tone was level, the words measured, the temper well hidden.

Kale smiled cockily. "I did a little checking on that looker you rushed out of the bar the other night. I know you've got her stashed within grabbing distance. Maybe she's the reason you stay so cool. Maybe if I had some of that…" The rest of his sentence was lost as he suddenly gasped for air. Sully was over the table, his hand around Lowrey's throat, fingers flexing menacingly.

"You don't really want to continue this line of conversation, do you, Lowrey?" Sully asked tonelessly. The man's dark eyes widened, and his hands came up in a vain attempt to break the hold. Sully's fingers tightened, and color washed into the other man's face as he fought for oxygen. "Because it really isn't healthy for you." A tinge of suppressed fury entered his voice as he advised lowly, "We're not going to talk about that woman, and you're not even going to *think* about her. My life, my business. Understood?" He waited for the man's frantic nod before slowly releasing his grip and sinking back in the booth. He sipped at his cup of coffee while Kale coughed and sputtered, gasping for air.

"You...you're a lunatic, you know that?" Kale wheezed. He drew in several deep breaths, his fingers soothing his throat. His eyes glittered angrily. "You're becoming just as crazy as those lowlives you do business with."

"Present company included, I presume."

"You're perfect for this job," Kale said bitterly. "You really are a bastard."

"Yes." There was no humor in the smile Sully gave him. "I really am. I'll let you know when I hear from Conrad again. You'll get your part in the action. But I set the terms."

"You always do," the other man muttered bitterly.

Sully smiled grimly. "That's because I'm in charge, friend. You seem to have a problem remembering that." He reached into his pocket and threw some bills on the table, noting Kale's involuntary flinch at his sudden action. The show of fear gave him no pleasure. Sliding out of the booth, he stood and said, "I'll be in touch," then turned and strode away.

He waited until he was back in his apartment before he allowed himself to examine the scalding burn of fury in his gut. His anger, however, wasn't directed at Lowrey, but at himself. As he showered away the day's sweat and grime from his job, the cold taste of guilt pooled in his mouth.

He turned off the water and stepped out of the small enclosure, drying off with abrupt, almost violent motions. He savagely welcomed the burst of pain in his battered ribs. He ripped away the saturated bandage and discarded it. After a quick examination of the pinkish wound, he decided to leave it bare. He'd known he'd taken a chance bringing Ellie here, to his building. He hadn't seen any other way at the time, and dammit, if he had a chance he wouldn't choose differently. She'd needed him, and he'd helped her the only way he'd been able to.

He'd never considered a time limit, although he'd realized that Ellie's stay next door would have to be brief. But first she'd needed time to heal, and then time to get a job. And then...

And then what, Sullivan? he jeered at his scowling reflection in the tiny mirrored cabinet. And then you just got used to having her around and convinced yourself that there was no harm in her staying? That you could successfully keep her existence from anyone with a reason for nosing around?

He padded from the bathroom to the tiny bedroom, his big muscled body moving without a sound. Carelessly he raked a hand through his dark blond hair, before fastening it back in a short ponytail. He drew on underwear, a pair of faded jeans and a ribbed white tank undershirt. Jamming his feet into a pair of dilapidated sandals, he reflected on the fact that there always seemed to be a price for indulgences. He'd given in to his own need to have Ellie close, for just a short time, and by doing so he could easily have placed her in danger. If Lowrey had discovered her existence, then any number of people could have. The thought of Nushawn trailing her here turned his blood to ice.

He took his keys and carefully locked his apartment. He didn't care what Ellie had to say about it; this was one decision he was going to make for her. He was going to go out, buy a newspaper and find her another apartment. One in a better part of town, with a higher class of neighbors and a cruiser that actually patrolled the street once in a while. A place away from him. A place where she would be safer.

His mouth quirked in a humorless smile. With Ellie across town, they'd both be safer. He moved down the hallway, his ears automatically attuned for any sound coming from her apartment. He was several paces past her door before he stopped and retraced his steps. This time he listened, really listened, and what he heard had the scowl returning, full force.

Silence.

There was no TV, no radio, no sound of Ellie moving about. He couldn't hear her fixing supper, taking a shower or the faint whir of the throwing wheel she had tucked in a corner of the living room. She wasn't home.

He took a quick look at his watch; it was eight already, even later than he'd thought. She was always home by six-thirty, even if she stopped to pick up something to eat. He knew her routine, and it was branded on his mind.

He pulled his keys out and selected a copy of the one he'd given her the day he'd moved her in there. Without compunction, he opened the door and walked into her apartment. It was warm and humid inside, the window unit rattling as it churned out its pitiful efforts to cool the air. It took only a few seconds to ascertain what he already knew. She wasn't there.

He roamed around her small living room. This was ridiculous; Ellie had a right to her own life, and she certainly could decide to change her routine on a whim, if that's what she chose. He knew it was the recent mention of her by Kale that had his instincts twisting with anxiety now, but he wished like hell that he knew where she was.

The window unit sputtered, gave a death rattle and went still. Swearing, Sully strode over to it and gave it a sharp bang with his palm. Unlike on some previous occasions, it failed to respond to that method of resuscitation. His hands on his hips, he surveyed it with all the frustration he was currently feeling. The urgency of his earlier plan for the evening abruptly vanished. Apartment hunting could wait for now. There was no way he was going out while she was missing.

He crossed to her tiny kitchen and yanked open the drawer next to the stove. There, in a neat little bundle, was her meager collection of tools. He grabbed them and returned to the air conditioner. Already the warm air in the apartment was turning more moist, and he could feel his undershirt clinging to him. Kneeling down in front of the unit, he used a screwdriver with barely restrained violence, removing the front panel and setting it ungently on the floor.

He knew he was overreacting. He had no reason to trust Kale, but he didn't think the man would tell anyone about Ellie. At least not yet. He was still jockeying for a high-profile part in the next deal Sully ran for Conrad; hopefully his ambition would keep him silent for a while longer. Grease smeared on Sully's fingers as he thrust them into the dirty coil of the air conditioner. The thought failed to settle his unease. If Kale had found out about Ellie's proximity, there was no telling who else had, or could. He had to get her out of here before someone on the street became too nosy and decided that Sully might be made vulnerable through her. He couldn't do his job with the constant worry of protecting her, as well. He just hoped like hell that she wasn't in need of protection right now.

One hour, he thought grimly, as he carefully cleaned the coil and tightened it again. He'd give her an hour before he went out looking for her, although he hadn't the slightest idea where to start.

And he'd give himself one week. He gave the bolt he was tightening a vicious twist. One week to find her another apartment and move her to a place where she'd be safer, more secure. One week to return to his accustomed solitary way of life.

The wrench slipped, slicing a shallow groove across the fleshy pad of his finger. Blood welled rapidly, but he barely noticed the pain. He was too busy fighting the deeper agony inside.

One week. One week to cut her out of his life again.

Chapter 5

"Where the hell have you been?"

The snarled words, coming from what should have been an empty apartment, startled her, and Elizabeth dropped the sacks she'd been carrying, grasping the doorjamb for support.

Sully stepped out of the shadows in the small living room, a wild pendulum of worry and relief swinging inside him. Although he had no idea what had caused her unusual departure from her normal schedule, the sight of her temporarily allayed his fears. She was obviously all right, although not fully recovered from the scare he'd just given her. Which was nothing, he thought grimly, compared to the one she'd put him through.

Leaning against the doorjamb, she drew a shaky breath. "You're going to put me in an early grave, Sullivan." Bending to retrieve her sacks, she missed the sudden bleakness in his eyes. "With your unexpected appearances, you'd be a smash working with Copperfield."

She dropped her parcels on the love seat, then went back to close the door. Turning to face him, she continued, "Am I to assume from your cordial greeting that you've been waiting for me?"

Tamping down the fear and frustration that had been roiling inside him for the past hour, he lifted a shoulder. "When I checked, you weren't home. Then the air conditioner gave out, and I've been fixing that."

She seemed to really look at him for the first time, and noted the towel he held clenched in one hand. He waited tensely for her to demand to know why he'd come in her apartment in the first place, mentally readying himself to counter her curiosity. But the question never came. Instead, her gaze slid away. She offered a murmured "Thanks," and turned back to her packages.

He stilled, his eyes narrowing. Her movements were awkward, and her manner self-conscious. But there were other differences, more obvious ones.

"What'd you do to your hair?" New bangs teased her forehead, flirting with her dark brows.

She sent him a quick glance over her shoulder. "Cut it." She reached up and released the pins, allowing her hair to topple from its knot. But it didn't cascade to her waist; it fell to a length that just brushed her shoulders when she swung her head. "Do you like it?" Her voice held a hint of anxiety.

Feeling like he should tread carefully without knowing why, he countered, "Do you?"

She ran a hand up to her nape, and let the shorter strands trickle through her fingers. "Yes," she said decidedly. "It feels…free."

His gaze fixed on those strands, and his palms tingled. He could still feel its silkiness when it had been crushed in his palm. To distract his hands from the urge to repeat that action, he transferred the packet of tools from one hand to another, and back again.

"I went shopping, too," she said unnecessarily. She smiled a half embarrassed, half pleased smile. "As a matter of fact, I'm wearing one of my purchases."

She bent over to retrieve the sacks she'd dropped. One had partially spilled its contents, a brilliant tangle of lace and silk. A heat owing nothing to the humid air arrowed deep within him, and a very familiar need coiled in his gut.

"I felt like celebrating tonight. Help me?"

With eyes made deliberately blank, he examined the bottle of champagne she held up. "What are we celebrating?"

She moved to the kitchen to take two glasses from the cupboard, and wrestled with the cork on the bottle. When it popped, the champagne bubbled up and over the narrow neck. Ellie put her lips to the bottle and dammed the flow.

Razor-edged lust sliced into him. The need to escape was just as primal as the need to protect, both her and himself.

"We are celebrating—" she held the bottle high, before lowering it to pour the sparkling liquid into two glasses "—new beginnings."

He remained rooted in place, and she approached him, handing him a glass. His fingers opened to take it, being careful, very careful, not to touch hers. He watched her sip, watched her nose wrinkle as the bubbles tickled it and took a savage breath. One drink. He owed her that much.

Taking a healthy swallow, he asked, "Did you win the lottery?"

She shook her head, and he watched, fascinated, as the ends of her hair swirled across her shoulders. "Better. Much better. I might, just might, have someone interested in stocking some of my pieces."

His pleasure was simple and genuine. "Good for you, Ellie. Who is it?"

She finished the champagne in her glass and crossed to

the kitchen to pour herself some more. "A friend of Monica's. He's got a very upscale shop, just minutes from the gallery. Sells all kinds of handmade gifts, crafts and such. He said he'd take a look at them. I know I shouldn't get my hopes up but..." She raised shining eyes to his. "This could be the break I've been waiting for, Sully."

He'd never grown used to the emotion that overcame him at the sight of her, dreams in her eyes. He didn't have a name for it, but it filled a place in him that was usually empty and cold. "You deserve it, kid. I've always known you were talented."

She laughed then, and drank recklessly. "Let's just hope that Simon Boze thinks so."

He cradled his glass in his palm as she finished off the contents in hers. "Maybe we should go out and do this in style."

"I don't want to go out." She brought the bottle to him and tipped some more champagne in his glass, before refilling her own. Then, kicking off her sandals, she sat down on the carpet, leaning against the love seat. "You can help me celebrate right here."

"If you don't take it easy with that bottle, tomorrow your head's going to feel like a jackhammer's taken up residence."

She merely smiled at him, noticeably more relaxed than she'd been when she'd entered the apartment. Toasting him with her glass, she said, "Just this once, I'm willing to take that chance."

He drank, while reflecting on what else he could do. "We need to get some food in you."

"I bought some meat, cheese and crackers. If you ask real nicely, I'll let you cut them up."

He crossed the room and dug through her bags cautiously, finally finding one with a market's name emblazoned across it. He was as familiar with her kitchen as he was with his own, and before long he had a plate loaded with slices of summer sausage, cheese and crackers. He took it over to her and set it on the floor in front of her. Not trusting her to eat without persuasion, he took the glass out of her hand, set it out of her reach and sandwiched some of the cheese and meat between two crackers. He handed it to her silently.

She was surveying him with amusement dancing in her eyes. "You sure know how to ruin a good buzz."

"Yeah, I'm a fun hater. Just eat."

She obeyed, taking the food he offered and sinking her teeth into it. Crumbs scattered over her lips, and Sully's body went tense. It would be so easy to dip his head, to clean those crumbs away with a swipe of his tongue. Too easy.

Releasing a breath, he got up and went back to the kitchen, needing distance to clear his head. He busied himself cleaning up the small mess he'd created when he'd prepared the food, and pushed her packages aside. He saw the envelope among the bags and picked it up. "What's this?"

She glanced up, diverted from the task of piling a slice of cheese on a piece of meat. "That, my friend, is the start of a whole new life."

His brows pulled together, and he reached in to take the papers out and scan them. Emotion shifted inside him. His eyes squeezed shut once, hard, then he opened them and directed a glance at the woman on the floor.

"I'm sorry, Ellie." The words were as difficult to say as they were to mean, and they sounded hollow, even to his ears. There might have been sorrow circling in the emotions swirling through him, but it wasn't for the fact that her marriage was officially over. It was for the pain he knew she was feeling. The relief that flickered inside him made him the worst kind of SOB. He pushed the knowledge aside. He was too aware of his own flaws to give them much consideration.

"You should be," she said, brushing the crumbs from her mouth. "You cut enough food here for a half-dozen people, and you haven't taken a bite yet. Are you trying to get me fat, as well as sober?"

He stared hard at her. He was a man unused to offering comfort, but she meant too much to him not to try. Slowly he returned to sit down on the floor across from her, leaning against the footrest of the recliner. "I know it's hard for you," he said, searching for words. "But you made the right decision. And I'm here." He stopped, made even more uncomfortable by her clear, direct gaze when it met his. His next words were little more than a mutter. "If you need me."

His heart hitched in his chest when she smiled at him, one of those brilliant, thousand-watt smiles that never failed to make him feel like he was going under for the third time. He tore his gaze away and dragged some oxygen into his lungs. And felt her hand cup his jaw.

"Sully." He didn't look at her, couldn't. He knew he'd see the tenderness of her voice reflected in her eyes. He remained motionless, every nerve in his body screaming with tension. His first impulse, as always, was to pull away from that soft touch. It would leave a lingering warmth in its wake that was impossible to erase, impossible to forget.

"You've always been there. You're such a wonderful friend. But you're wrong."

He reached up for her wrist and moved her hand away, even as he directed his gaze back to hers. When he released her, she slid her fingers down to catch his palm. Leaning forward, she said seriously, "You think I'm sad about the divorce being final. I'm not."

Her words almost diverted his attention from her fingers

linking through his. Almost. "It's normal to feel sad when a marriage is over."

"It was over six months ago. This just finalizes it. Thanks to Monica, I had several hours this afternoon to sort out just what I am feeling."

"And that is?"

She paused, as if considering her words. "Free. I've been building a new life for myself, but it was still like there was something hovering over me. Now that the divorce is final, there's this incredible sense of anticipation." A laugh bubbled out of her. "It's like I have all these paths open to me, and each one leads to a new adventure. It's…exhilarating."

He pulled his hand away from hers under the pretext of reaching for his glass. Suddenly his throat was parched. "That's the champagne talking."

"Thanks to you, I didn't have enough champagne to let it do my talking."

He took a hasty gulp, blaming his dry throat on the heat in the apartment. Although his tinkering had restored the air conditioner to its normally pitiful level of function, its efforts against the midsummer Miami heat and humidity were barely adequate. But he couldn't quite delude himself into believing that this suffocating feeling, this sense of his skin growing too tight, was due to the weather. No, the cause of those sensations sat a mere foot away, surveying him with wide, earnest brown eyes.

"I owe you so much."

Her words slammed into him, through him, leaving a ragged trail of pain. "No," he said with barely restrained violence, "you don't."

"But I do. Denying it might make you more comfortable, but it doesn't make it less true. I'm not exactly proud of the person I became while I was married to Carter."

"Your ex-husband is an arrogant ass. You're not to blame for his being a skirt-sniffing hound."

Her lips curved slightly, and she raised the glass to her face, pressed her cheek against its coolness. "I gave up control to him. He couldn't take it. I had to give it to him. That's hard to forgive myself for." She raised her earnest gaze to his. "Do you believe that everything happens for a reason, Sully?"

The glass had left a path of glistening moisture on her cheek. He knew from exquisite memory just how soft the skin there would be. It took all his control to divert his attention back to her words.

"No," he said flatly. "Things happen because of other people, or nature. There's no fate or luck involved. They happen. We just go on."

She cocked her head, as if weighing his words. "But we have to learn from what happens, don't we? So we avoid making the same mistakes over again?"

She was talking about lessons. Yeah, he'd learned plenty over the years. How to dodge a fist, how to drink enough water to fool your stomach into thinking it was full. And later, how to duck bullets, how to live a lie until there were even times he started to believe it himself. "Yeah," he answered finally. "Life is full of lessons."

She nodded. "Exactly. As much as I hate what happened to me while I was married, it's worth it if it makes me stronger."

He snatched the glass out of her hand and drained it, considered hurling it against the wall for a satisfying smash. The act would match his mood, savage and destructive. He didn't like to think about Ellie's marriage, didn't like to think about the hurt and pain she'd suffered before she'd picked up the pieces and moved on. And she'd done just that. It wouldn't have mattered whether he'd found her that day in the mall or not. She had a core of strength in her that she was only now beginning to recognize, but one he'd been aware of ten years ago.

She began to laugh, and his gaze jerked to hers. She covered her mouth with the back of her hand, but giggles escaped nevertheless. "It just occurred to me," she said between gasps, "that if Carter marries Robbie—that's his associate's name, by the way, short for 'Roberta'—she'll be...Robbie Robinson." She made an effort to stifle her mirth, but finally dropped her hand and let it shake her, doubling over with fits of laughter.

He watched her grimly. Hysteria, he thought, and for a fleeting moment felt panic. This woman's tears had the ability to completely unman him, but he couldn't leave her, alone and hurting. He reached out tentatively, almost drew back his hand, then forced himself to curl an arm awkwardly around her shoulder. "It's okay. It'll get better."

She shook her head, but the laughter still streamed out. "I'm not...it's not..."

His mouth flattened, and he went up on his knees, pulling her to meet him with his grasp on her shoulders. He cupped her head in his palm, guided it to his chest and skated a thumb down her spine soothingly. He ignored the tiny pinpoints of heat that burst inside him at every point where they touched and clenched his teeth. He could ignore it for her. He *would* ignore it.

Her shoulders were shaking silently, and each small movement battered him with regret. Not for the end of her marriage to Robinson, but for Ellie. She hadn't deserved to be hurt the way that soulless bastard had hurt her. But he, better than anyone, knew that few of them got what they deserved. So he held her, aware that there was little else he could do. Just as there was little he could do about the punch of sensation her touch sent flooding through him.

When he felt her shudders lessening, he pressed a small space between them, and steeled himself for the sight of the tears he'd see on her face. Her lips still quivered slightly, but the smile they held was real. And although her eyes were bright, there was no sign of dampness in them.

Suspicion lanced through him, and his brows drew together. "Ellie..."

"Sorry," she said, making an obvious attempt at seriousness. "It just struck me as funny. You know Carter—he likes things very elegant and proper. 'Robbie Robinson' just doesn't sound..." Something in his face must have warned her, and she paused, eyeing him carefully. With a note of realization in her voice, she said, "You thought I was upset."

He muttered an oath, and dropped his hands, but just as quickly, she skimmed her palms up his chest to his shoulders. The muscles there were bunched tight. When he would have shrugged her away, her fingers gripped him.

"When are you going to believe me, I wonder?" she said in a whisper. The sound was silk, dragged across the sandpaper of his nerves. "I'm over him. I *am,* Sully. He can't hurt me anymore, because I won't let him." Her gaze melded with his, and he remained frozen in place, ignoring the alarms clanging in his head.

"You don't have to protect me anymore." Her lips curved, just inches from his. His breath was trapped in his lungs, and he felt as though he were strangling. "But thank you for trying."

The kiss she brushed across his lips was as light as down, and was merely an impulsive gesture from one friend to another. He knew that, but he couldn't prevent the response that rocketed through his system.

Her mouth hesitated, a fraction away, and for an instant he forgot to don that careful, blank mask that served him so well. When her eyes widened in shocked discovery, he knew she'd recognized the ravages from the simultaneous assault of pleasure and pain lingering on his face. His jaw clamped tight, and he moved to rise. But he was stopped by the return of her lips.

Every muscle in his body stiffened in disbelief. She was leaning into him, her mouth pressing against his in a shy, untutored way that had his senses roaring. While the first kiss may have been casual, this one was laced with something completely unfamiliar. He drew in her scent in a greedy, guilty swallow while he struggled beneath twin layers of desperation and temptation.

Because it *was* temptation, beyond what any reasonable man should be asked to bear, that gripped him by the throat now. He'd spent a decade avoiding even the most casual of touches from her. It took only the slightest taste to shred those careful restraints. Need, too long denied, bubbled up within him and boiled over in a froth of scorching intensity. He would go straight to hell for even thinking of taking what she was offering so sweetly. His arms clamped around her, drawing her off balance, and his hands slid into the cool, silky mass of her hair. He could already feel the flames of perdition lapping at him.

Because he kissed her back.

His mouth hungry and demanding, he returned her kiss with all the pent-up longing that had simmered inside him for years. Just once, a dim promise sounded in his mind. Just for a moment.

Her taste was sinfully sweet, and her flavor traced through his senses. His tongue stabbed into her mouth, and he swallowed her startled gasp. But then hers came to meet his, in a timid, velvet glide, and need clawed through him, hot and urgent.

He cradled the back of her head in one palm, and slid the other down the soft, silky column of her throat. He could feel her pulse scrambling beneath his fingertips, and the evidence of her excitement was heady. His own blood was pounding, hammering him from the inside. The thick, humid air in the apartment had glossed her skin with the barest hint of moisture. Without thinking, he tore his mouth away from hers to sip at the dampness at the base of her throat. It wasn't enough.

More. The need for more slashed through him like a ruthless blade. He'd never been a man to overheat, much less burn, but he was burning now, as if a lit match had been set to the short fuse of his control. This was Ellie. His longing for her had grown too deep, been buried too long. He wanted to lay her back and unwrap her clothes and feel every inch of her skin against his. He wanted to discover the different flavors she'd have, beneath her wrist, behind her knee and in the sweet, damp cleft between her legs. He slid the tip of his tongue up the cord of her neck and took her lobe between his teeth, all the while struggling to tuck that savage need back down out of sight. Back to where he'd always kept it hidden, secret and burning.

Because this was Ellie.

He could no more follow this path than he could physically hurt her. Because the end result would be the same. He'd long ago come to terms with the kind of place he could have in her life. He'd set the boundaries cautiously, and he was comfortable within them. If he'd chafed at times under the corrosive pain of wanting more, he'd learned to accept it. His role in Ellie's life was as her friend, her protector. And even though the ball of heat lodged in his belly threatened to erupt, he had to protect her from this. From him.

A shudder racked him, and he released her lips, then found himself momentarily sidetracked by the hint of perfume behind her ear. Dragging her scent into his starved lungs, he closed his eyes for an instant, bracing himself for the feeling of loss that would follow the instant he pulled away.

Then Ellie's fingers slipped inside the narrow straps of

his undershirt and tangled in the hair on his chest. Sully's breath hissed out as a thousand points of flame burst beneath his skin. He threw his head back and fought for control.

The way she was touching him was both heaven and hell. It was more, far more than he'd ever let himself hope for. He had an illogical need to soak up the dizzying experience like a famished man, unsure of his next meal, devouring the food before him. He was letting himself in for a lifetime of torment, because now the memories would linger, of the softness of her fingertips over his rougher skin, the flick of her fingernail against his nipple, making his breath shudder. The memories would surely be enough to drive him slowly insane.

"Ellie." His voice was raspy with checked passion, passion that threatened to combust when she opened her eyes slowly. They were cloudy with desire, and the sight was like taking a fist to the gut. He'd imagined them like this a thousand times—would remember them so countless more. It took a strength of will he hadn't known he possessed to go on. "We need to stop."

Her gaze searched his, and the moment stretched, hung between them. As if she was unaware of their movement, her fingers continued to stroke and knead his chest, his shoulders, his biceps. And he knew his response was transparent.

"You want me," she whispered, her tone a little drugged, a little awed. "I didn't believe it. I don't think anyone has ever really wanted me before."

He closed his eyes as the vulnerability leaked through her words and squeezed his heart. His next words were tinged with desperation. "This is a mistake."

Her touch slowed, gentled, until it was an unbearably sensual glide. Her eyes drifted shut again, and she whispered against his lips, "I've made my share of mistakes, Sully. This doesn't feel like one of them."

Her mouth opened on his, and his lips were just as eager, making a mockery of his earlier words. He had a faint, wild thought that he had a cartoon figure on each shoulder, one an angel and one complete with horns and tail, each urging him toward different actions. He was very much afraid the demon was winning.

He returned her kiss with a hint of the violent emotion that had been dammed inside him for a decade. Her lips opened readily under his, returning his kiss with an unchecked, passionate need that nearly undid him. Her fingers tugged frustratedly at the hem of his undershirt, and then, when she'd released it from the waistband of his jeans, her hands slid up his torso. He swallowed her purr of feline pleasure.

Too late he tried to stem her actions as she dragged the undershirt over his head. While he was still untangling his arms, her fingers were releasing the thong that kept his hair tied back.

He took a huge, ragged breath. It was impossible, he thought dimly, as she rubbed her mouth over his, fingers entwined with the hair at his nape, to give her what she was asking for. He couldn't bear to be the cause of any more hurt in her life.

He caught both her hands in one of his and drew them down to rest between their bodies. Leaning his forehead against hers, he braced himself for the tearing agony of moving away from her. But she wiggled her hands from his and released the first button on her dress. Every muscle in his body froze. His eyes were shut; he didn't dare open them. But he knew as surely as if the sight were burned on his brain what she was doing. Barely daring to breathe, he felt the movements of her fingers as they moved again. Quick, impatient motions as she released the next button and the next. They slowed as the next one was slid from its hole, and stumbled a little over the next. His lungs were seared; he needed oxygen. He dragged in some air while her image danced behind his closed eyelids. The fragrance that was uniquely Ellie filled his senses. The warning signals shrieking inside him were no less insistent, but he gambled with one more moment. One more touch. Just one.

He smoothed his hand down the satiny line of her throat, pushed her hair back to follow the path with his mouth. Her taste was a kick to his system, a sinful flavor that pumped straight to his blood. Her gasp stoked his own reaction. Then his lips met silk, and immediately, involuntarily, his eyes opened.

His strangled oath was a curse, a prayer. She was wearing one of the frothy silky things he'd glimpsed in one of the sacks. A lacy border ran along its top. The lace clung to the skin above her breasts, and with shaking fingers he pulled it away and replaced it with his lips. Her hips jerked at the contact, grazing his stiffened manhood, where it was restrained behind his jeans. This time he couldn't prevent a groan.

The sides of her opened dress framed her torso. He didn't know the name of the invitation she was wearing; surely it was invented for the pure deviltry of driving men crazy. A one-piece pink garment, all silk and lace, it teased at the shadows and curves beneath. Narrow straps, barely more than ribbons, were all that held it in place, and it was obvious she wore nothing beneath it.

He couldn't seem to swallow around the boulder-sized knot in his throat. Even squeezing his eyes shut again didn't help. The sight of Ellie encased in bits of lace and silk was emblazoned on his mind.

She moved against him then, and his eyes snapped open. Impatiently she shrugged her dress off her shoulders, and let it slide to her hips, where it caught in a momentary resistance to gravity. Then she leaned forward and pressed against him, and nothing separated them but a tempting amount of silk.

Need streaked through him, making a mockery of his earlier intention. One arm clamped beneath her hips, and he pulled her closer, higher, so he could drag the dress down her legs to discard it. Then she was close, as close as she could be, closer than he'd ever dared let her. And still it wasn't enough.

Her hands explored the muscles of his back, tracing each vertebra and following their descending path. Her fingertips grazed the skin just inside the waistband of his jeans, making his body jolt against hers, then shudder.

Perhaps if she'd shown even a hint of hesitation, he would have been able to hold to his original intention and let her go. But her mouth was greedy, and her hands were never still. She charted every inch of his chest, tangling in the mat of hair there, teasing at the nipples. The muscles in his shoulders and arms were tested and stroked, and the softness of her cheek was rubbed against his far rougher chin, dragged back and forth over and over, as if she couldn't get enough of the sensation.

His hand discovered the silky expanse of thigh he'd uncovered, and he stroked the smoothness there. She was soft, incredibly so, and he could feel the taut whisper of muscle beneath the skin. His fingers grazed higher, nearer to her core of heat. Her breathing stuttered as his caress grew bolder, and she pressed closer against him, the tips of her breasts stabbing against his chest, separated by only the sheer fabric.

"Ellie," he muttered, burying his face into her hair. Desire stabbed through him, piercing deep. Tremors rippled between them, passing from one to the other. Need had never taken this form before, never been honed to such a keen edge. He wanted every inch of her; he wanted the satisfaction of knowing that she craved him just as desperately. With every shiver, with every gasp, she was telling him she did.

He cupped her silk-clad bottom in both hands, squeezing the rounded curves, fingertips skirting the lacy edge. He sat back and brought her between his thighs. Using his teeth in a primitive taste for flesh, he dragged one ribbon down her shoulder and uncovered one tautly beaded breast. Her gasp tangled in her throat when he drew her nipple into his mouth, and lashed it with his tongue.

"Sully." Her voice was pure sex, drugged, filled with longing. His eyes slitted open, and the sight of her threatened to peel away the veneer that restrained his violent need. Her fingers were twined in his hair, and her back was arched, that dark mass of hair spilling over her shoulders. Watching Ellie in pleasure was unspeakably erotic. The fading light sheened on her damp skin, making it gleam. She was innocently responsive, every touch, every shiver spasming her face, her reaction impossible to hide. He wanted more. He wanted to watch her face as he drew her higher, ever higher, then he wanted to watch her shatter. He wanted to see her as he slid inside her, wanted to watch her as they both rode the crest of pleasure until they crashed together.

His fingers cupped and stroked and smoothed, the fingers just grazing her damp heat. Ellie let out a throaty moan as he pressed one palm against the moist silk covering her mound, his fingers rubbing. He found a row of snaps there, loosened them, and then her heated flesh was bare to him. His fingertips dampened with her moisture, he slid them over her in a firm, repetitive motion that sent her hurtling over the edge.

Her hips twisted against his touch, and his name was a strangled cry on her lips. The sound of it filled a void he hadn't known he had, fed a fire that was burning out of control. When her body would have relaxed against him, the rush of fulfillment weakening her limbs, he slid a finger inside her and shuddered as her inner contractions worked against it. She moaned again, and twisted against his touch, pressing rhythmically against him. He pushed the silky garment up over her hips, pulled the other strap down her arm, so the pink froth of fabric caught below her breasts. Then he dragged her chest against his, closing his eyes at the exquisite sensation.

"Sully," she moaned against his mouth, her fingers clutching, tight and frantic on his shoulders. "More."

The word was a demand, a plea, and he could no more deny her than he could himself. He released her, wringing a frustrated whimper from her lips, and undid his jeans. Her hands went to help, and her eager touch made him groan out loud. He shimmied the jeans over his hips, down his legs, then stopped her before she could dispense with them altogether. He fumbled with the contents of his pocket and drew out the packet of protection. It was almost rendered unnecessary when she made a soft sound of discovery and wrapped tender, curious fingers around him.

He endured the sweet torment for only seconds. Already he could feel the tightness coiling, the red mist swimming before his eyes. It couldn't be over. Not yet. He finally understood how a man could need a woman until she was a keen-edged addiction, a fire in the blood. As the greed welled inside him, he moved her hands away and finished the ritual, then reached for her again. His mouth on hers was just short of savage, as all his hunger sprang forth from where it had been tightly leashed.

Her breath came in low whimpers. His own felt like it was burning in his chest. He'd never known a need could be so fierce, the desire to give and take so brutally keen. He leaned his back against the footrest of the recliner, then arranged her thighs to straddle his hips. Her eyelids fluttered open, her confusion at the position obvious.

With an arm around her hips he lifted her, and guided his shaft into her wet heat. Every muscle clenched when he heard her cry out, felt her delicate inner adjustments to his invasion. With great heaving breaths, he dragged his eyes open and focused on her. Every flicker of reaction showed on her face, every flash of emotion. She was moving against him, and with his hands on her hips, he held her steady as he thrust hard up inside her.

Her ragged cry mingled with his harsh groan. Her eyes flew open, glazed and huge, to lock with his. Her lips trembled as she tried to speak, but there was only another shuddering moan. His world narrowed until she was the only point in it. She was all he could see, all he could feel. His hips pistoned steadily against her, and the flush of arousal hued her chest, her throat. She twined her arms more tightly around his neck, and the sound of his name trembling on her lips drew him closer to the peak.

"Let go, baby," he urged, his voice harsh and ragged. "Just let go. Ellie." Her name was a prayer on his lips. "Sweet Ellie."

He pressed her hips firmly against him and drove upward hard, deep, and she screamed his name. There was primitive pleasure in the bite of her nails on his shoulders, of her body straining, shuddering against his. He watched the climax contort her features, felt the frantic contractions of her lower body, and something burst inside him. His hips pumped against hers with ferocious demand as he allowed himself to follow her, hurtling headlong into pleasure.

Chapter 6

It was the humidity in the air that finally awakened her. Elizabeth twisted on the bed, her eyes fluttering open at the sense of discomfort. She lay still for a moment, gauging her surroundings groggily. Her air conditioner wasn't powerful enough to push any cool air into her bedroom, and the ceiling fan did little more than circulate the humidity.

She pushed her tousled hair back, pausing for a moment as her fingers rediscovered the new length. When she disentangled herself from the bedsheet, her eyes came fully open. She was naked.

The discovery brought her completely awake, her memory restored. Her gaze swept the room, though she'd already sensed it was empty. There was no sign of Sully.

She went to the closet and took out a short-sleeved, thigh-length robe and slipped it on, tying it quickly. She went out and looked in the kitchen, the living room, but she was alone in the apartment.

Releasing a breath she hadn't been aware of holding, she

leaned weakly against the wall. Sully. Her mind grappled with the memories of last night. The mental images were enough to suffuse her with a heat that owed nothing to the temperature.

The emotions swirled and eddied within her, each one receding to be replaced with the next. Embarrassment, shock and secret, sweet slivers of delight accompanied each mental fragment. She'd acted completely out of character. Her senses had been altered, but not by the alcohol. They'd been altered by Sully himself.

Her eyes slid shut, seeing again that flash of hunger on his face, so sharp and keen it had pierced her, as well. For that one second, just for an instant, she'd caught sight of a mingled pain and pleasure so intense it had taken her breath away. And though their first kiss had been steeped in gratitude and friendship, the second one had been so much more.

She drew in a deep, shaky breath. As unusual as her actions had been last night, there was no regret mingling in the welter of her emotions. Maybe there was something more compelling than the sight of a man, *her best friend,* looking like he'd die for the chance to touch her, but she couldn't imagine it. It had been enthralling, tempting and so sexy that even the memory had the power to send fresh shivers of pleasure through her.

Her eyes opened, and her head tipped back to rest against the wall. She could be dishonest with herself and pretend that last night had resulted from a combination of too much champagne on an empty stomach and the effects of receiving the divorce papers. But she'd promised herself long ago not to fall into the trap of self-delusion ever again. Last night had happened because she'd wanted it to. And, perhaps even more amazing, because Sully had wanted *her.*

Touching him had been an incredible opportunity to run her hands over that broad torso and freely examine the jut of bone and sinewy muscle. His skin had burned beneath her fingertips, seeming to come to life in her hands the same way the clay formed and shaped to her touch.

There had been none of the props Carter had always used to orchestrate their lovemaking, no candles or soft music. Just need, edgy and fierce, which had passed from Sully to her, and back again. She'd never before experienced a touch so urgent it hinted at roughness, from a man visibly fighting at control. Although she could feel her face wash hotly at the memory, she'd taken a great deal of pleasure tempting Sully to give up that control, and had reveled with him in its loss.

Her arms slipped around her waist and hugged tight. If she tried hard enough, she could almost feel the hard clasp of Sully's arms. Which was silly, of course, because Sully was *gone*.

Why had he left, she wondered, and what did his absence mean? It had only been a few short hours ago that he'd last reached for her, tucking her beneath that hard, muscled body and sliding deep within her again.

She brushed her hair back from her face with a shaking hand, remembering easily the renewed rush of desire, the racking pleasure. Each time he'd been above her, she'd felt surrounded by his size and strength, yet curiously protected. But at the end it had been her arms sheltering him, his harsh groans sounding in her ear, her hands soothing his shaking body. There was no shame in the memories of last night, only quicksilver darts of delight. With the exception of her mother, Sully knew her better than any other person in the world. Last night had brought them closer than mere friends, and there could be no turning back.

A splinter of unease stabbed her then. It was Saturday, so neither of them had to worry about work, but he could have had an errand to run. It was possible that he had slipped from her bed and gone home to shower and change, but the longer she thought about it, the more troubled she grew.

What if he hadn't left because he had to, but because he wanted to?

Her teeth worried her bottom lip. Sully was unpredictable in any circumstances. She couldn't guess how he would feel about this change in their relationship. She may not have recognized just what it was Sully felt for her until she'd surprised it on his face last night, but she'd been troubled enough in recent weeks with similar thoughts of him to realize that their relationship had been headed into uncharted territory.

The unease intensified, and a frown formed between her brows. Every bit of intuition she had told her that it hadn't been need that had driven Sully from her bed while she lay sleeping. What it was, she was very much afraid, had been guilt.

Her eyes slid closed, and she let her head lightly bang against the wall. Although she had no regrets about last night, she could well imagine that Sully would have. He was too entrenched in his imagined role as her protector not to feel like he'd relinquished the role by making love to her. He'd use that guilt as a buttress between them, and he was a master at constructing near impenetrable fortresses around his emotions. He'd pull away from her.

The thought of losing Sully's friendship sent sheets of ice over her skin. Bereft. That's what she'd be without him in her life. Although he kept large portions of himself strictly walled off from the world, she'd lay odds that she was closer to him than he'd ever allowed anyone else to be.

Determination stiffened her spine. She wasn't going to let him drift away from her, and she wouldn't allow last night to affect their friendship. If it had been the lovemaking that had scared him away, then she'd ruthlessly cull that aspect from their friendship. She ignored the sharp pang at the thought. No matter how satisfying, how magical last night had been for her, she was mature enough to realize it might not have meant the same for him. And it wasn't worth pursuing if it was going to cost her the one thing she valued above all else. Sully's friendship.

Her plan of action decided, she pushed away from the wall to head for the shower. She was going to find Sully and force him to talk about his feelings. And it would be tough going, because getting him to talk at *all* was a chore. But they'd have this out, one way or another, because they had too much to lose otherwise.

Elizabeth was halfway to the bathroom when she heard a sound in the hallway outside her apartment. She reversed course immediately. If it was Sully out there, she wanted to catch him before he could leave. Or before he could hole up in his apartment.

She pulled the door open and stepped through it, almost colliding with the man poised in front of it. Her head tipped back, her eyes widened and her mind went abruptly blank.

"Carter," she said faintly.

Carter Robinson, Dade County's most promising young prosecutor, smoothed an imaginary wrinkle from his discreetly pin-striped suit and gave her a grave smile.

"Hello, Beth."

Faint annoyance rose at his use of that nickname. She'd never cared for it. On the heels of that thought came another. A suit? On a Saturday, in Miami, in July? Only Carter would dress for court to visit his wife.

His *ex*-wife.

"I'm sure you're surprised to see me here." One hand slipped halfway into his pocket, the movement too studied to be casual. He was the picture of a rapidly rising young professional. Where was a photographer for *GQ* when you needed one? she thought cynically. Her gaze slid beyond his shoulder to the door of the corner apartment. She wondered if Sully was behind that door, and she wondered what he was feeling. Was he remembering last night? Was he wishing it had never happened? Or that it would happen again?

"I'm sorry for coming by unannounced, but I'm on my way home from a breakfast appointment, and it was imperative that I speak to you."

Elizabeth's gaze jerked away from Sully's door and fastened on Carter's face. It took a moment longer for her concentration to shift, as well. "I'm sorry, Carter," she said politely. "But I was on my way out."

His brow arched. "Before you've dressed?"

Her gaze fell to her attire, and she felt a flush blooming. Self-consciously she tightened the sash on her robe. "I meant I was just getting ready to go out."

"Surely you can spare a few moments, Beth," he said persuasively. "I can guarantee you, this is important. For both of us."

With one final glance at Sully's door, Elizabeth reluctantly stepped back and allowed Carter to precede her into the apartment. Once the door was closed, she felt a measure of impatience creep in. How long would it take to get rid of the man? Long enough to hear him out, she imagined, to discover whatever it was he wanted.

And he did want something, or he wouldn't be here, wouldn't be calling her "Beth" in that ingratiating tone he used when he needed something from her. That was probably why she'd grown to detest the name. He'd preferred to call her "Elizabeth"; it was more dignified, she imagined, more befitting the wife of a proper young attorney. He'd only shortened the name when he was trying to persuade her that something he was intent on doing was in her best interests. The ploy had worked for a time, *a long time,* she acknowledged wryly, and once she'd begun to see through it she had gotten a little more stubborn. In the face of her resistance, his manner had always changed quickly enough, first to lecturing, then to cool and remote in the blink of an eye.

He'd seated himself on the love seat, and was surveying her apartment with faint distaste. The sight was enough to evaporate the trace of uneasiness she felt at standing before him half-dressed. She banished the half-formed idea of excusing herself and going in for a quick change. This was her home, *hers,* darn it, and she wasn't going to let him make her feel uncomfortable. He was the intruder here, and the sooner she heard him out, the sooner he'd be gone.

And when he was gone, she could get back to her own life. To Sully.

"My God, Beth, I had no idea."

She perched on the edge of the recliner, being careful to keep the robe covering as much skin as possible. The edge of pity tinging Carter's voice set her blood simmering. Still her voice was politely inquiring when she asked, "Had no idea of what, Carter?"

He gestured to her apartment. "The manner in which you've been relegated to living, the depths to which you've had to sink...."

Something about the set of her head, the raise of her brows must have warned him, for he dropped his hand and concluded, "Well, I blame myself."

"Do you?"

He nodded his dark head soberly. "Of course. I should have checked up on you after you stormed out of our home that way. Instead of listening to your idiot lawyer blather about keeping my distance, I should have made sure you had the means to live comfortably. It never occurred to me that your wounded pride would stand in the way of asking me for the money you so obviously needed."

Taking a deep breath, Elizabeth silently counted to ten.

He blamed himself that she'd chosen to live in what he would consider squalor, but there was no acceptance of blame for what had driven her from their home, their marriage, in the first place. What kind of man would feel so horrified by her small but clean apartment, but feel no compunction about betraying his marriage vows?

Immediately the answer came to her. One who was no kind of man at all. One whose word meant nothing, to whom promises were as insubstantial as cotton candy. A man to whom wealth, power and their accumulation reigned supreme, to whom people existed merely as a means to an end. A man she was fervently glad to be free of.

"You're mistaking pride for confidence," she said tartly. "This place meets my needs. I didn't ask anything from you because I didn't want it. I still don't."

Her words didn't alter the expression on his face, and Elizabeth set her teeth. "You've cut your hair."

His tone was almost accusatory, and her hand went to the shorter length automatically. "I'm hoping it will be cooler."

"I prefer it long."

She shot him a disbelieving look. "Carter, what possible difference could your preferences make to me?"

He had the grace to look discomfited, and quickly changed the subject. "So tell me what you've been doing. You acquired a lawyer, and moved forward with divorce proceedings so quickly. I never had a real opportunity to discuss your plans with you."

Shaking her head in bemusement, she looked at the man she'd once loved. Married. Lived with. No doubt he'd managed to convince himself of the truth of whatever story he'd concocted for his friends and colleagues about the end of their marriage. A story that would render him some heartfelt sympathy and cast her in the guise of a troubled young wife who hadn't known her own mind. But it didn't really matter. Nothing about Carter Robinson mattered to her any-more.

The impatience was back; she wanted him gone so she could get back to the man who *did* matter to her. In ways she'd never imagined. "Why don't we just skip to the part where you tell me why you're here?" she suggested. "It would save us both some time. As I said earlier, I need to go out."

Annoyance crossed his finely boned features. "Can't we be civilized about this, Elizabeth? I wouldn't mind dis-cussing this over coffee, if you have it."

"Sorry, Carter," she lied, "but I don't. I haven't gotten to the store lately."

He fixed a gaze on her then, one she returned steadily. Smoothing his hands over the creases in his trousers, he settled more comfortably against the cushions of the love seat. "Very well. The truth is, our split couldn't have hap-pened at a worse time."

"I didn't know there were opportune times for discov-ering a husband's unfaithfulness," Elizabeth responded with mock politeness.

The polished handsomeness slipped a little, and his voice sharpened. "What I meant was, in the last few months I've received quite a bit of publicity. The press really devoted quite a bit of space to my recent trial."

He paused expectantly, but Elizabeth only shrugged and shook her head. She didn't need to feign ignorance. Fol-lowing Carter's exploits in the press hadn't been high on her list of priorities.

"It was a high-profile case. I was lucky to be assigned to it."

Luck, she guessed, had had nothing to do with it. Carter had never been content to leave his career in the hands of something so capricious. No doubt he'd done quite a bit of maneuvering behind the scenes to get the assignment.

He arranged his features into that boyish mixture of humility and pride that had once softened her. "I won a conviction against Councilman Stanton. Bribery, corruption, solicitation of illegal funds..." His voice was laced with satisfaction. "He's been stripped of his office, of course. Sentencing hasn't been determined yet, but he's heading for a long stretch in prison."

Because his expectant pause seemed to demand it, she responded, "I'm sure your superiors were very pleased."

He gave an exultant laugh, showing even, white teeth. "They weren't the only ones impressed. I've been approached by some extremely powerful people in the city. They want me to run for the vacant council position."

"Actually," Elizabeth said dryly, "I have no trouble at all picturing you in politics, Carter."

That brilliant smile flashed again. "Your confidence is nice, but premature. I'm just being considered at this point. However, if these individuals decide to back me, I'd be at a distinct advantage." After a brief hesitation he added, "Of course, I haven't yet decided whether I'm ready to leave the prosecutor's office. I'd have to balance my need to serve justice against the greater good for the city."

She managed, barely, to avoid rolling her eyes. Apparently Carter had been reading too much of his own press. Sneaking a look at the clock, she wondered how she could hurry him along. She somehow doubted that Sully was next door, but wouldn't be satisfied until she'd checked. And if he wasn't, she was going to drive herself slowly insane while she waited for him to return. But that prospect was infinitely more appealing than being driven crazy by Carter's self-serving monologue.

Reaching a decision, she rose. "Well, it was certainly interesting to have you come and share your news, Carter, but I really don't see what this has to do with me."

He leaned forward, his blue eyes intent. "It has everything to do with you, Elizabeth. If I am chosen as a city council candidate, the press is going to find you very interesting news.''

She went still, staring at him blankly. Then slowly, weakly, she sank back down to her seat. "Oh, Lord."

He nodded grimly. "Exactly. But this doesn't have to be too disagreeable, does it? All we have to do is work out the story between us, and be sure that you adhere to it exactly when you have to answer questions from the press."

"A story?" Anger bubbled just below the surface of her words. "I suppose the truth just wouldn't be appropriate under the circumstances, would it?"

His tone was reproving. "Now, Elizabeth, please be reasonable. You have as much to lose from making that unpleasantness public as I do."

Glaring at him she returned, "I don't see how."

Two hard knocks interrupted them, and before she could do more than stand, the knob turned and Sully walked into the room. Instantly her knees weakened. He'd gone home and changed. As usual his hard features were closed and remote. It was probably fervent imagination that had her believing that his gaze lingered on her a fraction too long. But there was no mistaking the steel in his voice when his attention shifted to the man seated in the room.

"What are you doing here?"

Carter's expression was not nearly as difficult to read. He'd never made a secret of his loathing for Elizabeth's friend. "I think that question would be more appropriately addressed to you. Elizabeth invited me in, and we were in the middle of a very important discussion." Suspicion laced his tone when he added, "What gives you the right to barge into her apartment?"

"That's enough." Her voice was sharp enough to draw both men's gazes to her. They reminded her of two dogs, circling and defending territory marked as their own. No, Sully would be more appropriately likened to a wolf—a creature who had long lived on the outskirts of polite society and who had no interest in the trappings of civility that marked most people. Without knowing why, she knew that he was dangerously close to pouncing, like a predator in sight of prey. She rose and crossed to him, putting her hand on his arm. It was tense with bunched muscles, and her fingers stroked soothingly.

"Carter stopped in to discuss something with me, that's all." She waited for his gaze to turn to hers. "I was looking for you."

Not a flicker of expression showed on his face, but his gaze was hot, lambent, when it moved over her. "Why don't you go get dressed?" His voice was a low rumble. When she didn't move, he urged, "Go ahead. I'll entertain your…guest…until you get back."

She didn't move until she felt the subtle relaxation of muscle under her fingertips. Then, when she sensed that the danger of the moment had passed, she dropped her hand and looked at Carter.

"Excuse me for a few minutes, would you?"

Both men watched her leave the room. Only after the bedroom door had closed behind her did Sully fix his gaze back on Robinson.

"What the hell are you doing here?" he snarled softly.

"My question to you, exactly. I suppose it was too much to ask that Elizabeth had developed a better taste in friends since we parted."

Because his fists itched, Sully unclenched them and tucked his fingers in his jeans pockets to keep them from reaching for the other man's neck. "Elizabeth had a need for her friends after what you did to her."

Robinson's features tightened. "You'd be the last one to whom I'd choose to explain the intricacies of a marriage."

Sully snorted. "Intricacies? That's a new word for it. Tell me, just how is Roberta, anyway?"

Wariness flickered over Robinson's face. "I can't fathom why you would have any interest in my associate's well-being."

Sully rocked back on his heels. "Well, it's true I've never met her, but I know her type. She seems to be a broad with her eye on the main chance." He scratched his jaw, which he hadn't bothered to shave that morning. "Of course, it wasn't her eye she had on you when Ellie walked in, now, was it?"

Robinson bounced from the love seat and took a step toward him. Sully's weight shifted to the balls of his feet as he readied himself, anticipating the man's attack, *wanting* it. How sweet it would be, finally, to have an excuse to plow his fist into that pretty-boy face. How long he'd waited for just such an occasion to present itself.

"You both seem to be getting reacquainted."

Ellie's voice was dry, and it filtered sluggishly through his haze of expectancy. He turned his head to look at her and his mouth went dry. She'd made a quick change; she obviously hadn't trusted them to be left alone long. She'd exchanged the robe for a one-piece short outfit that buttoned down the front. His gaze lingered overlong on those buttons, and a hot ball of need bloomed in his belly. He knew somehow that she wasn't wearing any more under that outfit than she had been under the robe.

She turned to her ex-husband. "Carter, I don't mean to be rude, but I really am busy today. I'd appreciate it if you'd go."

His jaw was rigid. "We haven't finished our discussion." Faced with her implacable gaze, his mouth tightened and he reached into his pocket and withdrew a single sheet of paper and held it out to her. "If the press comes around, stick with the facts outlined there and we'll be fine."

She didn't even glance at the sheet he'd handed her. "Facts?" she repeated dubiously.

"What makes you think she'll do you any favors, Robinson?" Sully drawled.

She sent him a sharp look meant to silence him. In recognition of it, he subsided. She'd changed rapidly since moving out of Robinson's house, not to the extent where she'd acquired a different personality, but enough to allow her natural traits full rein. If he wasn't so on edge at finding Robinson in her apartment, he'd be delighted to watch her exhibit that stubborn determination she was capable of.

Her attention went back to Robinson. "I don't need a script to tell the truth, Carter." She stemmed his protest with one hand. "If the issue arises, I'll simply tell them that we parted amicably because of irreconcilable differences." Her tone was dry. "That should be politically correct enough to stem curiosity."

Frustration stamped Robinson's face. "Elizabeth, I really believe I know best here. If you would just listen to me…"

"I don't listen to you anymore, Carter. I listen to me." She thumped herself on the chest for emphasis. "I make my own decisions, and I decide what's right. You're just going to have to trust me."

One side of Sully's mouth curled up in a satisfied smile as her words made a direct hit. Robinson looked ready to argue, but he clearly didn't want to do so in front of Sully. "Elizabeth, if you would be so kind as to send your…friend…on his way, we can continue discussing this in a rational manner."

The transformation that came over Ellie at his words caught Sully's attention, held it. It was as if every muscle in her body stiffened, and if he'd been a more fanciful man he'd swear there were sparks shooting from her eyes. She marched over to Sully and slipped her hand through the crook of his elbow. "My *friend* doesn't need to get on his way. He's home, or close to it. He lives next door. And you don't seem to understand." Her tone was fierce. "This discussion is closed."

Robinson noted the placement of that small hand on Sully's arm and his handsome features twisted. "I should have known." His gaze slid to Sully's. "Couldn't resist taking advantage of a vulnerable woman, could you? What did you plan? Move her near you and play on her emotions, thinking she'll eventually turn to you so you can..."

"That's enough, Carter!" Elizabeth's voice slashed through the tension in the room. She went to the door and opened it. "I want you to leave. Now." Her gaze was unyielding. Slowly, grudgingly the man moved to the door.

He stopped when Sully said, dulcet voiced, "Take my advice, Robinson...stay away from Ellie. I stood by while you trashed her life once. The next time you won't walk away."

Robinson turned around and smiled, a mere twitch of his lips, but his eyes were murderous. "My mistake was in not eliminating you long ago."

Sully bared his teeth in return.

"Believe me, better men than you have tried."

Chapter 7

Ellie shut the door behind Carter and leaned her forehead against its smooth surface. Sully found himself wishing the moment could stretch and expand until he had enough hours, enough courage, to face her. It was humbling to realize that he'd rather face a rain of bullets than this slip of a woman. Terrifying to admit that this was one of the few moments in his life when he'd felt true fear.

To give his hands something to do, he drew out a cigarette and lit it. The smoke he inhaled seared his throat, already inexplicably dry. He braced himself for the moment she'd turn to him, the hurt and accusation unveiled in her eyes. He told himself he was ready for it, but he knew he lied. How could he be ready to face Ellie when he hadn't been able to face himself in the mirror that morning? Like a coward he'd wanted to put a little distance between them until he *could* face her, but then he'd heard Robinson's voice in her apartment and thinking hadn't been part of the equation. He'd functioned purely on reaction, something he'd been a little too prone to lately.

"Well." She turned to look at him. "That was certainly interesting."

He drew the smoke deeply into his lungs, and his gaze narrowed. "How long had he been here?"

She lifted a shoulder. "Not long. Ten minutes or so. I suspect I would have had a more difficult time getting rid of him if you hadn't come in when you did."

He surveyed the glowing tip of his cigarette. "Then I'm not sorry I busted in on you. Last night you said you were through with him, so I didn't figure you'd want him here." He took another quick puff, and his gaze shifted, couldn't seem to find a place to land.

"I haven't changed my mind since last night. Not about anything."

Her words attracted his attention to her as surely as metal filings to a magnet. She relaxed her shoulders against the door and eyed him steadily. "I missed you this morning."

The smoke seemed to expand in his lungs, squeezing out the oxygen, and he coughed harshly, trying to restore air to those strangled organs. Her words were the last he'd expected to hear from her. Taking one measured breath, he tasted relief, and worse, hope, an emotion he had no right to.

Finding it too difficult to face her, his gaze dropped back to the cigarette he held. "I figured you'd need some time...." His voice trailed off and he swallowed the rest of the thought. Time to get over the anger, the hurt, the sense of betrayal. Time to find a way to tell him he'd shattered her trust, and to get the hell out of her life.

He put the cigarette to his lips and sucked in savagely. Time to tell him all the things he'd been telling himself ever since he'd woken up this morning with her sweet, soft body still draped over his. Time for him to find the strength to do the right thing. Finally.

He turned away, crossing to the ashtray. It was on a small

table next to the recliner, within reach for him when he was there. She'd always done that—tried to make things easier for him. He stubbed the cigarette out with short, violent motions.

"I don't need time, Sully." Her voice sounded softly behind him. "I've had over ten years."

His gaze snapped back to hers. She was surveying him with wide, guileless eyes. "Last night was a mistake," he said, his voice expressionless. He watched the hurt and the doubt flicker across her face, and a spear of despair pierced him. When he continued, the words were ragged and hoarse.

"You were vulnerable, and I took advantage in the worst way possible. I betrayed our friendship."

Now it was she who seemed to have difficulty meeting his gaze. "I just wanted to tell you…it's okay." Her voice stumbled, then grew stronger as she went on, still looking anywhere but at him. "I figured it out when you were gone this morning, and I understand your regret." Her fleeting smile was rueful. "I've never been the kind of woman a man finds exciting in bed."

In three quick strides he was before her, lifting her chin with a crooked finger. His face close to hers, he growled, "Did I act like a man who didn't find you exciting?"

Her gaze melded with his, and her eyes…damn her, her eyes went soft and dreamy, much like they'd been after he'd made love to her last night. Every time.

"No," she whispered, and the wondering, wistful sound of her voice rasped across the jagged edges of his conscience and caught.

He watched, entranced, as her lips fought a tremble. His thumb obeyed an edict all of its own when it skated lightly across the full bottom one, exerted just enough pressure to part it. Her mouth was close, so close to his, and the memory of how it would taste reared up inside him, inciting him to put the memory to a test, to make another.

He snatched his hand away and shoved it into his pocket. He walked to the barred window, putting a safe distance between them. And knowing all the time that it wasn't safe, wasn't safe at all. The entire city could be between them, and he'd feel the same compulsion to see her, talk to her. Taste her. She was seared into his mind, and last night had just carved the futile craving deeper.

"I went out to buy a paper to check out apartment listings." He gave a short, mirthless laugh. "God knows I've never agreed with Robinson before, but he's right about one thing. This neighborhood is no kind of place for you."

"Because it's close to you?" she asked shrewdly.

He forced himself to face her then, and hoped the truth of her remark didn't show on his face. "It was okay while you got on your feet again, but you're fine now, Ellie. You're ready to move on, and thanks to the divorce settlement, you've got the means to do it."

Although the sudden hurt on her face was enough to stab deep, he went on doggedly. "I mean, this neighborhood stinks. There was an armed robbery down the street last night, did you know that? It was the third this month. You don't belong here. You deserve better." He'd grown up in worse, far worse, and had lived like this for so long he didn't even notice it anymore. But having Ellie here was like watching a fragile flower bloom in the middle of a cesspool.

"Don't you do this to me."

Her voice was shaking again, but now it was threaded with anger. It was reflected in her eyes, in the jerky steps she took. "If you can't live with what happened last night, have the courage to say so. Don't just try to push me away, out of your life, so you don't have to deal with it."

He stared at her, remaining stubbornly silent. Like that

would be possible. If he'd had the courage, he'd have done it a decade ago. If he hadn't harbored selfish, guilty desires that had festered inside him for years, he wouldn't find himself now pulled in deeper, faster, than he'd ever thought to go.

"Sully." Her hand went to his arm. She took a deep breath, as if marshaling her defenses. "I value your friendship too much to let last night come between us."

He couldn't look at her. Her voice misted over him like fog, seeping through his senses.

"If making love with me was something you didn't want, *don't* want, then I can accept that. But if it's guilt that's making you pull away, then we have a problem. Because I won't let you, or anyone else, make decisions for me ever again."

He stared out the window. The view was dispirited—another equally dilapidated building, across a dingy alley. "You can't blame me for wanting to protect you."

"Yes, I can." He did look at her then, saw the passion light her eyes, the determination tilt her chin. "I can if your protective instincts are going to cost me my dearest friend. I won't let that happen. It's your decision whether we continue our relationships as friends, or as—" her voice faltered a little, but her gaze didn't "—as lovers. But one way or the other, our relationship will continue. So go ahead and choose."

Her voice held a hint of dare, mixed with vulnerability. He'd never seen her like this before, and it was all too easy to be captivated. Like a miserly man hoarding gold coins, he tucked this memory away in his mental collection of images of her—cheeks flushed, eyes bright, and the tough sound of her words at odds with lips that couldn't quite fight a quiver.

Swamped with emotion, his voice was low and strained. "My wanting you to find a better place to live doesn't have anything to do with last night.'' That statement, at least, wasn't quite a lie. ''I've been thinking about it for a while. Where you live has never affected us. It won't now.''

''Liar.'' Her hand dropped away. ''I know you too well, Sullivan. When someone gets too close, you shut down. You'll let the physical distance be the start of an emotional one.''

Desperation flared, igniting temper. Because the truth of her words stung, he dismissed them. ''That's bull.''

''No, it isn't. But I'll tell you what. I'll make a deal with you.''

He glared at her, his mind swirling with possible ways to convince her to leave. He couldn't tell her that being this close to him could be dangerous for her, and he *wouldn't* admit that she was partially right. ''What kind of deal?''

''I'll look for another apartment, if you promise that when I move, we'll still see just as much of each other. Still your choice,'' she added hastily, flags of color unfurling in her cheeks, ''what direction our...friendship takes. But one way or another, you have to promise.''

He turned away from her and propped his fist on the window jamb, leaning against it. Frustration had tension knotting his shoulders. ''You've got the wrong man. I don't make promises.'' What were promises, really, but a broken string of words handed to kids too young and gullible to know better? Meaningless phrases that turned to ashes in the light of day. He'd ceased believing in promises, or much else, when he was six. And he'd never uttered one. The thought of doing so now, to this woman, had panic licking up his spine.

Her reflection in the glass folded her arms across her chest. ''Then I'm not going anywhere.''

He looked out at the bleak view, but her image mirrored over it in the window. The way she did in his life. He'd always pretended that she was allowed to touch it on no more than the surface, just as her reflection rippled across the top of the glass. Last night had shattered that pretense forever.

There had to be a way out of this mess. Instincts honed from a lifetime of training told him that things with Conrad were about to take a deadly turn. Everything he'd been waiting for was about to break, and if he didn't get her out of here, there was a possibility that she could be pulled right into the middle of it.

He saw her reflection move closer, get lost behind his. Her touch was light, tentative. Her palm glided up his back to stop at his shoulder. It shouldn't have been enough to have the need pooling in his gut. He could already feel the heat spreading through his veins. He squeezed his eyes shut tightly for a moment, as the familiar wanting, guilt and desperation warred within him.

"All right." The words were ripped from his throat. "I already said nothing has to change. Your move isn't going to affect our friendship."

Her fingers shifted on his shoulder, gently kneading the skin there. "I think you forgot something." Her voice was soft, and much too close to his ear when she prompted, "We'll see each other as often as we do now."

"Yes."

The waiting stretched between them; she wasn't going to provide him with any more cues. The words had to come from him. They shouldn't have been so difficult, so terrifying to speak.

"I promise."

Sully pushed open the door stenciled with the words Parole and Community Services. He walked past the desk clerk, who gave him a barely perceptible nod. He wound his way through the tiny cubicles until he reached a hallway. He walked down the hall and stopped before room 121, and knocked once at the door.

It opened immediately, and the man who appeared reached out to shake his hand, observing him closely. "Sullivan. How's it been going?"

"Okay," he said laconically. His gaze went past Ted Baker, his "parole officer," to Kale, who was slouched in a chair watching them. "What's he doing here?"

"I'm part of this case, too, Sullivan," Kale retorted. "Much as you'd like to forget it."

Ted brushed a nervous hand over his thinning gray hair and quickly shut the door. He motioned Sully to a seat. "Gentlemen, working an interagency investigation is difficult enough without our getting territorial."

"This is a DEA case," Sully said flatly. "I had my cover set up eighteen months before customs decided to horn in."

"Customs has every right to be involved," Kale interjected. "Smuggling's our jurisdiction, remember. You guys should have consulted us to begin with."

"Customs' job is to cooperate with other federal agencies, Lowrey, not to sabotage them." The man flushed and looked away. The anger that had been simmering in Sully for days reached the boiling point, and he leaned forward in his chair. "If I hear from one of my runners again that you contradicted my orders, your part in this case will be over."

Both men ignored Ted's feeble protests. "You don't have the authority to make those kinds of decisions, Sullivan," Lowrey said.

"It's my ass on the line out there. This job is risky enough without you stirring things up. Forget about being a customs superhero and concentrate on playing the role assigned to you. I'd just as soon make it out of the case alive."

"Gentlemen, please." Ted's lined face was wearing a

light sheen of perspiration. He took off his thin gold-rimmed glasses and polished them thoroughly. ''O'Shea will be here any minute. Let's try to be professional.''

Not for the first time, Ted's fussy manner grated on Sully's nerves. The man was said to be a whiz with technology, but in this investigation he was the detail man, reporting directly to O'Shea. The thought of Ted's immediate superior had Sully subsiding. Collin O'Shea was head of operations for the Drug Enforcement Administration in Florida. He'd been brought in five years ago to clean up the state's DEA office and clear it of the charges of corruption that continued to taint it. He was tough, but he was fair. He'd been a hell of a field agent himself before he'd gone into supervision, and Sully respected him. The man hadn't forgotten what it was like in the field, and he went to bat for his agents. Because of the scope of this investigation, he'd been personally involved from the beginning, had handpicked Sully to be the operating agent.

He reached for his pack of cigarettes and drew one out, ignoring Kale's glower. Lighting it, he took a long drag. Because he knew it would annoy Lowrey, he blew a perfect trio of rings and admired them as they hung in the air.

''Do you have to smoke in here?'' Kale complained querulously. ''My asthma has been giving me fits lately. And secondhand smoke kills, too, you know.''

''Not reliably.'' Sully shifted the cigarette to his other hand, so the smoke trailed in a different direction.

Ted spoke up nervously. ''This is a public building, Sullivan. There are rules.''

''Where's a cop when you need one?''

The door opened then, and Collin O'Shea stepped inside. Sully knew the man had registered the tension in the room with just one quick sweep of his narrowed green gaze. ''Gentlemen.'' He nodded to each of the men, pulled up a chair, shrugged out of his suit jacket and loosened his tie.

Sully watched approvingly. That was another thing he liked about O'Shea. He might be a suit now, but he made no bones about finding the apparel confining.

"Talk to me, Sully." That piercing green gaze was turned in his direction. "What have you got?"

"Lowrey reported my last meeting with Conrad?"

"Of course I did," Kale interjected. His sarcasm was thinly veiled. "Go-between is my role, remember?"

"He told us. Got the date set yet?"

"Conrad contacted me today. We set a meeting for next week."

O'Shea regarded him silently for a moment. "Think this is it?"

"I'm pretty sure. That trip to Colombia was just to let the guy take a look at me. This should be the real thing."

"I want in on this, Mr. O'Shea," Lowrey said. He looked from Sully to the other man. "I've got just as much right to be at this meeting as he does."

"Not a chance," Sully replied flatly.

O'Shea frowned slightly. "I don't like the idea of you walking into that meeting alone."

Sully brought the cigarette to his lips and inhaled deeply. "These guys aren't a bunch of dumb dopers. They can't be, and run an operation this size. Bringing an unknown to a meeting this delicate would be like signing my own death warrant."

"I insist on being included."

Everyone's gaze went to Lowrey. The nervous energy came off the man in waves. "Where's Kennedy? Why wasn't he included in this meeting? I'm sure he'd agree with me." Kennedy was Lowrey's superior, a suit from customs, who, if he'd ever been out from behind a desk, had developed a highly selective memory about field work. His agency wasn't exactly immune to corruption, but he'd never be heard to admit it.

"Kennedy couldn't be here today," Ted put in.

Sully leaned back in his chair in disgust while the men argued. He'd never be accused of being a team player. He was a loner, solitary by nature, peculiarly suited to the job he did. He'd been paired on several occasions, however, with other sharp DEA agents. He wished heartily, for what seemed the thousandth time, that if he had to be given a partner in this investigation, it had been one of them.

He watched Lowrey unkindly. Instead, he was saddled with an inexperienced kid, still wet behind the ears, who was going to make a mistake because he was too damn ambitious for his own good. A partner he'd never asked for, had never wanted. God save him from interagency politics.

"I'll take it up with Kennedy myself," O'Shea said. He turned his attention to Sully. "You'll wear the transmitter." It wasn't a question and Sully didn't take it as such.

He nodded. He'd begun wearing the compact voice transmitter under his shirt once he'd earned Conrad's trust. It allowed the agents stationed nearby to hear and document his conversations.

O'Shea spoke to the other men. "Sully's right. I can't figure any other way for him. He has to go alone."

"I demand that you reconsider." Lowrey's voice trembled with fury.

O'Shea responded levelly, "I'll discuss my decision with your supervisor. We'll debrief again after the meeting." He nodded a dismissal to his assistant, as well, and Ted picked up a briefcase. He walked silently to the door and held it for Lowrey, who shoved past him without a word. Ted closed the door quietly behind them.

O'Shea turned back to Sully, one brow cocked. "Been busy making friends again?"

Unamused, he leaned toward the desk and stubbed his

cigarette out on a glass paperweight. "Kale's tracking mud on my case."

The other man grunted. "Be thankful you only have to deal with him. Tiptoeing around the egos of the other agencies involved is enough to give me another bleeding ulcer."

He was talking about interagency politics, a field agent's nightmare. The more far-reaching the ramifications of this case got to be, the more other agencies jockeyed for position to get a piece of it. Sully knew the kind of pressure that was being put on O'Shea, but also knew that sometimes an agent got more recognition from his superiors for showing up or embarrassing DEA than for the bust. That fact was enough to keep him wary of Lowrey.

"Do you know where the meeting will be held?"

Sully shook his head. "They'll pick me up."

"Cautious little SOBs," O'Shea muttered. He grinned wolfishly. "I brought a little something that will help, though." He dug in his pocket and took out what looked like a silver dollar, flipping it through the air to Sully. "For luck. You're going to need lots of it."

Turning it over in his fingers, Sully studied it, then raised a questioning gaze to the other man.

Slouching down in his chair, O'Shea crossed one leg over another. "Sweetest little tracking device you've ever seen, encased in what appears to be a genuine U.S.-issued silver dollar."

"Who'll be covering me?" Sully asked. There was always a team of backup agents lurking quietly in the shadows whenever he and Conrad did business. One of its tasks was to take pictures to be used as evidence when the case was broken; another was to listen to and record the conversations picked up by the transmitter Sully wore. Those agents would also provide his safety net, should the case go bad. He rarely spent time considering the fact that, by the time something went wrong, his backup would probably be too late to do him any good. That was a risk of the business; he'd accepted that in training at the academy in Quantico.

"Constantine and Hansen. They'll be able to follow you to hell and back when you carry that." He nodded toward the tracking device Sully was slipping into his pocket. His face grew serious as he added, "That's as safe as I can make it."

"You're the one who told me there's no safe way to do deep cover."

"That's right. So don't be a hero. I don't want to lose another agent. If this meeting smells bad, make an excuse and try to get the hell out."

Sully nodded. He'd known the risks when he'd taken this case, had known that few agents would have been willing or able to put their lives on hold for two years and chance a cover as deep as the one he'd taken. The knowledge came without rancor. The surroundings he lived in now weren't much different than those where he'd been raised. Better actually, then the last few places he'd lived as a kid, when his mother's age and life-style had taken their toll on the looks and body she'd always cashed in on. This assignment had been his choice; he hadn't thought twice about accepting it. It had belonged to someone with little other life, and nothing to lose. Which described him perfectly.

Had described him perfectly. A mental vision of Ellie swam across his mind. It would be stupid to believe that their one night together over two weeks ago would change anything between them. He wouldn't, *couldn't,* let it. She hadn't given him the chance to utter the apologies she deserved, had instead offered to continue a sexual relationship with him in the most innocently erotic way possible.

Sweat beaded on his forehead despite the efforts of the window air conditioner. A true depiction of hell wasn't scorching flames for all eternity. It was being given one night with the woman he wanted most in the world, but deserved the least. It was the mental reruns of every little detail: how small her body had felt under his; the stunned look on her face as the first orgasm had shuddered through her; the tight inner clenching that had milked his own climax. It was having her offer him everything he'd ever wanted, and never dared hope for.

It was having Ellie within reach, yet knowing that to take what she was offering would shatter the few illusions he still had about himself.

"Sully?"

He shifted his gaze to O'Shea's. "What?"

"Don't take any unnecessary risks. This case is getting to be a minefield."

O'Shea's words echoed in his head long after he'd left him. A minefield. One false step, and everything could be blown to bits. It was a good description of this investigation.

He lit a cigarette and peered through the smoke at the bus rumbling to a stop at the corner. It was bitterly ironic that the word described his relationship with Ellie even better than it did this case.

Chapter 8

Elizabeth dropped onto the love seat and surveyed her new home through exhausted eyes. Odd that she hadn't remembered how her puny belongings could take so much time to pack, and could be so troublesome to move. Boxes still littered the hardwood floor, some still taped, and others half-unpacked in an effort to find her set of tools. Sully was sitting cross-legged in the corner, putting her potter's wheel together.

The sight had a smile of satisfaction crossing her lips. Despite his promise, she'd been in no real hurry to move away from him, and had driven him half-crazy by rejecting a dozen places. Apartment hunting had forced them together. It had been her hope that the time would put Sully more at ease with the situation and with her.

Oh, he'd really hated it, she thought, the way she'd cornered him so neatly. She hadn't even known she was capable of such guile, but the prospect of having him disappear from her life completely had made her desperate. He was too important to her and, darn it, he needed her, too, whether he admitted it or not. She had a feeling that he let down his guard with her, more so than with anyone else. Although she didn't know what caused those defenses, she was certain that living without relief within the walls he'd erected would gradually consume him.

With anyone else she might doubt the promise he'd made, offered under duress. But she trusted his word implicitly. He might not have any experience with promises, but his word would be gold. Although she didn't flatter herself that he looked upon their night together as anything more than a mistake, she thought their friendship was important enough for him to want to keep her in his life, as well.

Wistfully her gaze lingered on him, enjoying the opportunity to look her fill. This apartment came with central air, a fact she could almost mourn now, because it meant that there was no reason for him to take off his T-shirt. Quick heat suffused her cheeks at the thought. Her lovemaking with Sully three weeks ago seemed to have eroded some of that prudishness Monica so often teased her about.

The realization didn't shame her. She'd grown accustomed to blaming herself for Carter's restrained lovemaking. She'd just assumed that she wasn't the sort of woman to drive men to rough hands and desperate need. But her experience with Sully had proved her wrong. He'd wanted her just that frantically, been driven to take her over and over. In doing so, he'd also managed to topple one or two of her inhibitions.

Of course, she mused wryly, her womanly self-esteem would have improved even more if he hadn't seemed to revert to their former relationship so effortlessly.

"Still want it right here?" Sully hefted the wheel and set it down in one corner.

She nodded her head in satisfaction. "Perfect."

As soon as the landlady had opened the door to this place, she'd known it would be hers. Gleaming hardwood floors without a carpet in sight stretched across an apartment easily three times the size of her old one. But it hadn't been the size that had captivated her; it had been the light streaming in through the triple set of windows.

She'd been able to picture her wheel in the corner where Sully had just set it, the kiln on the far wall. Her furnishings looked meager in the open area, but she was pleased to have the space to operate her wheel without covering everything in the room to protect it from spattering clay. Her drop cloth would save the hardwood floor, and she could work whenever it suited her now, and not worry about the cleanup afterward.

The phone rang then, startling both of them. It had been hooked up only the day before. She picked up the receiver, expecting to hear Monica's voice, then got a little weak-kneed when the caller identified himself.

"Simon, hello."

Sully watched her impassively as she carried on what was essentially a one-sided conversation with Simon Boze. He talked, she listened. Except for a dazed "That sounds wonderful" repeated several times, she had no memory at all of what she said.

"Next week, then," she repeated his parting phrase, and hung up the phone, stunned.

Sully approached her. "Good news?"

She slumped against the wall and looked at him blankly. "Simon's going to take them. Every piece. And not on consignment, either—he wants to buy them outright. And he wants to know if I have an agent. I don't even know where to find agents, or what they do, or... And he has a contact he said might be interested in more pieces...." Her eyes flew to Sully's then, panicked. "Oh, my Lord, I don't have any other pieces. I gave them all to him. What am I going to do when he asks again for more and I have to tell him that...?''

His low voice was soothing. ''If you need more, you'll make them. Just like always.'' He crooked a smile then, endearingly appealing because it was so rare. ''You made it, kid.''

She stared at him a moment longer, then reality broke through the haze and she let out a whoop. ''He bought all my pieces!'' She launched herself at him, and he had no choice but to catch her as she threw her arms around his hard middle and hugged tight. She was laughing out loud, and his answering chuckle was a rumble in her ear. ''You're not going to be able to stand me now that I'm a big shot, Sullivan,'' she teased, tilting her head back to look up at him.

He heaved a mock sigh. ''Yeah, I can see you're going to be a real pain.''

Her hair brushed against her bare shoulders as she shook her head dramatically. ''You'll be doing my bidding constantly, fetching and carrying for me....'' Another laugh gurgled out of her as her gaze swept her apartment. ''But then, that won't be much different, will it?''

Her gaze bounced back to his, inviting him to share the joke, but the amusement had faded from his expression. And his eyes...she swallowed once, hard, and suddenly her merriment faded away, as well. Because in his eyes was such longing, such intense hunger, that she was staggered.

Her heart kicked once, hard, then settled into a staccato beat. A solid ball of heat formed in her stomach. She knew now that it would take only a touch of his lips for that heat to explode, sending fiery ribbons unfurling through her system. Her head fell back, her eyes slid half-closed, partly at the memory, partly in invitation. Sully's hand left her waist and rose to hover near her shoulder. She forgot to breathe when he lifted the hair that brushed her bare skin and rubbed the strands between his fingers.

When the doorbell pealed, she started, moving closer to him. For an instant the heat from his body seared hers. He stiffened, then both hands went to her shoulders and he deliberately set her away. When she saw his face, she could have wept at the loss. The shield was firmly back in place.

She took another few seconds before turning around. It had been so easy for him to let her go, just a mental click, and he seemed able to shut those feelings off. And there *had* been feelings there, dammit, she knew she hadn't been mistaken. She may be naive, but she wasn't totally stupid. Although at this moment she felt both.

"Well, hello there." The feline purr could only belong to Monica, and Elizabeth turned reluctantly, pasting a wan smile on her face. Her friend was sizing Sully up like a horse breeder looking over a new stallion, and the analogy wasn't amusing. For the first time since she'd met her, Elizabeth had an urge to pluck out Monica's perfectly coiffed hair. Strand by strand.

"Careful. I don't think he'll stand for you checking his teeth."

Monica slanted a look at her, and what she must have seen on her friend's face had her eyebrows climbing. Her gaze went back to Sully, even more assessing this time. She flashed her perfect smile. "Hello, I'm Monica Pruett, single, unattached and very available. And you are...?" Her sentence dangled delicately.

Elizabeth tucked her fingers into the pockets of her shorts, where they wouldn't damage her friend's face. "Monica, this is Sully, a very good friend of mine."

Monica's gaze traveled between the two of them. "How good?"

Elizabeth's voice was firm. "Very good."

She made a moue of disappointment, then shrugged

good-naturedly. "I'd sure like to see where you find your friends."

Sully nodded to the woman, then crossed to pick up some boxes. "I'll just take these into the bedroom and stack them up for you."

"Good idea," Monica murmured, watching him appreciatively. When he was gone she said, "Quick, lock the door behind him."

"Monica, honestly," Elizabeth said shakily.

The other woman strolled into the apartment. "Hon, I'm just saying that particular type of man is perfectly suited for the boudoir." She craned her neck, scanning the rooms comically. "You don't have any other 'good friends' around here, do you? Ones who just might be partial to tall, gorgeous blondes with a weakness for muscles?"

"Sorry."

"Well, there's no reason for you to be sorry, Elizabeth. None at all. In fact, I'd say there's plenty of reason for you to…celebrate!" In one smooth motion she pulled a bottle of champagne from the bag she was carrying, and beamed a dazzling smile. "I talked to Simon earlier, and girlfriend, you have made it!"

Elizabeth returned her enthusiastic hug. Monica's real pleasure for her made her ashamed of her earlier uncharitable urges. "You found out quickly. I just talked to Simon myself." A thought struck her then, and she pulled back, a frown teasing her brow. "You didn't have anything to do with this, did you? I mean, when you called Simon…"

Monica waved her anxiety away. "I pulled the info out of him—you know how I am. But if you're thinking I swayed his decision in your favor, don't worry. This is his business, and I never had that kind of influence over him, anyway. Not that I ever gave it my all, you understand." One eye closed in a suggestive wink, and Elizabeth felt a pang of relief. She appreciated her friend having given her

Simon's name, but it was important to her that these sales be deserved, and wholly based on her ability.

Her voice was warm with sincerity. "Thank you so much, Monica. If it hadn't been for you, I never would have heard of Simon Boze."

Monica made a dismissive gesture. "I just pointed you in his direction. You had the talent, and that's the biggest part." She held up the bottle. "Where should I put this? It's partly for your celebration, and partly for a housewarming gift."

"We could open it now if I had any idea which box the glasses were in."

Monica walked over to the kitchen counter and set the bottle on it. "Nope, I can't stay. Have a hair appointment in about an hour, and then my masseuse is going to spend the rest of the afternoon working out the kinks I get from those damn high heels Nathan insists on." Briskly she walked back to Elizabeth, kissed her on the cheek and turned for the door. "But I will be back this evening to take you out to celebrate in style." She turned before leaving and added, as if in afterthought, "Feel free to bring tall, blond and studly in there along with you. I've never been one to believe that three's necessarily a crowd." Her smile smug, she sailed through the door.

Sully entered the room in search of more boxes, then straightened when he saw Elizabeth was alone. "Your friend gone already?"

"Lucky for you," she informed him. "I think she wanted to strap you down and clone you. Have any DNA you could spare?"

He frowned and muttered something about a man-eater.

"She's not, really." Elizabeth defended her friend automatically. "She's just been hurt and that's her...defense." She couldn't interpret the look he gave her, but she was struck again by how much her two friends were alike. Both guarded, in different ways, although compared to Sully, Monica was a rank amateur.

"She's taking me out to celebrate tonight," she informed him, "and you're invited."

He bent down and lifted two of the boxes, rising effortlessly and striding to her bedroom. "Can't."

"Scared?" She trailed after him.

"Terrified. But I really do have an appointment later." He put the boxes down with a grunt. "I don't know how long I'll be."

She stood aside as he passed her to get more boxes. There was something about watching a man work, she mused. All those muscles tightening and releasing. Sully's were gleaming with a light glaze of perspiration, and she went to the thermostat and lowered the temperature to the air conditioner. She didn't doubt that he would have found a way to refuse, appointment or no. After what they'd shared right before Monica came, he'd be backpedaling again, as fast and furious as he was able.

A tiny smile formed on her lips. An infinitely feminine intuition told her she no longer had cause to doubt Sully's feelings. Oh, he might still deny them, but that was twice she'd surprised that look on his face, desire layered over desperation. She'd told herself she'd been willing to give him his space, up to a point. If he insisted on a return to their platonic relationship, she'd almost convinced herself she could do so.

But not now. She wouldn't push, not yet, but eventually…once he got used to the idea… The smile lingered, wouldn't fade.

There would come a day in the very near future when Sully's willpower would be put to the test. She'd be willing to bet on it.

Sully's cheeks flexed as he pulled in smoke and held it for a moment, letting it fill his lungs. His gaze was watchful, missing nothing. The stores that lined the street had closed hours before. In the crime-ridden neighborhood he'd chosen, it was too dangerous to stay open after dark. The hooker and her client in the rusted-out car across the street hadn't come up for air for ten minutes. Idly Sully gave them only another five before the woman went on her way. A working girl couldn't afford to waste much time. The coked-up punk in leathers and chains who'd passed by twice hadn't done a good job of hiding his interest. He was sizing Sully up; wondering how easy a mark he'd be. Sully hoped the kid wouldn't try his luck. He didn't need a would-be mugger screwing up his plans.

Headlights speared through the darkness as a car turned the corner and came toward him. Sully took one last drag and dropped the cigarette, grinding it beneath the toe of his boot. Almost soundlessly the black car pulled up to him and stopped. The back door came open, and Sully ducked inside.

"Roarke." Toby's gravelly voice greeted him. He leaned forward and spoke to the driver, who pulled away from the curb, and headed for the freeway.

Sully relaxed against the Rolls-Royce's soft leather upholstery, and stared out the window. It was tinted; at night there was little to make out but a blur of lights as they moved swiftly toward their destination. He didn't give more than a fleeting thought to the device in his pocket. If it worked as well as O'Shea had promised, Constantine and Hansen would be trailing at a safe distance. If it didn't... He gave a mental shrug. Either way, he was walking into the lion's den alone.

He made no attempt to break the silence in the car. When he'd been contacted by Conrad, he'd arranged to meet near the freight company. It was a small thing, but he didn't want them to pick him up in his own neighborhood. He'd wanted to be as far away as possible from anyplace Ellie might venture.

They rode for nearly an hour. Sully thought they were heading toward the Keys. O'Shea's information said Conrad had a place in Key Largo. He could feel nerves make an appearance, collecting at the base of his spine. Tonight he would meet with the man Conrad answered to, the man responsible for no less than twenty percent of the cocaine smuggled out of Colombia into Miami. He'd worked for two years for this moment, and every instinct he had was honed to almost-painful readiness. Earning the trust of a man like Conrad paled in comparison to impressing the man's boss. Sully knew that if he failed to do so, he wouldn't be making the return trip home tonight.

The driver drove through security gates and up a long driveway before stopping before a one-story, sprawling white mansion. Floodlights were placed strategically around the grounds, their function as much for security as to highlight the home's magnificence.

Sully waited for Toby to get out of the car and open his car door. He followed the silent man up to the massive double carved oak doors, and into a cathedral-ceilinged foyer as large as his entire apartment. When Toby muttered, "Wait here," Sully obeyed, surveying the marble floor and inside fountain cynically. Conrad indeed lived well, better than Sully had expected. He crossed to one of the sculptures sprinkled about the foyer, and stared at it through narrowed eyes. It looked like a tangle of brass and copper to him, but if Conrad had it, it must be worth a small fortune.

"Roarke, welcome."

Sully turned, and clasped the hand Conrad extended to him for a brief handshake. "Mr. Conrad."

The man was dressed far less formally than Sully had ever seen him. With the tight-fitting black pants and billowing white open-necked shirt, he looked like what he was—a cutthroat, modern-day pirate.

"I hope you haven't eaten," he said, leading the way through a wide hallway. Sully glanced curiously at the walls, which were adorned with artwork befitting a museum. "I have a marvelous chef, and he's prepared lobster bisque and Peking duck, with a chocolate soufflé guaranteed to make you weep."

"Sounds good."

Conrad's laughter bounced off the high ceiling. "I can assure you, it will be better than merely good. I make it a point to settle for nothing less than the best."

The dining room was huge, and the dark, gleaming table would easily seat thirty. Only three places were set at one end, however, and Sully's attention immediately focused on the man seated at the head.

He wasn't tall. Although he didn't stand at their entrance, Sully estimated him between five-seven five-eight. His age was harder to guess. He was somewhere between fifty and sixty, with a halo of faded dark hair that circled his balding pate, giving him a saintly look. Until one looked at his eyes. Glittering slits of brownish gold, they were almost lost in the folds of his eyelids, reminding Sully of a sleepy crocodile. He didn't need the reminder that this man was potentially much more dangerous.

"Roarke." The man's voice was cracked and dry, like the sound of autumn leaves underfoot. "Sit."

Sully seated himself at the man's left, as indicated. He silently returned the older man's survey until he spoke again.

"Thomas has kept me informed of your progress. He's been very impressed with your talents."

Conrad displayed none of his usual smooth grace when he seated himself awkwardly in his chair. "It's with

Roarke's help that I've opened up new markets through Florida, Mr. Vargas, and he..."

That strange reptilian gaze shifted to Conrad, and the rest of the sentence died in his throat. His jaw worked uncontrollably, and he turned his attention to the servant who had just entered the room. Silence reigned until the man had put bowls before them and sidled out, as soundlessly as he'd entered.

Sully took a cautious sip at what he assumed was soup. Unlike any he'd ever had, it tasted like it had just come from the refrigerator. No doubt it was gourmet something or other, but he'd take a steaming bowl of vegetable beef over chilled mystery broth any day.

Replacing his spoon, he looked at the man next to him. "I get the feeling that pleasing Mr. Conrad matters less than pleasing you."

Vargas's eyes flickered. "You're an astute man. One hopes that you are as intelligent as you are talented. However, I dislike discussing business over dinner. I've always found it bad for the digestion. Let's enjoy our meal, shall we?"

Conrad had obvious difficulty relaxing enough to find pleasure in the food. As he'd promised, the meal was excellent, and after the first course, Sully ate heartily. Vargas, too, appeared to appreciate the dinner, although he spoke sparingly, and only to respond to Conrad's forced conversation.

After the dessert dishes had been cleared away, the same servant filled wineglasses to set before each man, then, leaving the bottle on the table, left the room. Vargas picked up his glass and swirled the contents gently. "You seem to have had remarkable success in your role for Mr. Conrad, Roarke." He took a small sip of wine, and closed his eyes appreciatively for a moment. In the next instant he was staring at Sully again, the brownish gold gaze strangely hypnotic. "I must admit to being a trifle impressed myself with the way you moved our packages out of Colombia." He drank again, his eyes never leaving Sully. "How did you manage it?"

Sully tipped the wine to his lips and swallowed. "If I told you all my trade secrets, you wouldn't have much need for me."

The man's face was expressionless. "Not very trusting, are you?"

Running his fingers along the stem of the glass, Sully countered, "I doubt either of us are."

Vargas inclined his head slightly. "Thomas."

Conrad started, his wine splashing dangerously close to the edge of the glass. "Sir?"

Without removing his gaze from Sully, Vargas said mildly, "That large man in your employ. The one at the door when I arrived."

Conrad looked from Vargas to Sully, then back. "Toby?"

"I didn't care for his manner."

Seeming at a loss, Conrad asked, "He...he was rude to you?"

"I didn't care for his manner," Vargas repeated. This time he did look at his employee. "Please take care of it."

Sully's muscles bunched as Vargas's meaning became clear. Conrad rose from the table silently, and left the room. Then the other man's attention returned to Sully, and he picked up their conversation as if there had been no interruption.

"I would imagine that one could learn many 'trade secrets' in a federal prison."

Taking a long swallow of wine, Sully answered, "A few."

"You were convicted of possession, were you not?"

Sully knew what had been in the file Conrad must have

compiled on him, as well as did the man before him. He'd helped design it himself. "Possession with intent to deliver. Five to eight, out in three."

"Let's hope you picked up enough tips there to help you avoid going back."

Sully's eyes met Vargas's over the rim of the glass. "Don't worry. I have no intention of getting caught again."

The man's glass was empty, and he indicated for Sully to refill it. "It doesn't matter, really," he said once the glass was full again. His gaze met Sully's. "You're much too valuable for us to allow you to return to prison."

A chill trickled down Sully's spine. Those words were much less comforting than they sounded. As this man's employee, he wouldn't be allowed to go to prison, wouldn't be given a chance to talk to the police. If things didn't go well, he'd join Toby, and no doubt a long list of others who disappeared completely.

And if his true identity were ever discovered, he could anticipate a painful, brutal death. The Colombian drug lords were noted for their cold-blooded ferocity.

Vargas shifted the conversation smoothly into business, as if he hadn't just threatened the life of the man seated next to him. "With Thomas's help and—" he inclined his head in Sully's direction "—with yours, my operation has become hugely successful. So much, in fact, that I'm looking to expand it."

Sully reached out and poured a healthy amount of wine into his own glass. "How so?"

"I take an enormous risk to bring my cocaine to your country, where it is sold to dealers, who, in turn, sell it at a ridiculous markup." He took a long drink from his glass and watched Sully closely. "Tell me, Roarke. How would you advise increasing profits?"

Feeling his way carefully, Sully said, "You increase profits by reducing production costs or raising prices. But raising prices when there is a plentiful supply not under your control only makes you less competitive." He stopped, his mind grappling to figure out the direction of Vargas's thoughts. Slowly he continued, "You could eliminate the middlemen, deal the drugs directly yourself." It would be unheard-of for Vargas to do so. With each additional link of the chain from producer to user, he'd increase his visibility, and thus increase his risk. But for the life of him, Sully couldn't tell what the man was planning.

A slight smile curved Vargas's lips, and he leaned back in his chair, cradling the wineglass in his palm. "You are as intelligent as Conrad has reported. And you are partially correct. Some of my associates have established new markets in Japan and Europe, and I have an interest in doing the same. But I also have a plan for a more direct pipeline to a U.S. market, which will eliminate many of the middlemen, and raise my profit margin, without substantially increasing my risk."

"And that market would be?"

"The Midwest." The crystal teardrops adorning the chandelier overhead prismed the light, throwing a rainbow over the fine glassware on the table below. "The appetite of that population has been slower to increase, but as the coasts go, so goes the Midwest, is that not true?"

Inclining his head, Sully murmured, "So I've heard."

"The heartland of your country is crying out for what we can supply them. And by selling directly there, I estimate we can increase our supply into the country by ten percent, without driving the price down."

Sully thought about it for a moment. "It will be costly to develop a direct pipeline to the Midwest."

Vargas shrugged. "One must look at the big picture. A kilo that costs me one hundred dollars to produce is worth fifteen thousand when it arrives in the United States. A dealer buys it and takes it to the next city, and sells it for twenty-five thousand. If I take that ten-thousand-dollar profit per kilo for myself, I can afford a few more employees, some extra costs. Once the route has been established, if supervised well, I stand to make a tidy sum.''

''Where do I come into this?''

''You were suggested by Thomas as the man to set up that pipeline for us. I wanted to meet you myself before deciding.''

The longing for a cigarette was powerful. ''And what did you decide?''

There was a long pause, in which Vargas sipped from his wineglass, and surveyed Sully over the rim. ''You'll do, I believe,'' he said finally. ''You'll do.''

It was apparent that Vargas had discussed all the business he intended for that night. Sully followed the man to the front door. There was no sign of Conrad, but when Sully stepped outside, he saw the same car he'd arrived in waiting for him. A man he'd never seen before stood at the back passenger's door.

He was halfway to the car when Vargas's voice stopped him.

''Roarke.''

Sully stopped, looked back over his shoulder. Conrad had appeared at the door in back of Vargas, alone and visibly shaken. ''Be sure you don't disappoint me.'' A moth dive-bombed past the Colombian's face and was batted away. One of the security spotlights caught him in its beam, and seemed to envelop him in an unholy glow.

''I don't care to be disappointed.''

The debriefing was only slightly less harrowing than the meeting itself. After Sully had been dropped where he'd met the car, he'd immediately started walking. Six blocks away he ducked into a tavern and wound his way through the tables to a room in the back. Ted answered the door when he rapped on it, and Sully entered the crowded room. A denim-clad agent named Hathaway, with whom he'd worked years ago on a heroin buy-bust clapped him on the shoulder.

"Way to go, champ." He crooned the next words. "Was it good for you?"

Sully finally lit the cigarette he'd been longing for all evening. "Any one's good that you walk away from, right?" The man laughed and slipped outside the room. He'd make sure no one unauthorized came near the back room while the meeting was in progress.

Dropping into a chair, Sully surveyed the people in the room. Kennedy was there this time, seated by Lowrey, along with Ted, O'Shea and two individuals Sully didn't recognize. One of them, Ziesmer, was introduced as a high-ranking DEA official. The other man was the head of Florida's Customs Service Special Investigative Division.

Sully gave a silent whistle. The big guns all seemed to have an interest in this case, and the fact couldn't help but make him nervous.

"Have you heard from Constantine and Hansen?" he asked O'Shea.

The man grinned. "Your good-luck charm worked perfectly. They were never more than a mile from you. From the location they gave, you must have been at Conrad's estate."

He unbuttoned his shirt and loosened the adhesive tape he'd used to hold the transmitter in place. "Tell me the damn T-4 worked."

O'Shea crossed the room and lowered himself to a chair beside Sully. "Constantine said you were coming through loud and clear."

"He filled you in?"

O'Shea nodded. "He gave me the highlights. But I want to hear your take on it."

Sully proceeded to tell the now quiet room exactly what had transpired that night. He wasn't interrupted until he got to the part of Toby's disappearance. O'Shea looked at Ted. "Get word to the other agencies, the local police. When that body is found, I want to be notified immediately." Ted nodded, and O'Shea gestured for Sully to continue.

When he'd finished, the men in the room were silent for a moment. "This Vargas has got guts, I'll say that," one of the suits muttered.

"A man can be made pretty fearless when he has powerful friends backing him," Sully said to O'Shea. "I'd sure like to know who those friends are."

The other man nodded. "Maybe pinning down the real identity of this Vargas will give us some hints." He turned to a briefcase he had on the table and snapped the locks open. Taking out a file folder, he handed it to Sully, who flipped through the pictures inside. Halfway through the pile, he tapped one.

"There's your man."

O'Shea took the photo and studied it, the other men in the room gathering around him. Turning it over, he said, "Well, 'Vargas' is one of his many aliases. His real name is Enrico Mendez. Born in Cali, Colombia, he owns an import-export business there."

"I'd guess he's university educated," Sully said. "Maybe even in the States. His English was almost flawless."

"You win the gold ring," O'Shea replied. "Graduated from UCLA. We'll do some checking on just how often he's been visiting the States."

The talk in the room turned to how much cocaine could be seized when the case went down. Excitement simmered at the possibility that the case might have connections to El National Cartel, a rumored organization believed to rule whole countries and control millions of lives. Sully barely managed to hold his tongue. They had no evidence linking Mendez, alias Vargas, to the cartel, nor any firm evidence that the cartel even existed. He let O'Shea make the argument.

"Let's not let ourselves get sidetracked. This investigation has always been more than a buy-bust. We're going after the top people in the organization, and right now that's Vargas."

Sully scrubbed both hands over his face, tuning the voices out. His apartment beckoned like an impoverished oasis, and he felt a sudden longing to go home. That no longer meant Ellie. She wouldn't be next door, wouldn't be anywhere nearby. An entire city lay between them, and he tried to tell himself that was a good thing.

He'd been pretending to himself all these years that he could exist on the sidelines of Ellie's life and that it would be enough. But their night together had proved him a liar. It had taken only the opportunity to touch her for him to forget the careful boundaries he'd always observed. The ease with which she shredded his control scared the hell out of him.

"Sully."

He jerked his attention to O'Shea, who was standing close to him, ignoring the discussion going on in the room. "You did good tonight, buddy. We're going to have to be twice as careful now to be sure this case doesn't unravel on us. You can't think of any loose ends, can you?"

Sully thought of Ellie, across the city in her new apartment. The distance had never seemed greater, and represented more than mere miles.

"No," he said bleakly. "No loose ends."

Chapter 9

Elizabeth looked at her bankbook again. The thrill hadn't lessened despite her having gazed at it for over an hour. Depositing Simon's check had made her feel like the riches of the world had been handed to her. The opinions of friends, and earlier, of instructors, were warming, but this first check was a milestone of a different sort. She let herself daydream for a few moments of a time when she actually could support herself with her pottery, and quit her job at the gallery.

The smile on her lips grew rueful. She was a long way from that time, if, indeed, it ever came. But this first check marked a step forward in her career, and yet another milestone in her path of independence.

She looked at the phone then, tempted yet again to call Sully and share her news with him. She'd told herself she wouldn't push, and she hadn't. But, oh, it had been hard to back away, even a little. In the week since he'd helped her move, she'd had to be satisfied with a quick phone call from him when he'd been on his way out of his apartment.

It was telling that in this time of her greatest success, the person she most wanted to share it with was Sully.

Quickly she crossed to the telephone and dialed his unlisted number. She waited impatiently as it rang three times before the machine turned on. Without leaving a message, she hung up. Talking to a machine was no match for speaking to Sully himself.

Her doorbell pealed then, and when she took the precaution of looking out the peephole, she mentally groaned. Her ex-husband stood in the hallway, tapping a file folder against one suit-clad leg. Drat the man, she'd been quite happy not to have to deal with him at all in six months, and now he'd inflicted himself on her twice in three weeks. It occurred to her suddenly that he'd seemed to have little trouble discovering her new address, and her eyes narrowed.

She pulled open the door. "Carter," she said flatly. "Again."

"Beth." He offered her that toothpaste-ad bright smile that had so dazzled her years ago.

She leaned against the doorjamb and crossed her arms. "You didn't seem to have any trouble coming up with my new address. Would you like to explain that?"

The smile increased in wattage. "Wouldn't you be more comfortable inviting me inside? This may take a while."

She deliberately misunderstood him. "Shouldn't take too long to describe how you found me." Her smile was mocking. "Even for a lawyer." Because her gaze never left his, she saw the quick flare of irritation in his eyes.

"We employ all kinds of investigators in our office, Elizabeth. Discovering your new address wasn't even a challenge for them."

She drew in a breath, released it slowly. "You sicced the county's investigators on me? Isn't utilizing their services for a personal matter a complete misuse of county funds?''

''Not when I've discovered that the man my ex-wife has long associated with is a known criminal.'' He paused, as if to enjoy drawing the moment out. ''Your John Sullivan.'' Flicking a glance over his shoulder at the couple walking down the hallway, he inquired, ''Are you sure you don't want to discuss this inside?''

He took her silence for assent, and brushed by her to enter the apartment. Elizabeth wiped suddenly wet palms on her shorts. Never before had she had the sensation of actually being able to feel her blood pressure rise. The heat of anger sprang up nerve endings and spread through her entire body. Even her ears seemed to burn.

She shut the door behind Carter with more force than necessary, and turned to lean against it. He was making himself comfortable on the love seat, taking rapid inventory of her new home.

His gaze met hers. ''I'm happy to see that your taste in living quarters has improved since the last time we spoke.''

''Explain.'' Her voice shook with the rage gnawing away inside her. ''Try to explain why you would come here and trash the most decent man I've ever met.''

Carter's voice was cool as he crossed one leg over his knee, carefully avoiding wrinkling his trousers. ''Really, Elizabeth, one would think you doubted my motives.''

''Believe me, you don't want to know what I think right now.''

His smile never wavered, but his eyes turned gelid. ''Very well. I came to warn you about your *friend.* Seems I've been right all along about what an unsavory individual he is. My office ran a check on him and found out he has quite a past.''

''You bastard.'' She all but spit the word as she clenched her fists and fought the urge to spring toward him. Temper sang up her body, and her muscles fairly vibrated with it. "Anyone is fair game to you, aren't they? No insult is too slight, no offense too petty not to avenge."

Disapproval was in his voice, on his face, when he replied, "I'll blame the deterioration of your vocabulary on the company you've been keeping recently. This new attitude of yours is most unbecoming."

She took a long, deep breath, and worked on banking the fury. Temper had never been an adequate weapon with Carter. He was too cool, too remote. It only served to point out the difference between emotion and logic. *His* logic.

"All the information is right in here." Carter gestured with the file folder. "Imagine my surprise when I was told that the only other tenant on the floor of your old building wasn't called John Sullivan at all, but someone by the name of Roarke. This thug that you consider your friend has lied to you since the beginning, Elizabeth, and not just about his name. He has a long history of crooked dealings, but there was no need to dig through those, once I found out about the three years he spent in prison for possession with intent."

"Your information is wrong." There was no doubt, no hesitation in her voice. There may have been times in their friendship when she hadn't seen Sully for months, times he'd explained he'd been moving around. But always, at some point, he'd contacted her again.

The time frame aside, Sully simply wasn't capable of the kind of crime Carter was describing. He had a basic decency about him that he tried to hide from the world. She thought he did a good job of hiding it from himself most of the time.

She studied Carter as dispassionately as her mood would allow. Her ex-husband had obviously gotten Sully mixed up with someone else, perhaps a former tenant who had lived in his apartment previously. But there would be no way to convince Carter he'd made a mistake. The two men had always detested each other, now more than ever. Dread was making a belated appearance, and curling through her stomach. She wondered to what lengths her ex-husband would go to make trouble for the man she cared about.

"What do you want, Carter?"

He cocked his head, and folded his hands across the file folder that lay on his lap. "Want? Why, Elizabeth, I'm surprised you'd ask. I'm only telling you this because I worry about you." He let the silence stretch between them. "You understand, I hope, that it could be in the county's interest to take a closer look at the doings of a known drug dealer." He gave a small shrug. "Wouldn't hurt to ask some questions, talk to his parole officer and his boss, if, indeed, he even has a job."

Incredulous, she shook her head. "You mean plant lies and innuendos everywhere in his life, and see what sticks? You really are slime."

He leaned forward, his gaze steely. "Sullivan, Roarke—whoever he is—doesn't matter to me. He's a loser, a common criminal. If I have the opportunity to make things difficult for him, that's just a bonus. But you do matter. I asked you to do something for me a while ago, something quite simple." He settled back against the love seat, but there was nothing relaxed about his pose. "You refused."

An unnatural calm settled over her, icing her temper as his meaning became clear. "So there's a price for leaving Sully alone? Of course there is. With you there's always a price." Reaching a quick decision, she approached him with her hand extended. "All right, Carter. Let's see the story you want me to give to the media about our divorce." She fairly snatched the paper he took out of his breast pocket from his hand. Unfolding it, she read silently for a minute before giving an incredulous laugh. "You want me to tell the press that I'm psychotic?"

"Honestly, Elizabeth," Carter said reprovingly. "You never used to have this penchant for exaggeration. All I'm suggesting is that you tell any reporters who inquire that you terminated our marriage because of an emotional illness. That gives both of us a great deal of sympathy in the press, I believe." He lifted a hand in a casual gesture. "You can tell them you're receiving therapy, if you like."

She gave herself a quick shake, as if to dispel the mixture of amazement and fury tangling her insides. "Well, I can certainly understand why you don't want me to tell them the truth. It's difficult to put a positive spin on adultery, isn't it?" She crumpled the paper in her hand. "Forget it. Telling the reporters that we divorced because of irreconcilable differences will be hard enough for me to manage. You should consider yourself lucky that I'm agreeing not to tell them more." The smile she gave him was poisonous. "Much more."

"You're missing the point." The snap in his voice warned of rising temper. "'Irreconcilable differences' are meaningless words that satisfy only the divorce court. The media will be looking for the real reasons behind the failure of our marriage. You're going to give them one."

"You mean you want me to back up the story you've already been telling," she guessed shrewdly. His silence was all the answer she needed. Torn between anger and amazement, she surveyed him as if he were a stranger. Because that was exactly what he was to her. She'd never really known him, never realized what he was capable of. "You must want that city council position very badly."

"Oh, I have no intention of running for city council," he said calmly.

"What?"

He allowed himself a self-satisfied smile. "It's the publicity I'm after, Elizabeth. When contacted by the press, I, of course, will say I'm flattered and seriously considering

the offer. After several weeks of speculation, I'll regretfully
withdraw my name from consideration.''

"Why?"

He was clearly enjoying her baffled expression. Fingers
linking across his chest, he said, "There is a much larger
prize to be considered here. City council would be a short-
sighted move. District Attorney of Dade County...now,
there's a prize which could prove a valuable springboard
to real political office."

"Of course," she murmured cynically. "I wasn't aware
Marvin Postal was planning on stepping down." Postal was
the current holder of that office.

Carter made a dismissive gesture. "Whether he is or not,
I plan to be positioned to replace him. My name will already be well-known, and I'll have widespread support in
the community."

She went to the door and opened it. "Get out," she ordered flatly. "I don't want anything to do with you or your
sordid little schemes."

Carter's face set, then he slowly rose and walked to the
door. "If that's what you want, Elizabeth. Of course, if you
don't cooperate, I'll be forced to make things extremely
uncomfortable for your friend. But that's your choice."

Her fingers clenched more tightly around the paper he'd
given her. She wished she could doubt his intentions, but
she knew he'd follow through on his threats. Sully would
suffer because of her. The thought was intolerable.

"Think it over, Elizabeth." His voice was low, and he
trailed one finger carelessly down her cheek. "Underesti-
mating me would be a serious mistake. Don't ever doubt
how much misery I can bring to your life with just a snap
of my fingers. And to your friend's life, as well."

He moved away, and then hesitated. Turning back to her,
he slapped the file folder against her chest. "Go ahead and

keep this. I think you'll find the facts quite compelling. I'll call you tomorrow for your answer.''

When Sully returned to his apartment, there was nothing he wanted more than a long, cool shower, whiskey and a hot meal. If he had to choose, the shower and meal could wait, the whiskey couldn't. He'd just spent the past hour and a half with Conrad, soothing the man's nerves. The man was anxious for Sully to please Vargas with his plans for the pipeline. When he'd left him, Conrad had seemed a bit calmer, but there was still an edge there that had been absent in their previous dealings. Sully could smell fear on the man.

Conrad was terrified of disappointing Vargas. If Sully failed in his task, Conrad would be held responsible, as well, since Sully had been his recommendation for this job.

He smiled grimly. Conrad would be held responsible, all right. And so would his superior. Sully was going to personally see to that.

He removed the voice transmitter, wincing as he tried to loosen the tape without taking chest hair with it. He walked into the tiny bedroom and taped it beneath the dresser until he could get it back to Kale. He was edgy about keeping anything around that could blow his cover if someone got suspicious and tossed his apartment. O'Shea had ordered Lowrey to keep Sully's DEA credentials, as well, for that very reason.

He went to the kitchen and emptied the change from his pocket onto the scarred countertop. The silver dollar lay among it. Sometimes, he reflected, plain sight was the best hiding place of all. As he reached for the cupboard that held the glasses, a knock sounded on the door. Swiftly he moved to answer it. He hoped it was Lowrey. The sooner he got the transmitter out of here, the better he'd feel.

But it wasn't the customs agent at his door; it was Ellie.

Without returning his greeting, she entered the apartment, a file folder clutched tightly in her hand.

"Moving you to a better neighborhood loses its benefits if you're going to come by unescorted." He watched with resignation as she moved through the small apartment, shrinking it with her presence until she was the focus. He'd been unable to rid the place of her image, her scent, the last time she was here. Today would be no different. Hours, days later, he would still be able to visualize every step she took in here, everything she touched.

He rubbed a hand over his day's beard, remembering suddenly his need for a shower. Out of the corner of his eye he noticed the message light on his machine flickering, and he frowned. The machine was rarely used. Ellie had always refused to use it, and the one person who would hadn't called for months.

Ellie was moving through his apartment aimlessly, and still hadn't spoken a word. For the first time he let himself really look at her, and what he saw had the worry changing direction. Her face was pale, her movements jerky. But it wasn't nerves he saw reflected on her face. He'd seen her in a temper before, had been the cause of it only recently. This was more than mere temper. Her eyes were dark, lethal, and warned of a storm in progress.

"Looks like I'm not the only one in need of a whiskey," he said in an unconsciously soothing tone. "Why don't you sit down and let me fix you something."

She whirled around to fix her gaze on him then, and something in his gut tightened in response. He doubted she'd even heard his words.

"Carter came by to visit me again."

The name was enough to loose a burning blast of jealousy through his blood. The last time her ex-husband had dropped by, she'd been dressed in a thin, silky robe, only minutes from the bed she'd shared with Sully. He hadn't been able to do anything about the possessiveness that had leaped through him when he'd seen them together, so he'd relegated it to the back of his mind. But that didn't mean it hadn't lingered there, unresolved and simmering. "What'd he want?"

She held the file folder out. "To give me this." She slammed it down on the small table next to his recliner and turned to pace again. "And to issue threats."

Sully reached out for the folder and flipped it open. He perused the contents quickly once, then again more slowly. Tension rapped at the base of his skull. Robinson, the son of a bitch, would have to be dealt with. He was capable of the cool reason to fashion that thought, despite the hot flash of panic circling in his stomach. How to deal with Ellie was a different matter altogether.

He never lifted his eyes from the papers in his hands. She was on the move again. Pacing around the TV, lamp and recliner, she angled toward the window, as if driven by raw nerves.

He closed the file, and set it carefully down on the table. "Looks like he's been busy."

Quickly her eyes flashed to his, and her fists knotted. "It's not true."

He watched her, his expression deliberately blank. "How do you know?"

The look she gave him could have been directed at an extremely dull-witted child. "I know."

The sole certainty in her answer was an iron vise squeezing his chest. Trust was something he'd lived his life without, something he'd often doubted existed. To be presented with hers so unquestioningly made him want to throw his head back and howl. An undeserving man was never so humbled as when offered something he had no hope of repaying. He looked down into her dark eyes.

"Did you actually think I believed him, for even one minute? Carter lies as easily as I breathe. That—" she jerked a thumb at the folder he'd laid down "—is just an example. Either he made it up, or his investigators confused you with someone else."

Now he was the one to turn and move. It was an excuse to not have to face her.

"He's going to make trouble. I agreed to play by his rules if I have to talk to reporters, but he's driven with ambition, Sully. And he doesn't care who he has to use along the way. I don't trust him not to go ahead with his threats, to talk to your boss, or..."

He stopped and looked at her. "Wait a minute," he ordered, his voice harsh. "Are you saying you made some sort of deal with him?"

Her gaze dropped, then she angled her chin, as if preparing for a fight. Her next words guaranteed she'd receive one. "I think it would be best." She lifted a shoulder. "It's nothing major. I just promised to go by his little script—" distaste flickered across her face "—and in return he'll back off and leave you alone."

In frustration he scrubbed both hands over his face, then dropped them to glare at her. "Why in God's name would you agree to do anything to help him?"

"Because," she shouted, "he can hurt you!" She lowered her voice with visible effort. "Because I know him. He's going to try and twist whatever he can get and use it to make your life miserable, just because you've been my friend. You don't deserve that, and I won't allow it to happen."

He felt like he'd been sucker punched. The thought of her dealing with her ex-husband, for him, was enough to send waves of sickness to his throat. "I don't need protecting, Ellie. I'll take care of Robinson in my own way." His voice was rough with strain. "I don't want you having anything to do with that bastard." Especially not on his account.

She released a breath, and rubbed at a point between her brows. Swiftly she told him of her entire conversation with Robinson, finishing by saying, "Sully, his threats are real. He'll bend the truth, make up whatever story suits his purpose, and he's got the power of the district attorney's office behind him." She put a hand on his arm and shook it for emphasis. "He's not above using his office to further his own goals."

He swung away from her, unable to think with that small hand resting on him. Robinson had managed to unearth the cover the DEA had manufactured for Sully. The list of arrests, the conviction, the time served in prison had all been carefully planted to convince Conrad, and ultimately, Vargas, that Sully was who he said he was. That in itself shouldn't be a problem, if that's all he'd uncovered. Especially since Ellie hadn't believed the story her ex-husband had told her.

Unfamiliar emotion threatened to swamp him. Emotions caused by her generous gift of faith in him. With every fiber of his being he wanted to be able to reciprocate, to prove that he was worthy of that simple expression of trust. Never had he been more tempted to tell Ellie the truth about his life, his job. Never had it been more dangerous for him to consider doing so.

Nerves dampened his palms. This investigation had already brushed against her once. Unbidden, mental fragments of memory flicked across his mind. Images of the packages that had been sent to the agents he'd worked with in Mexico, each one holding a piece of Alberto Ramon.

The man hadn't deserved to be kidnapped and brutalized simply because he'd supported the DEA's cause. But savagery was a way of life among men like the ones Sully investigated, and there was no way he'd risk Ellie.

He forced himself to put aside emotion and concentrate on logic. A part of him was actually looking forward to confronting Robinson. His fingers curled into his palms. The man had a lot to answer for, not the least of which was trying to use Sully to manipulate Ellie.

Though she hadn't made a sound, he felt her behind him and turned to meet her. The fury that had carried her had passed, and suddenly she seemed so transparent that he could pass a hand through her. For the moment he pushed aside his plans for Robinson. Right now it was more important to take care of her.

"Why don't you go in and find that whiskey. It's in the cupboard to the right of the sink. Two glasses," he called after her as she moved reluctantly toward the kitchen.

Once she was diverted, he strode to the machine and pressed the button. He listened to the whir and clicks of callers who had hung up. The last caller had left a message. However, it wasn't the voice he'd half expected to hear.

He reached out and clutched the table until his knuckles were white as the disembodied voice echoed from the machine. "This is Greg Windham of the Jacksonville County Hospital. I regret to inform you…"

He listened to the message, stabbed at the button, rewound the tape, listened to it again. The machine turned off automatically when it was over. Still he didn't move.

Ellie found him like that, still bent over the machine, silent and still. She set the two glasses down and hurried over to him, her hand going to his shoulder. "Sully, what is it?"

It took a long time for him to answer. It took even longer

for him to consciously uncurl his fingers from the edge of the table. ''It's my mother.'' His voice was empty, devoid of feeling.

''She's dead.''

Chapter 10

Carter Robinson pushed open the door to his office the next morning, and stopped short in the doorway, his jaw dropping open in surprise. The man leaning back in the padded-leather desk chair, with his long legs propped up on the desk, shot him a slow, wicked grin.

"Hey, Carter," Sully said laconically. "Nice office. Colors are a little femmy for my tastes. Seem to suit you, though." With great deliberation, he selected a cigarette from the package in his pocket and lit it. His first perfect smoke ring hung in the air before he added, "Let's face it, a man who blackmails a woman isn't much of a man, is he?"

After a moment Carter closed his mouth and entered the room in one long stride. The etched glass in the door, with its carefully stenciled lettering, shook as the door slammed behind him. "What the hell do you think you're doing here, Sullivan?"

Allowing himself a measure of satisfaction at the wariness on the man's face, Sully took his time answering. "Paying you a visit. Sort of an unexpected one. The kind you like to pay to Ellie."

The flicker in Carter's eyes was almost infinitesimal, but his voice was smooth when he responded. "My relationship with my ex-wife is none of your concern."

Sully took the cigarette from between his lips and exhaled. "Now, that's where you're wrong, Robinson." He bared his teeth. "You made it my business when you tried to use her friendship with me to manipulate her."

"I don't have time to listen to you rant." Carter turned and pulled open the door. "I'm calling for security to remove you from the building."

"Why don't you do that, Carter?" Sully invited softly. "I don't mind letting a few more people in on this conversation if you don't."

The other man's hand tightened around the doorknob. After a long moment he shut the door again. Facing Sully, he said, "Say what you have to say, then, and get the hell out. You think I'm afraid of you? A burned-out street narc? I only wonder how the DEA can tell the difference between you and the men you investigate."

Sully gave a slight smile. He'd figured that Robinson had discovered his job with the DEA, as well as his cover, and the man had just confirmed it. With his contacts in the district attorney's office, it wouldn't have been difficult. "You've been a busy boy, haven't you, Carter?" His smile faded as he ground his cigarette out on the polished-oak desktop. "Makes a person wonder just how you'd explain to any interested parties just why you went looking for that information." His next words were cold and deadly. "Information you had no authorized reason to access in the first place."

Carter gave him a superior look and leaned casually against the door. "You're an incredibly slow learner, Sullivan. That doesn't come as a complete surprise, you understand, but I did give you credit for having a bit more imagination. You can't begin to comprehend the contacts I have at my disposal. Or just how much damage I could do with the information I acquire.''

Sully surveyed him silently for a moment. The man had to be desperate to pull a stunt as stupid as this one. Ambition did that to a man, he supposed. Made him deaf and blind to everything but his goal.

Leaning forward, he picked up a sleek silver letter opener that was lying on the desk. Holding the tip of the blade in his fingers, he flipped it up in a quick spiral, and then caught it again. He repeated the action absently, all the while staring at Robinson.

"Exactly what did you hope to gain by going to Ellie last night?'' he asked, with real curiosity lacing the words.

The man shrugged. "Apparently Elizabeth has already shared the gist of our discussion with you. I hadn't counted on that,'' he mused. "I knew better than to expect that she'd actually believe what I told her about you. She's hopelessly naive. But I did think the little martyr would agree to my plan to spare her dear friend—'' he sneered the words ''—any trouble. She gave me more difficulty than I'd anticipated. She's changed.''

"Yes,'' Sully murmured, thinking of the inner strength Ellie had slowly rebuilt. "She has.''

"It doesn't matter.'' Robinson's fingers played a quick tattoo against one pant leg. "She'll still cooperate.''

The letter opener flew in a dizzying arc between Sully's hands. "How do you figure?''

"Why, you'll encourage her to do so, of course.'' Robinson's smile was smug. "Because otherwise I'll tell her about the job you've taken such pains to keep from her. You could say that's my ace in the hole. Not that Elizabeth is a snob, far from it. But she does set an ingenuous store by honesty, doesn't she?''

Sully sent the letter opener spinning, then snatched it out of the air. Robinson's words struck a chord he wished he could deny. Yes, honesty was important to Ellie, but the truth wasn't going to come from this man. When the time came, Sully would tell her himself. And somehow he'd make her understand why it had taken him so long to share the truth with her. Somewhere he'd find the words.

Carter made a show of glancing at the slim gold watch on his wrist. ''You've wasted enough of my time, Sullivan. Get out. Just make sure you and my ex-wife do exactly as you're told, and I'll keep your secret. Maybe.''

His last word was strangled in his throat as the letter opener flew through the air and lodged in the wooden doorframe six inches from his ear. Robinson's gaze slid sideways and regarded the still-vibrating missile, the color draining from his face.

''I don't think that's the way we're going to play this, Carter,'' Sully said sotto voce. ''I never have responded well to threats. And I'm afraid where you're concerned, I have a long list of grievances.'' Regret tinged his next words. ''But, although nothing would give me greater pleasure than beating the hell out of you, this time I played by your rules.'' He cocked his head consideringly. ''Of course, I changed them some.''

Robinson finally tore his gaze away from the letter opener and looked at the man before him. ''You're crazy.'' His voice was dazed. ''You really are a madman if you think I'll let you get away with this.''

Sully was on his feet and looming over him with a speed that made the other man blink. ''You're not listening, Carter, and you're going to want to listen, because I'm only going to explain the rules once. Ready? You won't contact Ellie again. No calls, no more visits, no more information leaks. Pretty easy rules, really, but just in case you have trouble remembering them, I took the precaution of having a little talk with Postal before you came in this morning.''

The remaining color in Carter's face slowly drained. ''Marvin Postal? Why would you do that?''

''Ellie told me everything, remember? And our district attorney was very interested in your plans for replacing him.'' Sully shook his head in mock wonder. ''Those political types are paranoid as hell, aren't they? I'm afraid your popularity factor in this office was zero by the time our conversation was over. I'll be surprised if your boss doesn't have you back arguing the purse-snatching cases after this.''

''I can talk to Postal. I'll convince him—''

''You'll try. But that press you've been receiving will do most of the convincing, I think. Something tells me you're going to be way too busy to bother Ellie or me again. But if you ever do forget the rules, I can always drop a hint to Postal about your digging into confidential DEA personnel files.'' His grin was wolfish. ''You could say that's my ace in the hole.''

With both hands on Robinson's shoulders, he moved the man aside and opened the door. Before he passed through it, he stopped and turned back to Robinson. ''Oh, and by the way, I met your…associate while I was waiting for you.'' He closed one eyelid in an insulting wink. ''That woman sure does look like she'd know her way around your briefs.''

Sully shifted in his seat, trying yet again to find a comfortable position for his legs. He'd never get used to flying. He didn't mind the idea of being inside several tons of steel hurtling through the air, miles above land. But he disliked the closed-in feeling, the seats mere inches apart.

And right now he wasn't all that thrilled with the amount

of time it gave him to think. It had been easy to keep the disturbing memories at bay while he'd attended to countless details. He'd taken leave from work, and contacted Conrad to let him know he'd be out of touch for a couple of days. Then, once he'd taken care of Robinson, he'd had to call Ted.

He hadn't looked forward to the man's reaction, but the agency had to know about any threat to the investigation, even if Sully did think his visit with Robinson had put an end to it.

"You've got to be kidding me!" Ted had croaked into the phone. "You're telling me a two-year investigation might go down the tubes because of a jealous husband?"

"Ex-husband," Sully had corrected. "The woman is an old friend of mine, and I helped her out. For some reason Robinson has never been my biggest fan."

"Imagine that." In the silence that had stretched, Sully had visualized Ted whipping off his thin gold rims and polishing them with his customary fussy care.

"Well, it sounds like you contained the worst of the damage," he'd finally said grudgingly. "I'm going to let O'Shea know about it and see what he has to say. Is this the same woman Lowrey mentioned?"

"I don't know. What did Lowrey say?"

"He said you were hung up on some woman you had living beside you. If that's the case…"

Sully had taken a deep breath and exhaled slowly. "Lowrey needs to do better research."

But Ted had pressed on. "You don't think there's a problem?"

Lowrey would have a hell of a lot to answer for the next time Sully met with him, but he didn't think that was what Ted was referring to. "There's no problem," he'd replied. And that had been the end of the conversation.

He slanted a gaze at the "problem" in the seat next to

his. Ellie had her face turned toward the window, seemingly fascinated by the clouds below. He hadn't been able to shake her from the idea of accompanying him. He'd told her bluntly and more than once that she wasn't welcome. But the lady could resemble a velvet bulldozer when she had her mind set on something. She'd made plans quickly aloud. She had time off coming, she'd said. She'd call Nathan and tell him not to expect her until Monday. That would give them a long weekend to make arrangements for his mother. When he'd flatly rejected her help, she'd seemed to let the matter drop.

And today she'd been waiting for him at the airport.

He'd tried logic, then icy silence. Neither had changed her mind. Sometimes when he encountered that quiet determination of hers, he felt like he'd been ambushed. She was normally so sweet natured it was always surprising to bump up against her will.

Six months ago he would have cheered at any sign that she was regaining her old spirit, but not in this instance. The idea of having Ellie along when he brought this bitter, ugly chapter of his life to a close was violently distasteful. He'd been raised, for lack of a better word, alone—had found the filthy streets outside his home a slight improvement over what went on inside it. He hadn't wanted her to guess the origin of the darkness that was always a heartbeat away, that some days felt like it could swallow him whole.

He settled back into his seat, his gaze brooding. He'd never tried to explain where he'd come from; he knew too well how much the boy had shaped the man. Now she'd see for herself, and he didn't know whether to be sorry or glad.

He may have inadvertently found the surest means to convince Ellie to stay a safe distance from him. The muscle in his jaw went taut. Somehow the thought wasn't as satisfying as it should have been.

* * *

Elizabeth scurried to match her steps to Sully's long strides. He opened the back door of the taxi he had waiting, and she slid into the back seat. He followed her in, and gave the driver the address to the Jacksonville County Hospital. Then he'd settled into the corner of the seat and gazed out the window.

He'd been taciturn the entire trip, and seemed to get more so by the minute. They'd taken the time to unload their luggage at the hotel he'd booked. She'd expected an argument from him when she'd announced her intention of accompanying him to the hospital, where his mother's body was being held, but it had elicited little more than a terse nod.

She watched him from the corner of her eye. He seemed shrouded in solitude. He may as well have been alone in the vehicle; she was effectively shut out. She'd often damned that ability of his even as she'd wondered at his need to develop it. If she let him, he'd completely cut himself off from her. She wasn't going to allow that to happen.

Sliding closer, she slipped her hand in his larger palm, where it lay unmoving on one hard thigh. He stiffened, but didn't turn to look at her. She laced her fingers through his. Although he tensed at her touch, he didn't pull away, and she felt a small measure of satisfaction.

The driver pulled up in front of the hospital, and raised his gaze to the rearview mirror. "You gonna be long or you want I should wait?"

"Wait," Sully answered tersely. The word seemed to be aimed at both the driver and herself. He opened the door and got out.

"I could come in with you," Elizabeth said hesitantly. She saw the way his fingers clenched on top of the car door, saw the subtle shift of muscles in his back as they tightened in response to her words.

Steeling herself for a rebuff, she was surprised when he said, without looking at her, "Yeah, okay then. C'mon."

She waited quietly at his side while he talked to the elderly woman at the front desk, who then went to fetch a nurse. A young man in his twenties with thinning dark hair and an unsuccessful attempt at a goatee introduced himself, and then they were led down a quiet, tiled hallway. The man stopped in front of a steel door and pushed it open.

"You'll have to positively ID the body before I can release it," the man said. Consulting a piece of paper in his hand, he went to one to the squares that lined the walls and opened it, pulling out a gurney. He folded the sheet back, and Elizabeth swallowed a gasp.

The woman lying on the gurney bore no resemblance to her son. Hair that had once been blond was liberally streaked with gray. Her skin hung slack on prominent bones, as if the flesh inside had been wasted away. Elizabeth's gaze lowered, then fixed. Faded, thin marks traced down the woman's arms, and across her chest. Needle tracks.

Sully's voice seemed to come from a distance. "Yeah. That's my mother."

The nurse handed a clipboard and pen to him. "I'll need her name for the record, sir, and your signature verifying that you identified the body and gave us permission to release it."

He jotted down the information and scrawled his signature on the line indicated, then handed the clipboard back to the man.

"And where would you like us to release the body to?" the nurse inquired next.

Taking note of Sully's blank look, the man went on kindly, "If you're unfamiliar with the area, I can get you a list of funeral homes in the city."

Sully nodded, and he and Elizabeth followed the man

out of the morgue and back down the hallway. After selecting a funeral home from the list the man found for him, there were other papers to sign. A lone plastic bag was offered to Sully, containing his mother's personal effects.

Without looking inside it, Sully grasped it in one hand. "I'll need to know the home address she gave you when she was admitted."

The man looked puzzled. "You don't have it?"

Elizabeth watched Sully go rigid. "Not her current one, no."

Shuffling some papers, the nurse bent and wrote the address down on a piece of notepaper and handed it to Sully. He turned abruptly and headed for the doors, not waiting to see if Elizabeth followed. This time she had to jog to keep up with him, and was slightly out of breath by the time she slid in the taxi.

She allowed the silence to settle as they rode to the address the nurse had written for them. She didn't reach out to him this time—not because she didn't want, *need*, to comfort him. But because she knew her touch wouldn't be welcomed, knew that Sully was teetering on the edge of a dark, jagged precipice. The man at the hospital hadn't seemed to notice anything amiss, or at least, nothing more than a grieving relative. But if he'd looked at Sully, really looked at him, how could he have missed the terrible rage in his eyes, the way it seemed to come off him in waves? She didn't know who or what the rage was directed at, but she promised herself that before the day was over he would tell her.

Staring out the window, she watched as the buildings and neighborhoods gradually slid into deterioration. The houses got smaller, more ramshackle. The buildings grew more run-down. Taggers had spread their graffiti on every available surface. Trash littered the sidewalks, and derelicts sprawled against the buildings. There were no children in sight, if one discounted the small groups of toughs dotting the street corners. Occasionally one of them would gaze at the taxi as it went by with sullen defiance. None of them looked older than teenagers, but the look in their eyes was one of aged hopelessness.

Their cabbie was visibly nervous by the time they arrived at the address. "I'm not gonna be able to wait this time," he muttered, his gaze darting to either side. "This neighborhood just ain't safe, ya know what I mean?"

"Yeah." It was the first word Sully had spoken and it was without inflection. He took some bills from his pocket and handed them to the man. The door had barely closed in back of them when the taxi squealed away.

An old woman sat in their path, peering up at them between dirty, stringy bangs. "Got some money? I need me some money. Ya got some? How 'bout it?" Elizabeth started when the woman tugged at her purse. "How 'bout it, lady. Ya got some money?"

Sully reached around and released the woman's grasp. He steered Elizabeth around the woman, who continued to mutter behind them, and up the crumbling brick stoop.

The lock on the front door had long been broken. They entered the building, and Sully pounded on the first door to the right. It opened only a crack. "Whaddya want?" The voice was wavering, querulous.

"Landlord."

A gnarled finger pointed across the hall, then the door slammed shut again. They crossed the hallway, and Sully rapped on the door. "I need to see the landlord."

A woman in a dirty flowered housecoat appeared in the doorway. Fingers as thick as sausages were clutched around a shedding Siamese cat. Eying them both suspiciously, she asked, "You cops?"

"No. I'm here for Marcy Sullivan's things."

She took her time looking him up and down. "She dead

then?'' He nodded, and the woman swore. "Owed me two months' rent, she did. Coulda let that apartment half a dozen times, but always she said she was gonna get me the money. Well, she ain't gonna get me the money, now, is she?'' The cat meowed a protest as the woman's clasp grew tighter.

"How much?''

At Sully's question, the woman's face went from angry to sly. Looking them both over carefully once again, she said, "I get four hundred dollars a month, so that'd be eight hundred to call it even.''

Elizabeth opened her mouth to protest hotly. From what she'd seen of it, the entire building should be condemned. And the thought of the old biddy trying to take advantage of Sully, especially now, had protectiveness rising. Before she could speak, Sully moved a step closer to the woman.

"How much?''

The words were the same, the voice still expressionless, but the woman darted a look at his face and swallowed visibly. Retreating a couple of steps she muttered, "Two hundred a month.''

He reached into his pocket, drew out his wallet, and handed her some bills. She fumbled with something inside the door, and gave him a key. "Room 401. Top floor. Just leave the key inside when you leave.'' She stepped back inside her apartment and slammed the door.

Ellie followed Sully up the rickety stairway. Noise barraged the senses. There was a baby crying in one of the rooms, and the sound trailed after them to the next floor. On the fourth floor a loud argument was punctuated with the sound of fists meeting flesh. There was an angry shout, and something shattered. He fit the key into door 401 and looked down at her. "Welcome to the Ritz, kid.''

Pushing the door open, he stepped through and Elizabeth slowly followed. There was only one room to the apartment, with a tiny kitchenette fit into a corner. A dirty mattress lay on the floor, and the rest of the place was littered with clothes and debris.

She stood in the middle of the room, looking at the sum total of his mother's life, and felt an incredible sense of sadness for a life wasted, for a woman she never knew.

"She wouldn't have had much," he said distantly. "Best we can do is clear the place out." He picked up a box lying on the floor and dumped its contents on the mattress. A syringe rolled onto the floor. His gaze caught hers. "Must have kept it for old times' sake. Heroin was always her drug of choice, but when all her veins collapsed, she turned to crack."

His voice was matter-of-fact, as if he were discussing a ball game, but his eyes... Elizabeth looked into his eyes and knew she was looking into the pits of hell. She pushed aside the sickness at the realization of what he was telling her and sank to her knees beside him. "Let me help you. We'll put all the clothes in the bag, and anything you want to keep in this box. Make a pile of things to throw away."

She turned and quickly picked up the clothes strewed on the floor, wincing once or twice when something skittered from beneath them. When she'd finished, she went to the closet and opened it. There were a few more blouses on hangers, so she took them out and placed them in the sack. Spying a box on the shelf above the rack, she stretched up and retrieved it.

Elizabeth eyed it curiously. It was taped closed, and obviously hadn't been opened for a long time. The tape was dark with age, and cracked. She carried it over to where Sully was sorting. From the looks of the piles, he hadn't found anything he wanted to keep.

"What's that?" he asked.

"I don't know. I found it in the closet. Maybe it has her valuables in it."

He gave her a terrible parody of a smile and said, "Any valuables she ever had were sold long before I was born. By the time I knew her, drugs were her most prized possession."

Her gaze met his, held. "Tell me," she invited softly. She braced herself for his withdrawal, and the pain it would bring. He looked at her from enigmatic eyes, and that smile that really wasn't a smile faded. She saw the denial on his face, even before he voiced it. Then he looked away, and a muscle jumped in his jaw. She'd resigned herself to the fact that he'd shut down, again. Then his voice sounded, harsh and strained.

"This place isn't much different from most we lived in towards the end. At first, though, we at least had running water, real appliances." He stopped, his gaze roaming around the small apartment. She knew he wasn't seeing his mother's last home, but a series of his own.

"It didn't matter. We never stayed in one place long. She always said the way to keep people off our backs was to keep moving."

"What kind of people?"

He lifted a shoulder. "Cops. Do-gooders." He slid a glance at her and elaborated, "Social services. And then there were always the landlords who got ticked when rent wasn't paid. Which it often wasn't. Marcy stuck most of what she earned in her veins."

She struggled to imagine the life he was describing for her. It was a dark and desolate picture. "How did you live?"

"I was hungry a lot, until I became an accomplished thief." His eyes were shuttered. "I was a wise kid. Learned to walk miles to steal in better neighborhoods. People there had more to lose, and felt sorry for kids like me. Of course, it helped that I was big for my age, and quick. I dodged most of the trouble that could have come my way. Slugged my way out of the rest.''

She sat perfectly still, absorbing his words, and more, the tightly leashed emotion behind them. She'd known he hadn't had an easy life. The evidence was there in his eyes, in the constant guard he wore. But coming face-to-face with it now hurt unbearably. She ached for the little boy in tattered clothes who hadn't known if he would eat each day, or when. She and her mother hadn't had much after her father had died, but at least they'd been able to keep the house. And her mother's job, while not high paying, had kept groceries on the table.

''What kind of work did your mother do?''

''She worked on her back.''

Abruptly he rose and went to the window and stared out. Elizabeth knew he wasn't seeing the squalid street below. His gaze had turned inward. ''I don't know how old I was when I figured out what that line of strange men in and out of her bed meant.'' He shrugged. ''Five or six, I guess. I was always supposed to stay in the bathroom when she had 'guests,' or in the closet. Didn't take long before I preferred the streets. She told me once that she'd named me for my father—john. When I figured out what that meant, I started going by 'Sully'.''

Slowly, reluctantly he turned to look at her then, and froze. ''Damn you, don't you cry, Ellie. I don't need you crying over me.''

She made no move to wipe away the trickle of tears tracing down her cheeks. ''Yes, I think you do,'' she said shakily.

He turned away in a violent movement. ''Pity doesn't change anything.''

She rose and went to stand very close behind him, close enough to feel the heat radiating from his body, but not touching. Not yet. "Pity might not change anything, but caring does. I care, Sully. I always have. And because you can't cry, I'll do it for you." She leaned against him then, her face pressed against the taut muscles in his back, her arms linking around his waist. He was rigid in her embrace, but she didn't let go. She wondered if he really thought she couldn't see the scarred-over hurt beneath the anger.

She hurt desperately for the little boy who'd gone to bed hungry at night, lullabied by the sounds of addicts and johns. She'd wondered at that careful shield of his. Now she knew its cause, and it quite simply broke her heart.

"Why did you stay?" she murmured against his back. "There must have been someone you could have gone to…a teacher…the police."

"I was taught to spit at cops and dodge the suits. I went to a lot of different schools the way we moved around. At least it meant a couple of free meals a day. And it wasn't home or the streets." His hands went to hers and unleashed them, stepping away as if her touch was suddenly painful. He paced in the little room, kicking at the debris on the floor and sending the insects below it scuttling.

"She was getting more paranoid at the end. Always accusing me of stealing her stash, or hiding it. I only tried that once—when I was a kid. Flushed it down the toilet, and she beat me until I could barely walk. Taught me that people can't be saved, if they don't want to be. And she didn't want to be."

"And yet…you stayed."

He was silent while he reached for a cigarette, lit it. It was half-burned-down before he spoke again. "I stayed. Around, anyway. She was getting herself into more trouble by then. She'd been a looker, but the drugs took their toll on her physically and mentally. I needed to get some odd jobs to come up with bail money for when she'd get picked up for prostitution. She'd always come home shaken, full of tears and promises.''

The reason, she thought sickly, for his reluctance to make a promise, any promise, to her. She wondered how many had been made and broken by his mother. Enough to cause him to doubt, to teach a young boy distrust.

He took a quick, deep puff of the cigarette, then dropped it to the floor and ground it out. "Let's get finished up here and go."

She bent down and folded up all the clothes and put them in the sack. "Is this to be thrown away?" she asked about the pile he had in the middle of the mattress. When he nodded, she placed the things in the empty box, while he picked up the debris littering the floor. "What about this other box? Are you going to open it?"

His back to her, he answered, "Go ahead."

She ripped off the tape and opened the flaps. There were some documents inside, and a few pictures. She picked up one of the snapshots, curling at the edges. A little boy with a shock of white hair dressed in a pair of shorts, solemn and unsmiling. Her lips tilted. Sully. She didn't need the name printed on the back to recognize the still, waiting air that had existed even when he was—she checked the back again—seven years old. She riffled through the photos, ignoring the yellowed documents for the time being. There was one of Sully as an infant, and a few more taken up until the time he was eleven. One showed him with his mother, who was holding up a hand to ward off the camera.

She took out the packet of documents, and noticed a few more snapshots on the bottom of the box. She picked them up and studied them, turning them over to read the back. "Did you have any relatives?"

He looked swiftly through the cupboards, then brought

handfuls of trash back to the box they were using to discard it. "If I did, I never knew them. Why?"

She turned to look at him, the photographs still in her hands, questions in her eyes. "Then who were Jed and Cage Sullivan?"

Chapter 11

Sully surveyed her impassively. A streak of grime marred her skirt, picked up, no doubt, from her position kneeling on the filthy floor. He'd expected to see horror in her eyes at his story; he'd steeled himself to face her revulsion. Pity was almost as distasteful.

Pity would have been simpler to overlook, to walk away from. But Ellie had offered more than that. When he'd seen those tears sliding down her cheeks, tears for him, the tight knot in his chest had loosened a fraction. It was then he'd realized how much he'd been anticipating a much different reaction. By telling her more, far more, than he'd ever told another soul, he'd expected to see her cringe away. It probably would have been easier for both of them if she had.

He strode over and took the photographs from her and studied them. The first depicted a toddler and an infant. In the next the boys were older. His mother was holding the younger of the two, and the other boy was standing beside them. He turned them over. They were both dated before his birth. He handed them back to Ellie and shook his head. "I can't figure it. My mother was from Nebraska, but she came to Florida when she was eighteen. We had no relatives that I ever heard about."

Ellie held up the packet of documents, and he took them from her, and flipped through them. There was his mother's birth certificate, complete with her parents' names, Henry James Sullivan and Marilyn Denton Sullivan. He was unprepared for the jolt the names gave him. They were unfamiliar; Marcy had never spoken of her home, had only said her family was dead. But they would have been his grandparents. For the first time in his life he thought about family, and what it would have been like to have one. He couldn't imagine it. There had only been Marcy and him, and she'd always been more shadow than substance in his life.

"Is your birth certificate in there, too?" Ellie asked.

He shook his head. "I've got mine."

"Then what are those?"

He tore his gaze away from the certificate in his hand and looked at the next one. He stared dumbly for a moment, then comprehension punched through him and sent him reeling.

"Sully?"

When he didn't answer, Ellie rose and peered down at the document in his hand. "It's another birth certificate." Shock filtered through her voice, and her gaze flew to his. "For Jed Sullivan."

He turned to the next paper, certain of what he'd see, yet the sting of shock was fresh. "And Cage Sullivan. Birth mother Marcy Elaine Sullivan. Fathers...unknown." Just like his own read, he thought dully. There had been a lot of men through Marcy's life over the years, transient men who hadn't stayed for more than a month, a week, an hour.

Three of them had become fathers. He doubted they'd ever known it, or that they would have cared.

Checking the dates, he found that the boys had been older than him—Cage by two years, and Jed by almost four. Brothers.

The shaft of emotion that pierced him then went deep and burned. He'd always been alone. Marcy had been more a self-indulgent child than a parent, concerned with getting high, staying high and getting money for her next fix. It had never occurred to him to wish for brothers or sisters. He'd learned early you didn't ask, you didn't want. Disappointment was infrequent when there were no expectations.

He turned to the last sheaf of papers in his hand, and unfolded them. They were written in legalese, and he frowned, trying to make sense of them. He felt Ellie's hand on his arm, heard her indrawn breath, knew understanding dawned in both of them at the same time.

"She gave them up." His voice sounded dully in his own ears.

"They were taken away," Ellie murmured. She leaned closer to read the rest of the document. "They charged her with neglect. She probably didn't have many options."

He swung away from her. "She chose to sign over her parental rights rather than make the changes the court ordered. Everyone has options, Marcy just chose the drugs. She always did. Do you know how many treatment centers I've put her in over the years? Six. She only made it three days in the last one before she took off again."

He gave a humorless laugh that tasted sour in his throat. "They told me at those places over and over that the addict has to want to change. And no matter how much she cried and promised, she didn't want to change."

He prowled the small area, the tension coiled tightly inside him. "I'd set her up in an apartment, pay the rent on it and pay a nearby restaurant to feed her whenever she stopped in. I knew better than to send her money, or give her anything she could sell. But that last time I took her to treatment did it. When she ran, she ran from me. She went on her own rather than chance me trying, one more time, to help her.''

He avoided looking at her. Coming here had freed long-dormant memories. It hurt seeing Ellie here, more than he could ever have predicted. And because it hurt he lashed out, wanting to shock her. ''I didn't ask the hospital what she died of. I didn't have to. She had AIDS.'' He turned to her then, wanting to see the revulsion, the horror on her face. ''She was diagnosed five years ago. The only surprise is that it didn't appear sooner. Her life-style was about as high-risk as it gets.''

He waited then for the disgust to appear on her face. But she said nothing, and her expression never changed. Her gaze was steady on him and for a moment he forgot himself and wished he could take what it was offering. Comfort, sympathy.

He scrubbed both hands over his face. The room, the day's events were closing in on him. It was so easy back here to remember where he came from, and what he was, what he'd always be. A man who'd grown up suspicious of everyone he'd ever met, one who regarded trust as a luxury for dreamers and fools.

Ellie rose with the bag and the box she'd taken from the closet. ''I think we're done here.'' Her voice was calm, matter-of-fact. She handed him the bag and retained her hold on the box. ''Let's see if you can remember how to get us back to the hotel.''

He let her guide him out the door and didn't look back as she pulled it shut behind them. He didn't have to. The room, as with all the others like it, was branded on his memory. She talked all the way down the stairs. He couldn't concentrate on the words, but focused on the way her low, soothing voice seemed to cut through the sounds of arguments, the raucous stereo and the cries of the child that seemed to envelop them.

The old woman was still sitting in front of the building. Without a word he dropped the sack in front of her, then turned Ellie away as the woman started rooting through it. "We're going to have to walk a ways to find a taxi." His eyes cut to the group of gangbangers loitering on the curb, and he moved closer to Ellie. "Don't worry. We'll make it okay."

There was a different meaning in her eyes, in her voice, when she said, "I'm not worried. I have faith in you."

Her words brought a familiar jangle of pain and pleasure, but for once, just this once, he pushed the pain aside and let himself concentrate on the pleasure.

"You didn't eat much." Elizabeth got up and joined Sully at the railing of the small balcony outside his room.

"I'm not really hungry."

That's what he'd told her when they'd gotten back to the hotel and she'd suggested finding a restaurant. She'd decided to order room service instead. As far as she knew, he hadn't eaten at all that day, and the hours had been stressful. She eyed the remaining food on the trays that had been delivered by the hotel kitchen. If the time came when he was prepared to eat, she could order more. She just wished it would be as easy to fix what else ailed him.

It was agonizing to watch Sully hurt. A stranger might interpret his silence, his absence of expression, as a lack of feeling. But she knew better. Beneath the surface there seethed such a cauldron of emotions she wondered if he could even identify all of them. She doubted he'd had much practice at it. Left to his own devices, he'd tuck them away in the bruised corners of his mind, along with the unwanted memories he'd torn open for her today. The need to comfort warred with the need to make him lay some of those emotions out in the open where their sting would lessen with time. She took a deep breath and prepared for battle.

"What did you arrange with the funeral home?"

He leaned on his forearms and didn't look away from the tiny pool ten stories below them. "A graveside service tomorrow afternoon. Someone from the place will say a few words." His voice was raspy from the cigarettes he'd been smoking nonstop since they'd returned to the hotel.

He brought the one in his hand to his lips absently. "Marcy wasn't much for religion, so it didn't make sense to get a minister."

She turned and propped herself against the railing so she could watch his face. "Are you going to look for them?"

"Who?"

"Don't be annoying, Sullivan. You know who. Your brothers." Nothing like taking the bull by the horns, she thought. But left to himself, Sully would bury the information he'd learned today in that dark, tormented spot he shoved all unpleasant memories, safe from the light of day.

"There's no point."

She waited, but he said nothing else, seeming to find the tip of his cigarette fascinating.

"No point in what? No point in the Marlins playing out the rest of the season? No point in Congress continuing to fund Star Wars?" She waited a heartbeat, then added, "Or no point in letting yourself start to care about two brothers you never knew you had?"

His eyes did meet hers then, and irritation was visible in them. "Knock it off, Ellie."

"No, I don't think I will," she said with a calm she was far from feeling. She'd never pushed Sully deliberately before. It was a little like baiting a tiger. She knew that he wouldn't hurt her, but she couldn't be exactly certain what she'd unleash. "You can't tell me you don't wonder about them, about what happened to them. What are they like? Do they look like you? Have either of them made you an uncle?"

"That's enough."

The hint of warning in his voice had nerves prickling along her spine, but it didn't convince her to quit. "It wouldn't be that difficult to ask a few questions, would it?"

He stared hard at her, then shook his head slowly. Gradually he relaxed again against the railing. "Adoption files are closed."

"You're assuming they were adopted," she said. Triumph reared up inside her. He had to have been giving it some thought to come up with that idea. "They may not have been. They could have remained in foster care until they were grown. Or if they were adopted, they may have opened the file themselves by starting a search for their birth mother."

"Drop it." Although his voice was even, the words sounded as though they'd been chipped from a glacier.

"I'm not going to drop it, Sully, and neither should you. You might have been alone all your life, but you don't have to be anymore. You have family out there somewhere. All you have to do is look for them."

"Family?" The disbelief in his voice lashed at her. "Because we share a mother? That doesn't make us any more a family than a litter of pups. I'll admit that I don't have much experience with the concept, but even I know that."

"So you're just going to give up on them." Her temper was beginning to simmer. "You're not going to make any moves to find your brothers, because then maybe, just maybe, you'd have to open a little of yourself up and let someone else inside. And that would be too much risk for you, wouldn't it? Sully, the emotional submarine. At the first hint of rough waters, your instinct is to dive."

His eyes had chilled to ice, but she didn't care. An unfamiliar recklessness was coursing through her. "You think I don't understand why you let me come with you today?"

He snorted. "Let you? I'd have had a better chance trying to stop an earthquake."

"I think part of you wanted me to see how you grew up." He stiffened a little, but remained silent. "You could have told me yourself any number of times over the years if you wanted, but you never did. You didn't want to today, either, so I can only guess that you had other reasons. What were they, Sully? Did you think I'd be so disgusted by what I saw here that I'd walk away?"

She saw the truth in the clenching of his jaw, the flicker in his eyes, and it hurt, it hurt unbelievably. "That's it, then." Her gaze dropped to the railing, which her hands were clutching, white knuckled. Consciously she relaxed them. "I guess you place me in the same category of those 'do-gooders' you once dodged."

"Don't be stupid."

"You're the one being stupid, Sullivan." Tears were forming a hot ball in her throat, and she hated it. She wasn't going to cry, not now. She'd much rather take a swing at his hard, stubborn jaw. "You're stupid if you think that your wreck of a childhood makes you any less than what you are. A decent man, who cares more than he wants anyone to know."

He brought the cigarette to his lips and inhaled. "Yeah, that's me. Saint Sullivan."

"Not by a long shot, buddy. But you're not exactly Satan's long-lost twin, either."

Very deliberately he drew deeply from the cigarette one more time, before dropping it to the ground and grinding it out. "We're not going to discuss it, Ellie."

She took a step closer to him, her chin angling up. "Yes. We are."

He turned and walked back into the bedroom. She trailed after him. "You aren't going to get rid of me. I'm not going anywhere. I wish you'd let yourself believe that."

His voice was emotionless. "You'd be better off if there was a little distance between us for a while."

"The way your brothers would be better off if they never knew of your existence?" she countered. "That'd be the easy way out, wouldn't it? Then you'd never have to let yourself care, never have to take a risk that maybe, just maybe, you could get something more from life."

"I've gotten everything in this life I've got coming to me."

"That is such a crock!" She strode over and tugged on his elbow. He didn't move, so she shoved in front of him, where he'd have to look at her. Have to face her. "Happiness isn't rationed. You have to reach out and take it when you find it."

"Leave it alone." His eyes were cold, but with a shimmer of anger that threatened to erupt.

"Or what?" Her voice dared him. "Or you'll slice me out of your life, as well as any chance you've ever had to be happy?"

He lowered his face close to hers and snarled, "I shouldn't have to slice you out of my life. You oughtta be running, baby. If you had the sense God gave a gnat, you'd be putting as much distance as you could between us, and then you'd keep it that way."

Satisfaction snaked through her, winding through the nerves. The lid was off his tightly controlled emotions. They were boiling now, churning out of him. "And why would I want to do that?"

"That room today was a mirror of every place I've ever lived. That neighborhood was everywhere I've ever been. You were out of place there, but I *belonged*."

"No. It's where you used to belong."

He started to whirl away, but she stopped him with a tug on his belt loop. When his eyes met hers again, the icy indifference was gone. She recognized the fury, welcomed it.

"You think because of what you saw today you understand all there is to know about me?" He stopped, raked a hand through his hair. "I'm not what you think I am. There are things I can't tell you, or hell, maybe I can, but I haven't."

It was hard to watch him wrestle with his demons. Poison still leaked from wounds he'd long thought healed. "You're the only one who can open that door," she said softly. "Take a chance, Sully. Let someone in." Before he could regain that rigid control he'd let slip, she slid her hand up his shirtfront. Muscles jumped reflexively beneath her palm. "Let *me* in." Her fingers trailed back down his shirt, then up again.

"Is it really that difficult?" She ignored his soft curse, and when he took a step back, she followed, keeping the touch intact. "Do you want to be alone the rest of your life, or are you just scared to take a chance?" She didn't know whether his start was in reaction to her words or to the finger that had slipped inside his buttonhole to touch scalding skin.

"You don't get it." The words were little more than a rasp, but she smiled, slow and serene.

"I think I'm beginning to." Her words should have distracted him from the button she released on his shirt to gain better access to his chest, but from his hissed breath she'd only partly succeeded. "I really think I'm beginning to." His hands came up to pull hers away, so she leaned closer and pressed her lips against the skin she'd bared. His heart was rocketing in his chest, thudding in her ear.

She took strength and courage from the sound. He looked like he was fighting a war with himself. Whatever feelings

the day's events had unlocked, they were raw now, close
to the surface.

She watched his throat work, then freed her hand from
his and traced the muscle that was jumping in his jaw. He
jerked away as if her touch scorched him and retreated a
few steps.

"You should go back to your room."

His words made her heart stutter for a moment, before
it began a rapid tattoo beat. He was looking everywhere
but at her, and for the first time since she'd met him she'd
swear he was wearing nerves. The air-conditioning made
the slight sheen above his lip unnatural, and his fingers
were clenching and unclenching, until he shoved them in
his pocket with barely restrained violence.

The gesture made her breath hitch with apprehension and
something else, something she'd only recently gained the
experience to identify as desire. For the first time she
thought about the dangers of baiting the tiger. Especially
one as hungry as Sully. She almost felt remorse at pushing
him so hard at a time he was most vulnerable. But vulnerability was rare in the man; vulnerability stripped layers
from those defenses until she could see what he strove to
hide from the world. Emotions, dark and turbulent, frothing
white water from a lifetime of being forced back deep in
the caverns of his soul.

And she'd have them. She'd have every last one of them.

"Make me."

His head whipped to hers and if she'd been able, she
would have smiled at the disbelief on his face. But her lips
couldn't fashion a smile, could barely control a tremble.
Her limbs felt heavy; she couldn't have left the room if
she'd tried.

"You don't know what you're asking for."

"I know what I'm *not* asking for. No soft lights. No
mood music. No careful little seduction."

He was completely rigid, the force of his control almost palpable. She approached him on legs that were inclined to wobble, and her fingers went to his shirt, stumbling over the buttons. He was still while she unfastened them, pulled the shirttail from his jeans. The only hint at the powerful battle waging within him was in the flare of his nostrils, the muscles quivering beneath his skin.

His words sounded strangled. "I can't give you what you need."

She studied that expanse of taut flesh before her, neatly bisected by its triangle of chest hair. Her hands slid up the smooth skin on his sides, fingers lingering over knots of scar tissue. Blindly she leaned forward, opened her mouth against him in a shocking need to taste flesh. His flavor shuddered through her, and he was forced to take more of her weight, as her knees grew weaker.

She never thought of it as seduction. Never imagined she could wrap its velvet chains around him, around them both. She only knew that however it had begun, she was tangled in a web of her own making. It was harder to tell the effects on him when they were blurred by her own yearning, clawing to get free.

"The only thing I need is you." The voice didn't sound like hers, the words thick in her throat. "Wanting me. Showing it." Her head fell back, too heavy for her neck. "Show me again, Sully."

She could actually feel the effort it took for him to remain rigid in her embrace. Could feel the shudders rippling across otherwise unyielding sinew and tissue. She heard the short, staccato breaths, felt his chest expand with each one.

And she felt it when that control snapped, when the blood raged through veins and nerve endings and muscles surged to life. His arms clamped around her with a force that should have frightened, but instead exhilarated.

The tiger had sprung.

His mouth covered hers with a bruising force that might have been terrifying if she didn't crave just that proof of his need, didn't return it with an answering greed. Other women might want pretty words and gentle hands. But right now, from this man, all she wanted was the hunger, clean and sharp. Unvarnished. A match for her own.

He wasn't careful when he pulled the sleeveless top over her head, yanked the skirt down over her hips. He had her bared to her camisole and tap pants within a matter of seconds. Her hands were just as frenzied. She pushed his shirt aside, and he shrugged his massive shoulders to let it drop from his arms. She got no more than the button undone on his jeans before she was caught in a dizzying twirl and tumbled on the bed. They rolled once, twice, before settling, him above her.

Damp flesh was pressed to damp flesh. Skin heated wherever it touched. His hands moved over her body, gripping, pressing, possessing. Hers were no more gentle. His mouth was streaking over her, and her body was vibrating under his. She was ravenous for every sensation he could give her, every peak he could drive her to. She wanted to feast on all the simmering, violent emotion he'd fought to keep chained for years.

Her teeth grazed his shoulder as her mouth went in search of his. His kiss was hot, avid, carnally explicit. She could taste the tang of the wine he'd had for dinner, the slightly bitter taste of tobacco and the dark, mysterious flavor that was uniquely Sully. His tongue swept her mouth, stealing her breath, then his lips moved lower.

Her neck bowed for the scrape of his teeth, the rasp of his beard. A gasp strangled in her throat as his mouth strung a burning line of kisses along the sensitive cord below her ear. His hands snaked inside her camisole and cupped her breasts. She murmured a pleased sound as his thumbs rubbed against the sensitized nipples, then his hands were gone. The lacy top was pulled over her head and thrown over his shoulder, and he lowered his mouth to suckle.

Rich, dark tendrils of pleasure twisted deep inside Elizabeth with each flex of his cheeks, each stroke of his tongue. Her heels pressed into the bed, and her back arched, straining to offer him more. Unconsciously her hands came up to fist in his hair as she held him to her. There was a wildness, a greed in him that struck a responding chord. If he was desperate, so was she. His impatience fired her own. The prick of his teeth against her skin had her blood churning thicker, hotter. She could feel the primitive, rhythmic pulsing just under her flesh.

One calloused palm skated down her side and cupped her thigh, stroking up again in one smooth movement. His fingers just grazed the skin where leg and hip joined, and nerve endings sang. She burned with the need to touch him, to show him even a fraction of the heat he'd generated. She pushed frantically at his shoulders until he raised his head.

His eyes were hot, lambent, with an edge of barely leashed urgency. He lifted away a little, so she was free to slick her hands over damp, heated skin. Out of control, she thought dimly. She was as out of control as he was, and reveling in it. She reared up and pressed tiny, nibbling kisses across his chest and throat. She was fiercely glad for the early-evening sun slanting in through the windows, making it possible for her to study his every nuance of reaction. She couldn't get enough of it, couldn't get enough of *him.*

Impatience bucked inside her, and her hands dropped to his jeans. She'd never known she could feel this kind of passion for a man, never known a man to respond in the same way. The hunger was honed to a painful edge. She drew the zipper down over the tight bulge in back of it before her wrists were braceleted.

"No, not now," he rasped in her ear. "Not yet."

His mouth careened down her torso, licking over tight, sensitized breasts, pausing to dip his tongue in her navel. Her hands were released and they dived into his hair. He could make her forget. He could make her think of nothing but the sensations slapping through her, each with enough force to send her reeling.

She could feel his heated breath between her legs, against the silk covering her. Her eyes had only a moment to flutter open as the panties were drawn down and his tongue traced the crease of her thigh. She gave a little sigh of contentment, a murmur of pleasure, then his mouth streaked to her center and that heat became an inferno. She cried out, shock holding her rigid, before the flood of sensation began to rise.

He tilted her hips to his mouth and devoured her, thrusting her deeper into the eye of the storm. The pleasure was razor sharp. The air was too thick to breathe; she had to fight it into her lungs. Each stabbing motion of his tongue had the tension drawing her body tighter and tighter until her body was a mass of quivering nerve endings and tearing needs. The heat and lightning were staggering her. A knot clenched in her stomach, and then the explosion rocked her, and she was crying out, shocked, shattered.

The climax left her limp. She floated down from its peak, her body weightless. Her eyes fluttered open, unfocused when she heard Sully's voice.

"More."

He shot her from relief to wanting with one sure touch. She could feel her inner muscles clenching around him greedily, and impatience reared again, chiseled by desperation. With every motion he had the ache spreading, until even her bones throbbed with it.

"Sully, please." The words sobbed from her chest, from her lips. Her fingers clutched at his shoulders, nails raking in a desperate attempt to force him to join her, to end it together. He stood and shimmied out of his jeans, taking time to protect her, then made a place for himself again between her legs.

He entered her with a powerful lunge that had her arching her back, striving to take him deeper. He dragged her legs over his hips to open her fully and thrust harder, driving twin moans from both of them.

Elizabeth could already feel the comet of sensation zinging through her body, see the kaleidoscope of color exploding under her eyelids when Sully stopped above her, within her.

"Open your eyes, Ellie. Look at me." His voice was low, urgent, little more than a growl. She forced her heavy eyelids open to see him, only him. The muscles in his biceps quivered as he braced himself above her. She was trapped in a cage of his making. There was nowhere she'd rather be. She stretched beneath him and felt him stir within her, and his eyes went dark. "I want to watch you." His mouth came down on hers, devouring. "I want to see you."

Their gazes locked, he began to move again, and immediately she could feel the sparks starting deep inside her. Her hands moved over him restlessly, across his shoulders, down his muscled back, over his hips. His head reared back. She could feel him go tense, and still he never looked away. He yanked her body up, plunged deeper, thrusting harder in a pounding rhythm that had answering sobs of need breaking from her lips.

Higher and higher they climbed. There was nothing else she could want, nothing else she could need. Just the feel of Sully's hard body. The sight of the savage hunger on his face, the unleashed need. Her fingers raked down his back, and she clutched him to her as she felt the first tremors of pleasure start to unfurl deep in her belly.

She chanted his name as the climax pummeled her, nearly sobbing the words. Because her eyes were open, she could see his face contort. The grip on her hips grew tighter, and as the sensations slammed into her, he gave a powerful surge of his hips and joined her in the free fall into pleasure.

Awareness returned in gossamer layers. Her eyes fluttered open slowly, to see Sully's face close to hers, his gray eyes smoky and demanding.

"Again."

Chapter 12

"Mr. Vargas is anxious for an update on your progress."
Conrad clasped his hands on the desk before him like a
well-mannered schoolboy.

Sully raised an eyebrow. "What did you tell him?"

There was the barest tinge of worry in the other man's
voice. "That things were going well." The anxiety became
more noticeable when he added, "They are going well,
aren't they, Roarke?"

Nodding, Sully reached for a cigarette. "I've got the
plans drawn up. I've refined them as much as I'm able
without knowing for certain which stops in the Midwest he
wants to make."

"Trucks, you said." Conrad's fingers clenched and unclenched against his knuckles. "Do you think they're a
better way to go than planes?"

Sully drew smoke in and held it as he considered the
man's words. "Better? Not necessarily."

Panic flickered across Conrad's smooth countenance.
"But you said…"

"I was thinking of safer. Cheaper. Trucks tend to be more risk free than rail or planes, simply because there are fewer people to involve. No landing fields, no rail inspections. Just some semis and drivers with valid commercial driver's licenses. The driver sends for the correct DOT labels, we supply him with some forged shipping papers and he's in business."

He leaned forward and used the ashtray on Conrad's desk. "Have you done much traveling across country, Mr. Conrad?"

The man looked puzzled at the question. "Of course."

"By car?"

"No. I fly if there's any distance involved."

Sully nodded. "If you did much road traveling, you'd know what I'm talking about. Trucks rule the highways in this country. They're everywhere and they have the capacity to haul huge loads. As long as it has the proper papers and labels, it's not overloaded and the driver obeys the speed limit, there's no reason for it to be stopped. A driver can travel from the Gulf of Mexico to northern Minnesota without being bothered."

Conrad brought his linked hands up and leaned his chin on them. "How big a load can one of these trucks carry?"

"A big semi could easily haul fifty-thousand pounds and still be below the legal limit." He watched, satisfied, as the man mentally calculated kilos into pounds.

"What did you mean by needing labels?"

Sully inhaled slowly, studying the man before him. The only other time he'd seen the man this edgy was when Vargas was visiting. The Colombian must be powerful indeed to strike this kind of fear in Thomas Conrad. Then he remembered Toby, and wondered if it wasn't Vargas's ferocity that had the other man running scared.

"Every truck has to carry a label of some kind indicating

the type of load it's hauling. A driver just sends to DOT for them. There's no hassle involved.''

"I assume there would be a hassle if the driver got pulled over and it was found he wasn't hauling what he's supposed to be.''

Taking a last draw, Sully leaned forward and stubbed his cigarette out in the ashtray. "But our drivers will be carrying what it says on their label. Or at least it will look that way.'' At Conrad's blank expression, he explained, "Mr. Vargas wants to distribute in the Midwest. That's farm country, right? Farmers need herbicides. The trucks will have permission to carry them. The herbicides these days come in packets. We'll get some of the empty boxes with the correct markings, plus we'll have a few boxes of the real thing. That way we can put a couple layers of the herbicides over the top of the packages of cocaine, in case anyone gets too interested.''

Conrad pursed his lips and contemplated the scenario Sully had just outlined, searching it for flaws. He wouldn't find any, Sully knew, and the knowledge brought him mixed feelings. He'd just given the man a very workable plan for smuggling great quantities of cocaine to the heartland, expanding their market substantially. But Conrad and Vargas would never have an opportunity to use it. He'd see to that.

"It really sounds like it could work,'' Conrad mused.

"It will work. The next step is to run this by Mr. Vargas. He's got some decisions to make. Does he want to buy the trucks himself and hire drivers, or does he want me to find people with their own rigs? How many trucks is he interested in?''

Conrad tapped his fingers against his lips. "As you say, we need input from Mr. Vargas on this. But if each truck has a capacity of fifty-thousand pounds, I would estimate that we'd require at least four semis.''

Sully did some quick mental math and then stared hard at the man. The sheer volume he was suggesting was staggering. And with the ten thousand dollars per kilo Vargas would make by eliminating the middlemen in Miami, he stood to raise his profits by the tens of millions. If his cover was real, he thought cynically, now would appear to be a perfect time to ask for a raise.

"When you speak to Mr. Vargas, tell him I'll need a bankroll to start the purchases."

"Of course. I'll get back to you soon after I've contacted him." Conrad reached inside his desk drawer and withdrew an envelope, which he held out to Sully. "Well done, Roarke. I think our employer will be pleased." A smile eased his countenance. "As a matter of fact, I think he'll agree with me that your plan is nothing short of ingenious."

"You're a mess."

Ellie tilted her head at him. "Did I ever tell you what it does to me to hear you talk so sweet? I just get gooey inside."

"Cute."

She stepped aside, and he entered her apartment. Maybe he hadn't engaged his brain before he'd spoken, but the word had been accurate. The sleeveless smock she wore was spattered with clay, as were her arms. She had a matching streak on one cheek. And if he wasn't mistaken, that was paint she was wearing on her nose.

He drew the logical conclusion. "You've been working."

"And you're smart, too," she marveled, teasing.

He looked down at her, mussed and untidy, with a hint of a smile lurking at the corner of her mouth. He wanted to take that mouth with his, wanted to seep himself in her taste again, until the dangerous ugliness he was immersed in faded away. He wanted to lay her down and rediscover all the sweet secrets of her body, drown in her, until they were both spent and wasted. And because he wanted it so desperately, he did nothing.

"And you're a smart-*ass,*" he noted mildly. He walked by her, studying the changes she'd made in her apartment. He nodded at the long worktable she had set up in front of the windows. "When did you get that?"

"I had it delivered during my noon hour yesterday." She wrinkled her nose. "Of course, that meant I had to rush home to let the deliverymen in and then rush back across town. I was an hour late and I thought Nathan was going to have a stroke. Not even Monica could save me from one of his famous lectures." She ran a hand over the smooth surface of the tabletop, transferring some paint to her fingers. She didn't seem to notice.

"It was worth it, though. Now I don't have to paint at the kitchen table. I've already done two pieces." She nodded at the kiln in the corner. "They're firing now."

He chose a paint-free corner of the table and propped his hip against it. "You've been busy."

She nodded. "When I hear from Simon again, I want to be ready with at least a half a dozen pieces. In case he wants to see them, I mean. If he does."

"He will." The quiet certainty in his statement seemed to please her, and she beamed at him.

"Are you thirsty? I'll get you a beer."

He glanced pointedly at her hands. "I think I'll get it myself, thanks."

When the phone rang, she made no move toward it, saying, "The machine will pick up."

He turned from the refrigerator and twisted the bottle top off the beer, taking a long swallow. Ellie added some water to the clay on her wheel, and then threw a damp towel over it.

As he listened to the caller's message, his mouth flattened. "The *Miami Herald?* How many calls have you been getting from reporters?"

She made a face. "That makes six. I've managed to dodge them so far."

He took a long drink from the beer, then lowered the bottle to gaze at her. "There's no reason why you can't talk to them. Tell them the truth. Carter isn't going to be bothering you anymore. I took care of him."

Her eyes went wide. He wondered what she thought he'd done to silence Carter. With a flicker of regret he considered that it hadn't been half of what he'd wanted to do. But it had been enough. Robinson was too concerned about his career to jeopardize it. And thanks to the little chat Sully had had with Postal, that career should be stalling right about now. Robinson would be too busy trying to resuscitate it to trouble Ellie again.

"Exactly...how did you handle Carter?" she asked.

"He likes to play games." He grinned wolfishly. "So I played a little hardball with him."

If anything, the worry on her face deepened. "You didn't do anything that's going to get you arrested, did you?"

He pretended to take a moment to think. The smile spread to his eyes when he saw the way hers narrowed at him. He finally took pity on her. "Nope."

She didn't smile back. "The last thing I want is to be the cause of trouble for you, Sully."

The concern in her voice had his chest growing tight. He still hated the idea of what she'd been prepared to do to protect him, while another part of him grappled with amazement that she would want to. No one else had ever shown him an ounce of her compassion; no one else had ever been allowed close enough to offer it. By some twist of chemical reaction, it was only *this woman* who mattered, only her feelings he cared about. He vaguely recollected from a distant biology class that all emotions started in the brain, but somehow that didn't seem true in his case. The emotion she pulled from him came from much deeper, more gut level. He no longer questioned the urge he'd had to maintain a connection from the first time they'd met. The pull had been instinctive, and inevitable.

Belatedly he answered, "Don't worry about it. Like I said, it's been taken care of."

Walking over to the recliner, he began to sit down. He heard a loud "Yeowl," and sharp teeth raked his backside. He jumped up. "What the hell?" A huge, angry feline hissed at him, and they glared at each other from narrowed eyes.

"Oh, no!" Ellie hurried over to them. "You didn't hurt him, did you?"

Incredulously Sully realized the question was directed at him. "I think I got the worst of it, thanks to the teeth on that baby mountain lion there."

She stopped in front of the recliner and sank to her knees, her hands going to stroke the cat's ruffled fur, unmindful of the fangs it was still baring at Sully. "There, now, sweetheart, it's all right," she crooned. She looked up at Sully half-apologetically. "For some reason he seems to have taken a liking to your chair."

Sully's eyes slitted. The beast was actually rubbing its head against Ellie's arms and purring, although the rumble coming from its big body sounded more like a Volkswagen engine.

"Where did you find it, Ellie?"

"Actually he found me. After work yesterday I was walking to the bus stop, and he dashed between my legs and almost tripped me. He'd been in a fight fairly recently—see his ear? It needed some attention, so I brought him home to tend to it."

"On the bus?"

"No, I had to get a taxi." She was scratching the big

cat under the chin now, and its eyes were half-closed in pleasure. Every once in a while it would open them enough to send a malevolent glance in Sully's direction.

Sully looked at the wound she was indicating. Indeed, it looked as if the beast had been on the receiving end of that particular battle, and it had just been one of many. The tom was a walking collection of far older war wounds. There was a gouge of fur missing from one side, where there was a knot of scar tissue. Its tail had a crook in it, and there were scars on its face and back.

"I thought he might be someone's pet, so I took him back today and released him where I'd found him, but after work he came right up to me again, can you believe it? I'm beginning to think he doesn't have a home, do you, big guy?" she murmured, running a hand over his fur.

"There's a shock."

She raised a questioning glance to him, and Sully elaborated. "It's no pet, Ellie, it's a mangy old tom. Probably been living in back alleys all its life."

His words seemed to please her. "That's what I've been hoping. I bought him a few things today, in case he wants to stick around."

There wasn't much doubt about that, Sully figured. The battle-scarred beast had enough street smarts to know when he'd found a meal ticket.

"Does your landlord allow pets?"

A guilty look crossed her face, and Sully had his answer. "He's not going to cause any problems, are you sweetheart? I call him 'Bill,' because 'Tom' sounded too trite and anything else just seemed undignified. Are you hungry, hmm?" As a matter of fact Sully was, but again, she wasn't talking to him. She stroked the cat one last time before rising again and hurrying to the kitchen.

Sully stared down at the huge ball of fur unkindly. "You and me are going to have to reach an understanding here,

cat,'' he muttered. ''This chair? It's mine. And so is she.''
He jerked his head in the direction of the kitchen, where
Ellie was opening a can of cat food. ''She might be a soft
touch, but I'm going to be watching you.''

The cat stood up and leaped gracefully to the floor, where
it shook itself, as if to rid itself of Sully's words. Then it
sauntered into the kitchen to enjoy Ellie's dinner prepara-
tions, and Sully reclaimed his chair.

It was ridiculous to feel jealous of an animal, he reflected
as he listened to the sound of Ellie's voice in the kitchen
as she talked to the cat. And even more ridiculous to feel
an odd sort of kinship with the fleabag. He recognized Ellie's strays; he was one of them himself. He could match
the beast scar for scar, and he'd be willing to bet they'd
both spent more time than they'd care to admit in back
alleys. Neither of them deserved Ellie's care and her loving
touch, but she offered them anyway, with that sweet generosity of spirit that constantly astounded him. Time spent
with her opened little pockets of peace within him. Time
spent with her made him greedy for more.

He tipped the bottle to his lips and drank. Greed was a
dangerous thing. It made a man disregard what he knew in
his mind, and focus on the want, the need. He'd never been
one to waste time on regrets, so it was troubling now to
realize how often his mind turned to them. With increasing
frequency he was finding himself wondering what it would
be like if he were a different sort of man, one with a job
that didn't deal in lies, and drugs and death. A man who
didn't need to fear bringing those things home with him.

Ellie came out to the living room and perched on the
arm of his chair. ''Well, I've got one beast fed—I suppose
I ought to think about you next.''

His arm snaked out and tugged her down in his lap. ''It's
going to take more than a can of cat food to satisfy me.''

The look she sent him was surprised and pleased, then

her arms twined around his shoulders. "You must be hungrier than I thought."

He focused on her soft mouth as it shaped the words, the softness of her body as it molded against his, and his mind freeze-framed the moment. If time could stop here, right now, he'd die happy, and figure it was far more than he deserved. He tucked the bottle beside him and took her face in his hands, slowly combing her hair back with his fingers, drawing out the moment. Tenderness etched an aching path through him. It was an unfamiliar emotion, but not an unwelcome one. Slowly he fit his mouth to hers, and she responded with all the sweetness that was so much a part of her.

Lazily, with thorough care, he drank her taste and explored the moist, dark secrets of her mouth. He let her flavor trace through his senses, swallowed her purr of pleasure. The slow melt she did against his body had his blood quickening, but he made no move to deepen the kiss.

When his lips lifted from hers, he leaned his brow against hers. Her lips were damp and parted, her breath coming in short bursts. "Do you have to do something with that clay?"

"Hmm...?"

The dazed, languid sound she made had satisfaction curling through his stomach. "The clay on the wheel. Do you need to do something with it?"

Her eyes were open but still uncomprehending. Slowly they followed the direction of his gaze. "I guess I should put it away." She looked up at him then. "Unless you want to use it."

"Me?"

Her lips tilted. "Yeah, you. C'mon. I'll show you." He released her reluctantly and helped her to her feet. She took one of his hands in hers and tugged. "Let's go, Sullivan. You're about to get your first lesson in pottery."

He let her pull him to his feet, although he still wasn't sure what she was about. Trailing after her, he stared down at the wheel, with the separate bench he'd seen her sitting at dozens of times before. He looked at her, and found her studying him.

"I don't have a smock that will fit you." Her face was bland when she added, "Maybe you should take off your shirt."

Seconds ticked by. "My shirt."

She nodded. "No use taking the chance of ruining it with spattering clay. And you don't need to worry about me being overcome with lust, either. Remember, I *am* an artist. The human form is merely a collection of lines and angles to me."

He saw the glint in her eye, and played along. "Okay, then." With one smooth move he pulled his T-shirt over his head and threw it in the direction of the couch. He noted with satisfaction that the detachment she'd promised was missing in the long, avid gaze she sent over his chest. "Now you."

That pulled her gaze back to his face. "Pardon me?"

His fingers went to the buttons on her smock, and she stepped back hastily. "That won't be necessary," she said with a hint of laughter in her voice.

He looked down at the wheel. "Now what?"

She reached down and turned the bench lengthwise. "Sit down." She pushed at his shoulders and he obliged, straddling the bench awkwardly. She sat in back of him and stretched her arms around his waist, her hands reaching for his.

"This isn't going to work," she muttered.

"I disagree." The warm notch between her thighs was pressed snugly against his hips, and her bare arms wrapped around his middle. "I think it's working great."

"Uh-uh." She got up. "Slide back." He did so, and she

settled herself in front of him, reaching around to catch his hands and bring them forward. She pulled away the towel covering the damp clay and dropped it to the floor. "Wet your hands in the water and then put them in the clay." When he hesitated, she took his wrists and directed them. "C'mon, don't be a baby. Afraid you're going to get dirty?"

"I don't know if this is such a good idea," he muttered.

"You'll be fine." When his hands were in the bowl of clay, she flipped a switch, and the wheel started with a gentle whir. She placed her hands over his. "Let yourself get used to the texture first. No, don't tense up. Relax your wrists."

The cat, finished with its meal, padded over and sat at a safe distance to watch. Sully could have sworn it was wearing a smirk below its whiskers. "Ellie, I don't know..."

"Close your eyes," she ordered.

"What?"

"Close your eyes. You're thinking too much. Right now all you need to do is feel."

Reluctantly he did as she requested.

"Now relax. Feel the texture. Picture shapes in your mind."

Texture. Shapes. They filled his mind as ordered, but it wasn't the clay he was concentrating on. Instead, it was the feel of her hair as he leaned forward, his head above hers, her hair tickling his chin. The shape of her waist against his arms, the glide of her hands against his as the slick, wet clay slid between their fingers. Unconsciously he moved closer, dipped his head to inhale more deeply the fragrance that was uniquely Ellie.

"Good. Now open your eyes and watch our hands."

Again he did as she requested and watched fascinatedly as the damp clay began to take shape under their fingers. With the gentle guidance of her hands on his, sides began to form on the clay in front of them. Ellie dug out the center with her fingers.

He moved his head until it was beside hers, pressed his lips against the sensitive area below her ear. A quick shudder ran through her.

"The clay responds to each movement of your hand." Her voice was breathless. "Each action gives it a different shape."

His mouth cruised down her neck and lingered at the spot where it curved to meet her collarbone. Her skin quivered beneath his lips, responsive as the clay she'd mentioned. From memory he knew she would respond to each small touch of his hand, as well. A gentle brush, a long smooth stroke, and her skin would heat beneath his palm. His heart thudded as he remembered the shape of her breast in his hand, the smooth curve of her thigh, the hollow of her lower back.

Her neck arched to give him better access, and he took immediate advantage by nibbling his way to her jawline. Her fingers never moved from his, and the clay swirled around their hands. Her hair trailed over his shoulder, and it only took a turn of her head to meet his lips, only took a touch of her mouth to pull him down into a pool of sensation.

Her lips molded to his, and her tongue tasted of wild, sweet delights. Her taste churned through him, chugging in rhythm to the pounding in his blood. Her mouth was soft under his, but made its own demands. He tilted his head to better oblige them.

Freeing his hands from hers, he pushed them under the loose smock she wore and discovered warm, silky skin beneath it. Her breasts were bare, and he cupped them in his palms, shaped them just as her hands still shaped the clay it was steeped in and ran his slick fingers over her nipples. She went boneless and molded against him, her hands stilling, her head heavy on his shoulder. Her hands went to his wrists, and she traced those cool, wet fingers over him.

This was art, he thought dimly as his mouth ate at hers. A woman who gave until a man didn't know where he stopped and she began. Each time with her it started the same, the slap at the senses, the rush of desire, a fresh onslaught of pleasure. And each time was unique. The twist the passion took, the unexpected curves and turns, from wild, violent need to dark, languid arousal. He tore his mouth away from hers to bury it at the base of her throat. Each time new. Each time a rebirth.

Her hands slid up to cover his, and he raised his head. Her eyes fluttered open, then she glanced down at the clay that had toppled from their inattention.

"A masterpiece," she murmured, her voice faint and dazed.

His eyes never left her. "Yes." They were the masterpiece, what they created together each time they touched. He felt like a guilty thief, hoarding a stolen treasure, knowing he had no right to it. Caring less by the day.

He leaned forward and flipped the switch off, rose and picked her up easily in his arms. Her breath was a gentle sigh against his mouth. He didn't release her until they stood in the shower, his back to the pounding spray. He drew the smock over her head, the shorts down her thighs and let them lie on the bottom of the tub. His now wet jeans were more difficult to manage. Ellie helped push them over his hips, and then he was lifting her again, pressing her against the cool, wet tiles and sliding into her with one smooth stroke.

He pulled her legs tighter around his hips and braced himself with one hand against the tile. Pressing farther up inside her, he let the pleasure create anew.

Long after darkness had fallen, long after Ellie had slipped into slumber, exhausted and peaceful, Sully lay awake in her bed. She was cradled in his arms, her cheek pressed against his chest, her hair fanned over his shoulder. Sleep didn't beckon. He stroked the velvety skin along her back, lightly enough to avoid awakening her.

These were the times that were the most dangerous, when logic retreated and reason was difficult to summon. In the night, with this woman in his arms, her warmth reflecting his own, things had a way of seeming simpler than they were. He'd never been one to believe in hope, but there was no denying that it burst forth in moments like this one, made him think foolish, improbable things.

Like maybe the luxury of dreams wasn't just for other men. Maybe there was a chance, just a chance, for him to have a normal life. Maybe it wasn't a fool's prayer to believe in a future that included Ellie.

The darkness had a way of shrouding the doubts, making the realities of his life fade to shadows. One word continued to swirl across his mind like clouds of mist.

Maybe.

Chapter 13

"You look as smug as a cat with a pitcher of cream," said Monica, sidling up behind Elizabeth. She kept a practiced eye out for Nathan. "Anything you'd like to tell Auntie Monica?"

A small smile crossed Elizabeth's lips. "I have a few more pieces ready to show Simon."

"Yeah, right. Like that's enough to put that satisfied look on your face. C'mon, 'fess up, Elizabeth," she wheedled. "You're positively glowing. Only one thing can be responsible for that, and it's a three-letter word that starts with *M*. Could it be that hunk you've got locked in your bedroom?"

Elizabeth's head jerked. "I do not have him—anyone—locked in my bedroom."

"Then you ignored my advice, and a perfectly wonderful opportunity."

Letting loose an involuntary laugh, she said, "Honestly, Monica, you're incorrigible."

"Yes, I am. I'm also insatiably curious. So tell me all about it. It's that positively yummy guy I met at your apartment, isn't it? Is he as delicious as he looks?"

"You make him sound like a hot fudge sundae."

Monica's brows rose. "Now that you mention it, I'd bet he would look great wearing nothing but a little whipped cream."

Elizabeth's cheeks fired. In a war of double entendres with her friend, she was definitely outclassed. "You should be writing for *Playgirl*."

The other woman tilted her head, as if considering the suggestion. "You know, I think I could. What I lack in writing skills, I more than make up for in imagination. But don't think I can be sidetracked that easily. What gives with you, kiddo? You're positively glowing."

Elizabeth sent a look around the gallery. It was a slow afternoon, and Nathan was closeted in the office with the door shut. Although there really wasn't anything for her and Monica to be doing right now, their boss liked them to appear busy. She strode to a closet and came back with a couple feather dusters.

"Here," she said, handing one to the other woman. "Make yourself useful. Nathan will be checking on us any minute."

Monica followed Elizabeth around, wielding the duster on the display items in a desultory fashion. "I'm waiting."

Elizabeth bit back a sigh. "It is Sully, yes."

"Well, well, well." Her friend looked impressed, and a little speculative. "I have to admit to being supremely envious, and a bit surprised. Until I met him at your place, I never would have pictured you with someone like him."

Protective instincts rushed out in a torrent. "What's wrong with Sully?"

"Absolutely nothing, from what I could see, and believe

me, I was looking. Actually, I guess a guy like him is any woman's type.''

"I've known him since college. It's just recently that we…that he…''

Monica waited, and when Elizabeth stumbled to a halt, she gave a peal of laughter. "Honey, you can't even talk about it without turning four shades of red. I'd have thought a few nights with your Sully would have loosened some of those inhibitions of yours.''

Inhibitions. Elizabeth considered the word. They had certainly been part of her makeup until recently. Because she'd never experienced real desire from a man, she'd thought the lack had been hers. There had been a lingering fear that she was at least partly to blame for Carter's infidelity. If she had been more beautiful, more sexy, more experienced, maybe her ex-husband wouldn't have turned to another.

But her time with Sully was rebuilding her self-confidence in herself as a woman. She thought of long, endless minutes in the shower, their loving going from heated to tender, until the water had turned to ice, finally managing to cool their fevered bodies. Or of her legs straddling Sully, his fingers clenching on her hips as she rode them both to satisfaction. Despite what her friend thought, her inhibitions had definitely loosened. They simply didn't factor into the time spent with Sully. Restraint wasn't possible; thought wasn't clear. There was only the need, edgy and fierce, stabbing deep within her like a sharpened sword. Excitement, bubbling up in a froth of sensation. The erotic sexiness of watching Sully's face, waiting for the moment when his control would shatter and the hunger take over. She wondered if there was a woman alive who could hold on to inhibitions, no matter how deeply ingrained, faced with that depth of desire.

"There you go, blushing again.''

Elizabeth turned her attention to the copper sculpture before her. "I think it's safe to say I've shed a few of my inhibitions."

"Well, good for you," crowed Monica, surveying her with the duster tucked under one arm. "And no matter how much I want to, I'm not even going to beg to hear every sweaty, sexy detail. I'm going to give you your privacy." She waited a beat before drawling, "Unless of course, you're dying to brag."

"Dream on."

Monica sighed lustily. "Oh, I will, I will. That's about the only recourse I have lately." Then she grew serious. "But I am happy for you, girlfriend. If anyone deserves a break in the man department, it's you."

Elizabeth smiled at her friend. "Thanks. I feel pretty lucky."

"Take it from me—you *are* lucky. I'm having a tough time these days coming up with candidates that fit my lofty standards."

"And those are?"

"Sane, employed and breathing."

The two women went into gales of laughter, bringing Nathan out of the office to look down his long nose at them.

"Ladies? Do you have a problem finding something to do?"

"No, Mr. Milway," Elizabeth said meekly, returning to the dusting with studious fervor. She waited until the door to the office was closed before she noted in an undertone, "You realize, of course, your standards actually apply to Milktoast."

She ducked the duster Monica sent sailing her way, and this time they kept their giggles low-key.

"Hey, hey, hey, lovely lady."

The familiar voice sent a whisper of dread racing up her spine, leaving shivers in its wake. Deliberately Elizabeth kept her gaze forward. She finished paying for her takeout food, picked up the container and headed for the door.

Before she'd gotten more than a few feet, her way was blocked by a young black man holding a pool cue and sporting a wide grin. Elizabeth searched her memory for his name. Nushawn, Sully had called him. He'd said he was bad news, but she wouldn't have needed the warning. It was there in the man's stance, in the attitude that fit him as sleekly as his skintight T-shirt.

"Get out of my way." Elizabeth kept her voice steady, despite the wariness prickling under her skin. She knew better than to show fear to a man like this. He'd sense it and take immediate advantage.

Nushawn raised his hands in a conciliatory gesture. "Hey, no sweat. I ain't gonna hassle ya, not me. I just wanted to let you know, I din't mean nothin' that other day. Din't have no idea you was Roarke's lady, ya know what I mean?" His grin grew wider, but the look in his eyes was calculating. "Don't need that kind of trouble, no way, no how. You tell Roarke we cool, okay?"

She stared at the man uncomprehendingly. "What are you talking about?"

He seemed to a move to a beat heard only in his head. His entire body bobbed to the rhythm of it. "I mean your man, *the* man, Roarke. Tall dude, blond hair, mean temper." He gave a mock shudder. "I don't need me that kind of trouble, and since that time, Roarke, he looks at me like he wants to slice me in half. Dude could do it, too." There was a flicker of real fear in his eyes, and his grin faded a few degrees. "I just seen ya here, and thought I'd apologize." He sketched a half bow. "'Cause I'm a gentleman, ya know what I mean? Now, you tell Roarke Nushawn said he was sorry."

He stepped aside, but Elizabeth didn't move. She couldn't.

"I don't want me any kind of trouble with the boss man. Tell Roarke that for me, pretty lady. You hear?"

The roaring in her ears was deafening. Her feet moved without conscious command from her brain. Out the door. Down the street. Around the corner. The same path she'd taken that day with Sully.

With her body shifted into automatic, she waited for a bus, boarded it, sat down. Her mind was a jumble of half-formed thoughts and questions, and she seemed incapable of picking through them, of making sense of the recent scene.

There had to be some mistake. The words were a litany whispering inside her head. Nushawn had mistaken her for someone else...had mistaken Sully for someone else.

She gazed out the window unseeingly. But the two men had been too close for mistaken identity the first time she'd seen Nushawn in that bar. She'd wondered where Sully had come from so quickly, how he'd seemed to know Nushawn....

Nushawn works with me. She remembered Sully's words, but she'd assumed the man worked with him at the freight company. If the men worked together, surely Nushawn would know Sully's name.

And surely it was too much of a coincidence that he'd call him by the same name Carter had called him, when he'd come to her, spreading what she'd been certain were lies about Sully.

...someone by the name of Roarke...your friend has lied to you since the beginning, Elizabeth....

She sat perfectly still, unseeing, unaware of anything but the thoughts spinning inside her head like a whirlpool. The bus paused at her stop and then continued on. She never noticed. Nausea rose in her stomach, and tangled with the nerves collected there. Amid all the questions, all the snarled possibilities, one stood out with crystal clarity.

She'd thought she'd finally come to understand John Sullivan.

It had never been more apparent that she didn't really know him at all.

"Why were you sitting in the dark?" Sully asked as he followed Ellie into the apartment. She'd taken a long time to come to the door, long enough to send worry trickling through him.

"I was thinking."

He bent to switch on the lamp next to the couch. "You can't think with the light on?"

"You'd be surprised how illuminating the darkness can be."

He straightened, eyeing her carefully. "Something wrong?" The answer was clear. She stood facing him, her spine straight, her eyes distant. Instincts, honed by a lifetime on the streets, had unease snaking down his back.

"Yes, I think you could safely say that something is very wrong."

Concern sharpened his voice. "Did something happen?" He strode over to her. "Is it the reporters again? Carter?"

Her short laugh was devoid of amusement. "No, it wasn't Carter. It was a friend of yours. Nushawn, I believe you called him. He wanted me to deliver a message to *my man*. He wanted me to tell *Roarke* that he didn't mean any harm."

Comprehension hit him like a one-two punch. He hadn't recovered his breath when she said, "Nothing to say? How original."

Dread, and even worse, panic, were circling in his gut. "Ellie…"

"Before you start, you might want to consider that I'm in no mood to be lied to. I've had enough lies to last me a lifetime.'' Her voice was tight with suppressed emotion, and there was a flash of heat in her eyes.

''I've never wanted to lie to you.'' The words tasted false even as they left his mouth. He winced at the expression of disdain they brought to her face.

''You're lying now.''

He couldn't stand to have her watch him like that, wary and suspicious. It didn't make it any easier when he made a move toward her and saw her take a quick, barely discernible step back. Hurt exploded with the force of a fist punching flesh. He stopped himself, muscles quivering as he held them rigid. ''I know what you're thinking....''

She cocked her head, waiting, and when he didn't go on, asked, ''And just what am I thinking, Sully?''

When he didn't answer, *couldn't* answer, she gave a tight smile. ''Aren't you even going to tell me it's not what it looks like?''

He had to force air into his lungs. He felt like he was going down for the last time. ''It's not. It's...'' He swallowed hard, still with no idea of what to tell her. Years of living in the shadows had him grappling with the maze of truth and lies that made up his life, wondering how to shake off a lifetime of careful guard and offer her a piece of the truth.

When he left the sentence unfinished, she turned away, as if the sight of him was painful, and crossed to the trio of windows. ''It's narcotics enforcement, isn't it?''

A moment ago he'd searched for words; now he couldn't have spoken them if he'd tried. Strange that believing she thought him a criminal had been easier than dealing with the fact that she guessed the truth about him. A truth it was his job to hide.

His silence didn't matter to her anymore. She didn't even seem to notice it. ''What is it? Local police task force? DEA? Customs?'' She gazed out the window, her arms crossed around her middle in a gesture that spoke at once of hurt and defiance. "I figure something federal," she went on in that flat, emotionless voice he hated. "Policemen, even detectives, don't dive so far undercover they forget to come up for air. Of course, they wouldn't have had the experience with life in the streets that you've had."

Carefully, with the caution of a blind man on a freeway, he felt his way with her. "Most people would have drawn a different conclusion with the information you have." The light from the lamp was just bright enough for him to see the way her fingers clenched at his words.

"Oh, I have no doubt what Carter wanted me to think when he told me the story about a man named Roarke. It's a measure of his lack of ethics that he would twist the truth about you in an attempt to manipulate me." One shoulder lifted. "But I had a lot of hours here to think, to put the pieces together. Odd, after ten years, how few pieces there really were."

He closed his eyes for a moment then, and cursed the fact he'd been born a fool. "Ellie…"

Her fists jammed into the pockets of her shorts, and still she didn't turn around to look at him. "I'll admit that I considered quite a few scenarios, but I kept coming back to one thing—I just can't bring myself to believe that you're a criminal. Logically I know you couldn't have done that time in prison Carter spoke about, because we've kept in contact over the years. And I'm certain that there is no way on earth you'd be dealing in the kind of death that killed your mother, and robbed you of a childhood. That only left one other possibility."

Another time he would have basked in the expression of faith she'd made, but it was impossible to do so now. She'd delivered those words like she was dissecting his life under a microscope, with no more than clinical interest. Her detachment fanned the flickers of panic to flames.

Desperation fueled his words. "This doesn't have to matter to us."

She did turn then, and he winced at the look of sad incredulity on her face. "What *matters* is that I didn't find out from you. What *matters* is that you never trusted me enough to tell me. Not ten years ago, not a month ago."

His fingers itched; he wanted to touch her. He didn't dare. "I didn't keep it from you to hurt you. My job, my life, depends on keeping my cover. Telling you anything just puts you in danger."

But she was already shaking her head. "No, you're not going to pull that protective crap on me now, Sully. Not now. This doesn't have anything to do with protecting me, or anyone except yourself. It never occurred to you to tell me because there's still a huge part of yourself you keep off-limits. You've doled out little bits, but never enough to really let me know you."

He crossed to her then, if only to close the physical distance between them. She was pulling away without moving an inch, and he was suddenly terrified. "I was going to tell you, just as soon as this investigation I'm involved in is over. I just needed more time."

"More than a decade?" The disbelief in her question slapped at him. She let the question hang in the air between them. "If you'd ever had any intention of telling me, you'd have done it by now. I'd invaded every other part of your life, and this was the last part you had free of me, wasn't it?"

The quiet resignation in her voice tore at his heart. "It wasn't like that. I didn't know how to tell you. I mean, after all this time...."

"Yes." There was a wealth of meaning in that one word. "After all this time. It's no mystery to me, Sully. You didn't tell me because I'd already been allowed as far into your life as I was going to get. I believed you were starting to open up, but then, you had an ulterior motive for sharing what you did about your mother, didn't you? That should have been my first clue to how badly you wanted to push me away."

"I haven't been pushing you away. Just the opposite." Drum tight with tension, he swung from her and paced the room. "The job—it's difficult to explain. But I have good reason for not wanting you close enough to get involved in it."

"It doesn't matter anymore." The calm acceptance in her words should have been soothing. Instead, they shot him with slivers of fear. "You didn't tell me. That in itself speaks volumes more than words ever could."

Slowly, with dread in every movement, he turned to face her. She was looking at him, but her eyes could have been a stranger's. "You never considered sharing something that has been a huge part of your life for years. You never felt the need. That really tells me all there is to know."

Desperation, and a fear unlike any he'd ever known, burned hotly in his chest. "I've been working a deep cover for more than two years. I couldn't jeopardize the case. And I wouldn't jeopardize you."

A sigh seemed ripped from the depths of her, and her gaze dropped away. "It's been a long day." Her voice was quiet, but deliberate. "I'd like you to leave."

His hands fisted at his sides, but he already knew he couldn't batter through the wall that had sprung up between them. A wall of his own making. Panic sprinted up his spine, roughened his words. "Don't do this. I need you, Ellie."

Her shoulders stiffened, as if he'd dealt her a mortal blow. "You don't know how I wish I could believe that, how much I've wanted to hear it. But I have to protect myself. You're big on protection—you understand that, right? I can't..." Here her breath hitched. The sound sent lances of pain piercing through him. "I want you to leave now."

He felt like he was in a wind tunnel, with time and events zipping by him until they had no semblance of sense, of sanity. As if from a distance he watched himself walk away from the best thing in his life. Go to the door. Open it. It wasn't until he was standing in the hallway, with the sound of the door shutting behind him, that reality crept a glacier inch through the numb shell encasing him.

The feeling of helplessness that flooded him was unfamiliar; the hopelessness was not. He'd never been a man to dream until Ellie. It was the cruelest of jokes that having sampled just a small taste of happiness with her was going to make a return to his normal solitude jarringly harsh.

He forced one foot in front of the other, each step taking him farther and farther away from her. Tearing Ellie out of his life was going to leave a void he wasn't sure he could exist with. He wasn't sure he even wanted to try.

Chapter 14

The meeting was lasting well into the early hours. Sully rotated his aching shoulders and shifted in his seat. The cigarette in his hand added to the faint haze in the room. His glance slid over the dozen or so occupants and landed for a moment on Lowrey. Kale was loving this. It added to his fantasy that he was involved in a Bond-like adventure, instead of the same old bureaucratic BS.

Too bad he couldn't feel that same level of excitement—hell, what was being discussed involved him more directly than anyone else. He wished he could care, but nothing seemed to have much meaning since that day a week ago when his life had suddenly emptied of purpose.

He brought the cigarette to his lips and sucked in savagely, letting the smoke fill his lungs. He'd stayed away from Ellie, as she'd asked. The need to see her was a powerful lure, one he fought every waking minute. Only the threat of the pain that would burst anew at seeing the hurt on her face, in her eyes, kept him away.

Maybe if his life had been different, he'd have known what she expected, would have known how to give it to her. Perhaps if he'd had the experience of a family he'd understand the sharing that she'd spoken of. He'd never pondered that lack until now. Never regretted it so bitterly.

"What do you think, Sullivan?"

He hadn't been following the argument in the room, but there had been no need to do so. They'd been covering the same ground all evening. "Seems to me that it all depends on whether we have enough already to float a conspiracy charge against Conrad and Vargas."

All eyes turned to the short, round, balding man seated behind the desk. Division Chief Ed Paquin was a leading cocaine-conspiracy expert. It was his job to gather all the scraps of information, taped conversations, acquired evidence and mold them all together into an airtight case. He pursed his lips and leaned back in his chair, which emitted a protesting squeak. "You've got plenty to ensure multiple convictions for Conrad. But then, I assume if he was all you wanted, you'd have moved on him months ago."

"We want Vargas," O'Shea asserted. His green eyes glinted in the artificial light. "How close are we to getting him?"

The man considered. "The times he's entered the country correspond to the shipments Sully can attest to. A good lawyer will call that circumstantial. We've got Sully's taped conversation, which will be damning. I'd feel a hell of a lot better if we had some phone conversations between him and Conrad."

"He was too careful for that," O'Shea said. "Our taps didn't pick up anything, either on Conrad's office or home line. He's used safe phones."

"What are the chances Conrad would turn state's evidence and testify against Vargas?"

"I don't like that idea," Ted Baker protested. He'd been

listening silently up to that point. "We have enough to bury Conrad. What if we went after them both, promised Conrad a reduced sentence for his testimony, and Vargas gets off? Then we've got almost nothing to show for our efforts."

O'Shea looked at Sully. "What do you think the chances are of getting Conrad to flip on Vargas?"

Sully dropped his cigarette on the scarred tile floor and ground it out. "I wouldn't bet on it. I would have sworn Conrad was bloodless until I saw him with Vargas. He's scared of the man, clear through. He'd probably take his chances with prison. He'd figure he stands a better chance of making it out alive."

"Then we have to go ahead with the investigation," asserted Kennedy, the superior officer from customs. "I'd rather see us go after a shipment, as well as the men. I've said that before."

"A seizure isn't necessary for a conviction of conspiracy to distribute drugs," O'Shea said with the weary air of one who'd repeated himself endlessly.

"I know that," the other man snapped. Sully wondered if the interagency "cooperation" was about to unravel. He didn't envy O'Shea his part in smoothing the waters. "But it strengthens our case, and it makes headlines. I don't care what you say—headlines help."

Sully's lips twisted cynically. For every bust that ever went down, for every dead agent it cost, there were always plenty of suits to push themselves before the media and take the credit. Put a news camera before some of the damn bureaucrats, and they were like teenage boys in the back seat of their daddy's cars—no self-control, and no thought of protection for others.

"Kennedy's right," Baker interjected. "We might not like it, but our funding depends on our successes. And the better we publicize our big cases, the better for our agencies." He shrugged half apologetically. "Big cases attract

Washington's attention. We've put the resources into this thing. The more we have to show for it at the end, the better for everyone involved.''

"You're saying to continue the case until the next shipment,'' O'Shea interpreted.

"Any extra time gives your men opportunity to collect even more evidence,'' Paquin said. "That aside, you're going to want to pick up Vargas when he's in the country.''

"I say we move ahead with the investigation,'' Lowrey put in. "I don't know about Sullivan, but I'm not willing to pull out now.''

Collin O'Shea got to his feet and moved restlessly around the room. Sully watched him closely. Not for the first time that evening, he noted that the man looked the worse for wear. Too much time dealing with interagency frictions, he supposed. This case was taking its toll. Sully had never known him to belabor a decision this long before, but then, he'd never been involved in a case of this scope. He wondered if O'Shea had more riding on this investigation than Sully knew. Cases had made and broken state supervisors before.

He waited for the man's decision with an effortless ease that had nothing to do with patience. If he weren't here, he'd be back at his apartment. Alone. With nothing to occupy it, his mind had a way of transporting him back to when life had seemed to brim with the impossible, however briefly.

The trouble with happiness, he thought as he shook another cigarette out of the pack and lit it, was that it left such a void when it was gone. The emptiness caused by Ellie's absence was a gaping wound that would never heal. That reality squeezed his chest like a vise. If he hadn't disappointed her a week ago, he would have done so later, in countless ways. He'd prolonged the inevitable breakup, but it *had* been inevitable.

He squinted at the men in the room, some of them silent, others talking at once. His mouth tasted like a gravel truck had driven through it, the result of too many cigarettes and not enough food. He needed sleep, but that hadn't been visiting too regularly for the past several nights. As he waited for O'Shea to decide the future direction of the case, he began to give silent thanks for this job. Without it to occupy his mind, he would have gone out of his head already.

"Okay." When O'Shea spoke, the room quieted expectantly. "We're going ahead with the investigation. I want to be sure we have enough on Vargas to put him away." He looked at Sully. "When do you meet with him again?"

"Conrad didn't say. But I've gone over the plans with him already. Vargas is careful. I figure he'll want to hear them firsthand. We can't move ahead until he approves them, so I figure it shouldn't be much longer."

O'Shea crossed to Sully and contemplated him soberly. "You look like hell, Sullivan. You sure you're up to this?"

"You don't look so great yourself." Sully took a quick puff of the cigarette burning down in his fingers. "I'm ready for this. I'll do my job."

O'Shea nodded slowly. "Just be sure you do it with even more caution than ever, will you?"

Caution. Sully considered the word. It was the quality that had served to keep him alive all these years. It was a trait that kept senses alert, the inner guard raised. Funny, no matter how deeply ingrained that trait was, it had been no defense at all when it came to Ellie.

Ellie lay awake in the darkness, trying to force her mind to rest. It was useless; this would be another night she wouldn't sleep through. There had been enough of them in the past couple of weeks to recognize the signs. Rather than lying wakeful in bed for hours, she rose and padded out to her dark apartment.

Bill didn't stir from his cozy sprawl in the recliner. He'd turned up his nose at the bed she'd brought home from the pet store; it sat unused in the corner of the kitchen. He'd claimed the chair as his territory the first time he'd entered the apartment. The sight of him there never failed to bring a pang.

She went to the worktable that stood before the triple windows. It was full now, holding no less than eight new pieces. She'd worked tirelessly; indeed, when the midnight shadows had become too oppressive, she'd often risen and gone to her wheel.

She looked at the work without pride. They were good; she could tell that, but there was no joy in the knowledge. Only a kind of burning emptiness that seemed to stretch and expand more with each day.

The potter's wheel had provided a channel for her restless energy, each new piece a focus for her churning thoughts. As distractions, they'd provided only momentary relief. Once each piece had taken shape beneath her hands, been fired and glazed, the desolation had threatened to take over again, and she'd been driven to banish it anew. Anything rather than think of the man who had caused it.

She turned on a small lamp on the worktable and directed the beam. Bill roused and blinked irritatedly at her. She readied some clay and sat down at the table and began to work with it. Before college she'd actually preferred clay work using only her hands and tools. It hadn't been until her college courses that she'd begun to concentrate on improving her talents at the wheel.

A calm settled over her as she started to work the cool clay. Time flowed unnoticed as she twisted and smoothed, occasionally reaching for a tool to refine the shape coming to life in her hands. One hour melted into the next until exhaustion began to make itself known through burning eyes and an aching back. Her hands stilled, and she leaned back in her chair to relieve the ache.

She stared at the form she'd created. The clay was supposed to have taken her mind off the man who occupied it far too frequently, but even her subconscious seemed to have conspired against her. The wolf she'd shaped should have been a fearsome thing, yet, curiously, it was not. There was a fierceness in its gaze, a certain proud bearing to its head and an overall air of wariness.

Transfixed, she studied the form. How often Sully had reminded her of just such an animal, one circling a campfire, beckoned by the warmth but wary of the flames. How long had she worked to lure him closer to the heat? She wondered now if he blamed her for having gotten singed.

She wiped her hands on a damp towel with quick, furious movements. The anger and hurt his silence had cost her was still there, but there was no denying the emotional vacuum caused by his absence. She'd not only lost her lover, she'd also lost her best friend. She didn't know which caused her more pain.

There had been countless times in the past when they'd been out of contact for far longer. But then she'd never needed to fear that she wouldn't see him again, or that their relationship would continue.

She dropped the towel, then propped her elbows on the table, resting her forehead against her clasped hands. Sully knew how important honesty was to her. Discovering Carter's duplicity had shattered her. It was hard to forgive him for realizing that, and still being less than truthful with her. Understanding what he'd come from offered her a glimmer of understanding, if not comfort. Certainly he'd never had experience at giving or receiving trust, and even less experience with love.

Her head lifted then, panicked by the thought, but once

formed, it wouldn't be banished. She loved Sully. The realization brought dueling emotions of hope and despair. She'd planned to be more careful the next time she found love. She'd wait for a man whom she could trust, one who trusted her. That didn't describe Sully.

But then she hadn't really found Sully; he'd been there all along. Before her marriage to Carter, and during it. The night seemed a place for self-honesty, and if she were completely honest she'd admit that her friendship with Sully had continued through her marriage because he gave her something Carter never had, never could. The bond that had connected them so immediately when they'd met had proved more enduring than her marriage.

Destroying that bond brought her more pain than all of Carter's lies ever could. Because what she felt for Sully was deeper, far deeper, than anything she'd experienced with her ex-husband. Sully had far more capacity to hurt her than Carter ever could, because the depth of emotion was so much greater.

Elizabeth rose to pace near the windows. Lights dotted the horizon like little beacons of hope. She knew from experience that love, especially when it was one-sided, wasn't enough to sustain a relationship. And she was certain that despite Sully's real feelings for her, love wasn't among them. At least not in a form she could accept.

Her eyes swam with tears, tears she refused to shed. She'd picked an impossible man to fall in love with. One with no experience of the emotion, one whose job perfectly mirrored his childhood, with its intricate tangle of lies and distrust.

A part of her mourned the fact that she'd come so far since her marriage. Too far to settle for less than total love, total honesty. She'd regained too much of her self-respect to push any further. Sully would have to take the next step. He'd have to decide if she was worth risking that careful defense he'd fashioned to keep the rest of the world at a distance.

She stared out at the night unseeingly. He'd said he needed her. It wasn't enough. Love made her greedy; she wouldn't settle for less than everything he had to give.

Or she'd have nothing at all.

The weatherman had been predicting a relief from the brutal Miami humidity for the past week, but if anything the air seemed closer, heavier. Elizabeth hurried from the bus stop to her condo, looking forward to frigid air-conditioning and ice-cold lemonade. Despite her work in a climate-controlled gallery all day, the bus ride had been enough to wilt her. She mentally added a long cool shower to her list of priorities when she reached home.

She was fitting her key into the door of her building when she heard her name being called behind her. Looking over her shoulder, she saw a man coming toward her, his features half covered by the handkerchief he was using to mop his brow.

"Miss Bennett? I've been waiting for you."

Wariness flickered through her, and she turned, automatically looking to either side, checking for possible help if she should need it. The street was strangely empty for this time of day.

"Are you a reporter?" she asked warily. The stranger meticulously folded his handkerchief and slipped it in his suit pocket. "No, of course not." He approached her, reaching into his pocket again, this time bringing forth a leather case the size of a checkbook. He flipped it open so she could examine his badge and credentials. "I'm here to talk to you about John Sullivan, one of the DEA agents I've been working with."

DEA. Her breath clogged in her lungs, and her legs went abruptly weak. "Sully? Is something wrong?"

The man put his credentials away and regarded her soberly. "I'm sorry, Miss Bennett, but yes, there is. Sully was undercover and the case went down...there was shooting...he was hit."

The concrete beneath her feet abruptly listed, and she put a hand behind her to brace against the door. "Is he all right? Is he...?" *Alive* was the word she was trying to form. She wouldn't even consider the alternative. Dread oozed nastily through her stomach, and her heart reared to her throat.

"He's alive, yes," the man said hastily. "Gosh, I'm sorry for frightening you like that."

Panic and relief pendulumed crazily inside her, and for one nauseating minute she thought she'd be sick. She waited a moment for the feeling to pass, then raised her head and asked, "How badly is he hurt?"

"We think it's just a flesh wound, but of course, he's not letting any of us near enough to be sure." A grave smile showed on the man's face. "You know Sully. He's raising hell about going to the hospital, and refusing to leave the site until the arrests are taken care of. After the shooting he mentioned you." He shrugged self-deprecatingly. "I pumped him for a little more information before his head cleared. I hoped if I found you, I could take you to him, and you could convince him to go to the hospital, where he belongs."

It took a moment to sift through the conflicting emotions, but she grasped the most important information he'd given her and clung. Sully was alive. And he was asking for her. She took a deep breath and rose, locking her still shaky knees. "Take me to him."

The man rose, as well. "With pleasure."

Sully saw the man as soon as he walked out of the freight company. Frank was leaning against a late-model sedan parked at the curb, but pushed away when Sully approached.

"Boss wants to see you."

Sully eyed him warily. The first time he'd seen Frank had been at Conrad's estate, when he'd taken Toby's place and ridden with Sully back to Miami. Whatever his duties in the organization had been in the past, now he was a replacement for Toby in every sense of the word, serving as Conrad's bodyguard. Sully had always wondered what hand, if any, the man had played in Toby's disappearance.

"When?"

"Now." The man stepped aside and opened the car door.

Deliberately Sully wiped his forehead on his shirtsleeve. "I'm going to go home and wash off this grime first. Something tells me Mr. Conrad would rather see me after I clean up."

Frank moved into his path. "The boss said now."

Sully regarded the man through narrowed eyes. Conrad had been visibly nervous the last time he'd seen him. He wondered if the man needed more reassurance, or if this sudden summons meant something more serious.

He moved to shove by the man. "I'll come by after I've showered and changed."

Frank sidestepped to stay in his path, and moved his jacket back just a fraction, enough to show the holstered gun he was carrying. "Mr. Conrad gives me an order, I carry it out. He wants to see you. Now."

Weighing his options coolly, Sully made the only decision he could under the circumstances. He lifted a brow. "You make a good lackey, Frank. I guess the shower can wait, if Conrad's really that eager." The other man waited for Sully to precede him into the car, and then followed him in and slammed the door.

"Okay, Ernie," Frank said to the driver. "Let's go."

The car pulled away from the curb and into the Miami

traffic. Sully leaned back. "What's this all about? Conrad getting nervous?"

The man flicked a glance at him. "How should I know? I'm just following orders."

"Yeah, so you said." Frank didn't react to the subtle sarcasm, and Sully lapsed into silence. His instincts, though, were on full alert, adrenaline spurting through his veins. Conrad had always used Sully's pager to contact him before. His sending Frank to fetch him spoke of an urgency that had edginess prickling along his spine.

After several minutes Sully was able to guess their destination. They were headed toward a warehouse Conrad used as a distribution point after the drugs had been smuggled into the country. Here the shipments were split into smaller parcels and readied to sell to street buyers. Since there was no shipment scheduled that Sully knew of, the selection of the spot just stoked his apprehension.

Frank and Ernie flanked him as they walked into the warehouse. The interior was cavernous, dim and empty of activity. When the heavy door slid shut behind the men, Thomas Conrad stepped out of the shadows, his face wreathed in a professional smile.

"Roarke. Let me apologize for this hasty meeting. Something's come up."

"I figured." Sully made a point of looking around the warehouse. "What's going on?"

"Come with me," Conrad invited, indicating that he should precede him. "The office is this way. We'll be more comfortable there."

Sully's spine prickled as he stepped before the man. They went through a door, down a short hallway and entered a glassed-in office. Frank and the driver remained standing, but Sully waited until Conrad had sunk into one of the vinyl-covered chairs, then seated himself. He studied the other man beneath lowered lids, but there was nothing in Conrad's expression to cause him alarm. That faint air of edgy eagerness was there, the same one he'd worn since Sully had met with Vargas the first time. He looked out of place in the serviceable office wearing his Savile Row suit and Italian shoes, but didn't appear unduly agitated. Remembering the visible emotion on the man's face when he'd been forced to eliminate Toby, Sully felt himself relax a degree.

"Mr. Vargas has paid me an unexpected visit," Conrad said. He pulled up one pant leg carefully, and crossed one knee over the other. "I gave him a thorough rundown of the plans you developed for the pipeline. Naturally he'd like to discuss them with you himself."

"Why here?"

Conrad held up his hands in a gesture of genuine bafflement. "He likes to vary his comings and goings. He also insists on being apprised of every detail of his operation. He's never been to this warehouse before—perhaps he hopes to kill two birds with one stone on this trip."

Sully shrugged, as if the answer didn't matter. "He's in charge."

"I am happy that you remember that, Mr. Roarke."

Sully's head jerked around. He'd only heard that dry, rustling voice once before, but it was immediately recognizable. He rose, as did Conrad, as the Colombian came through the door in back of them. He gestured for the men to retake their seats, and pulled up a chair to face them. Then he turned his reptilian stare on Sully.

"Thomas has been most impressed with your ideas. He said that you have completed your plans, as far as possible, and need further input from me."

Sully inclined his head. "That's about it."

The smaller man rested his hands lightly on the sides of the chair and contemplated Sully. "I would like to hear for myself what you have come up with. You may proceed."

That still, waiting air continued, as Sully filled him in on the plans he'd outlined for Conrad, the ones that would, if the men weren't stopped, quite successfully establish a new pipeline of death into the United States's heartland. Other than a few questions, Vargas listened silently.

When Sully had finished, he said, "Very good, Roarke. You've been very thorough."

"As I told Mr. Conrad, there's nothing more I can do until you make a few decisions." Perspiration collected at the back of Sully's nape when fixed with that sleepy, predator look. "How many trucks will you need? Do you want to buy the rigs and hire some drivers, or find some drivers with their own rigs?"

"What would you suggest?"

Pausing, as if contemplating the question, he answered finally, "I'd use a dummy front to buy the trucks outright. Put some of your own men in as drivers. Take care of getting the proper licenses and labels yourself, rather than entrust it to someone who might not be as careful."

Vargas gave an imperceptible nod. "As you say. Great caution should accompany every aspect of our work. I believe you are right. I will buy the trucks. A half dozen of them should be sufficient. Thomas, you will see to it."

Conrad gave an almost invisible snap to attention when addressed, and nodded. He'd listened in almost avuncular indulgence to Vargas's approval of Sully's plan. Then his superior's gaze shifted away.

"You have been a great help to my organization, Roarke. Perhaps you can do even more."

Sully slouched farther down in his chair, giving an appearance of ease despite the keen-edged energy kicking through his veins. "I'll do what I can."

The man nodded, as if his agreement were no more than a formality. "I told you before that I intend to expand to

Europe and Japan. You may be of help in those particular projects, as well.''

Conrad straightened in his chair and protested, ''Mr. Vargas, I'm more than capable of handling those details alone.''

Vargas didn't even look at the other man. His oddly hypnotic gaze was trained on Sully. ''Well, Roarke?''

Sully gave a regretful shake of his head. ''Sorry, I don't have the kind of experience you need for that. I've never even been overseas.''

The man's hands tightened then released on the arms of his chair in a continuous rhythmic movement. ''You needn't have traveled abroad extensively to have acquired the kind of experience I'm looking for. I believe you'll be more helpful than you think.''

Returning the man's stare unblinkingly, Sully didn't answer. There was no way in hell he was going to provide this drug lord with any more ideas of how to spread his drugs and death to even one more victim. The first thing he'd do when he got out of here was try to contact O'Shea. He was rapidly becoming convinced that it was a mistake to let Vargas go unchecked for weeks longer.

He lifted a shoulder. ''I'll do my best, but like I said. I don't know much about Europe, and even less about Japan.''

At his reply, the Colombian relaxed imperceptibly. ''I think you underestimate yourself. You have proved to be wonderfully ingenious thus far. I know of no other man who could have accomplished what you have. Why, you managed to dupe Thomas, and that, as far as I know, is a first for him.''

His lips stretched in a dreadful parody of a smile. ''But of course, that's your job, isn't it...*Agent Sullivan?*''

Chapter 15

Not by a flicker of an eyelash did Sully display the splinters of ice those words shot through his bloodstream. "I guess I'm not following you."

Conrad frowned and straightened in his chair, but a wave of Vargas's hand stemmed his question.

"I'm sure you are." He reached into his inside suit pocket and withdrew a plain white envelope. With unhurried movements he withdrew its contents. "You're much too clever to deny the evidence I have here." He let the dull black leather case fall open to reveal the DEA badge with the gold eagle perched atop a gold globe, sunbeams radiating out to the edges. The official picture tucked in the bottom corner wasn't particularly flattering, but it was undeniably Sully.

Conrad's face went ashen. "What the hell is that?" he croaked.

Vargas didn't spare him a glance. "It appears to be Agent Sullivan's death certificate."

The nerves that had been tightly bunched at the nape of Sully's skull exploded, and fear sprinted down his spine. Lowrey. That scum-sucking son of a bitch. He was the one who'd been holding Sully's credentials. He was responsible for Sully being made as an agent. "I don't know what you think you've got there, Mr. Vargas, but any second-rate con can get his hands on a badge and shield realistic enough to look legit to civilians. I hope you didn't pay somebody for that."

There was no emotion on the other man's face. "Please, Agent Sullivan, do not try my patience. I paid a colleague of yours quite handsomely for the information that he offered when he contacted me. I know all about the investigation targeting my organization, just as I know about your identity."

Conrad sprang to his feet and grabbed the shield from Vargas's hand. "This...this is impossible."

"What is impossible, Thomas?" The malice in Vargas's voice was unmistakable. "That you were fooled so easily? That you paraded this undercover cop before me as a man worthy of rising in my organization? Were you really that stupid, I wonder, or should I be planning your death, as well?"

Conrad swung his terrified gaze from Vargas, to Sully and back again. "You've got to believe me, I didn't know...." Desperation flared in his voice, on his face. "He checked out! He worked for me two years before I..."

"You'd rather plead stupidity than duplicity, Thomas?" The dry words circled, like fallen leaves caught in a brisk wind, all the more deadly for their even delivery. "We'll discuss your failure later. Now, thanks to you, we have a situation."

He gave a slight nod, and Sully was yanked from his chair. Ernie held his arms behind him, and Frank ran his hands over his body in a quick, professional frisk. "He's clean."

Conrad turned to stare at Sully, his face twisted with fear and hatred. "You bastard, I'll kill you myself." With both his arms held behind him, there was little Sully could do to avoid the blow Conrad sent to his midsection. Thought receded and instinct took over. He sagged in the man's arms as if doubled over, then straightened with lightning speed and brought his foot up to catch Conrad beneath the chin, snapping his head back and sending him staggering.

His movements caught the men in the room by surprise, and he was able to twist one arm free and close his fist to deliver a roundhouse punch to the side of Frank's head. Ernie struggled to recapture his arms, and for a few seconds confusion reigned. It ended abruptly when Frank pulled his gun and tucked it beneath Sully's jaw.

"Die now or die later, cop," the man taunted, enjoyment visible in his chilly blue eyes.

Sully stopped, and this time when Ernie yanked both of his arms in back of him, he didn't struggle.

"Entertaining as always, Agent Sullivan," Vargas noted. "It's a pity you weren't what you seemed. I really could have used someone with your skills in my organization."

There was little doubt that his cover was in shreds, so Sully didn't bother pretending otherwise. "Sorry. My 'skills' have never been for sale."

"You've cost me a great deal of trouble, not to mention the money to pay your colleague for his information. I intend to get a bit more from my investment before we dispatch you to hell."

The mention of Sully's colleague, the one who had sold him out and sent him to a certain death, sent a renewed hot ball of rage racing through him. Blood from his split lip pooled in his mouth, and Sully spit it at Vargas's feet. "I'll meet you there."

The man regarded him unblinkingly. "What you will do, Agent Sullivan, is give us all the information you can about expanding my operations to overseas markets. I've been told that you have had experience working there. Undoubtedly you have facts that could prove invaluable to me."

Again the man's information was correct. Sully had been involved in a handful of DEA cases worked throughout Europe in the past few years, in countries whose governments had requested DEA assistance. But he had no intention of providing this man with any details.

"What do you need me for?" Sully asked. He was buying time, prolonging the minutes, the hours, until his death. His backup would have no reason to be monitoring the tracking device; the only meeting he'd had planned for today was with Lowrey, and somehow he didn't think he'd be raising the alarm. Even if someone did check the tracking device, and trailed him here, there would be no reason to expect that things inside the warehouse had gone terribly wrong. Not until it was much too late. "You've got my...colleague...in your pocket. Get the information you want from him."

"Unfortunately he lacks your level of experience and expertise in such matters," the man said with real regret.

A murderous rage, the likes of such he'd never known, coursed through Sully. How many people had fallen victim to this man's poison, how many had suffered addiction or death because of him? There were too many men just like him in the world, eager to make a living on other people's misery. People too weak or too hopelessly hooked to escape. People like his mother.

"I'm waiting for your answer."

Sully bared his teeth. "Bite me."

Even if the Colombian's grasp of American slang wasn't enough to interpret the meaning of Sully's words, the tone was insultingly clear. Frank stepped forward quickly and sent a series of blows to Sully's rib cage. With methodical precision, he delivered punch after punch, guaranteed to make sure no inch remained unbruised. The room was silent but for the sickening crunch of fists hitting flesh. The beating stopped painful minutes later, and only when Vargas spoke.

"Enough."

The words seemed to come from a distance. Colors cartwheeled behind Sully's eyelids. He tried to straighten, and the agony in his ribs was enough to announce they'd been broken. He blinked, trying with difficulty to open one eye that was rapidly swelling shut.

"This grows tedious, Agent Sullivan, and you are only prolonging the inevitable. But I took precautions in case you proved to be uncooperative. Frank, would you be so kind as to go fetch the delivery that came earlier?"

Frank flexed his fingers, straightened and grinned. "Sure thing, Mr. Vargas." He left the room.

As if from a distance, Sully heard Conrad say, "Mr. Vargas, what's this all about? If you had just seen fit to let me in on your findings, I could have taken care of this for you."

"You, Thomas?" The disdain in Vargas's voice was unmistakable. "Don't you understand yet that you are the cause of this unpleasantness in the first place?"

The door reopened behind him. The short, shallow breaths that had eased Sully's lungs suddenly stopped, when a body stumbled into the room.

His good eye widened in horror. All his blood stopped pumping and congealed in his veins. The horrors of the past collided to form a waking nightmare, and the proof of it was lying motionless on the floor before him.

"Ellie," he rasped. Terror-spiked adrenaline kicked in then, and he lunged forward, dragging his captor with him.

His only thought was to get to her, to prove to himself that she was all right.

Vargas's voice was dry and amused. "Am I to assume, Agent Sullivan, that you are feeling a bit more cooperative?"

If there could be anything worse to contemplate than his own imminent death, it was the sight of Ellie, crumpled on the dirty floor. Frank reached down and pulled her to her feet. Sully took rapid, automatic inventory. There was blood matted in her silky, dark hair and a bruise on one cheek. But despite the cold, lethal rage that swirled through him as he cataloged her injuries, relief rose with a suddenness that almost choked him. Her eyes were open. She seemed a little dazed, but lucid. Duct tape covered her mouth and bound her hands, but she was alive. For now.

He tore his gaze from her and fixed it on Vargas. He disconnected himself from the talons of pain clawing through his body, from the panic rearing inside him, and thought coldly, logically. The possibility of him coming out of this alive had seemed slim, but he couldn't accept that possibility for Ellie. He *wouldn't* accept it.

"Good, I see you recognize her. Your colleague assured me you would. Tell me, Agent Sullivan. Does her arrival make you any more eager to help me?"

The words jammed in his throat. He had to force them out to rasp, "You've made your point, Vargas. She's not a part of this—she never has been. Get her home safely, and I'll do whatever you want."

The man's laugh was silent. "You're not really that naive, Sullivan. You are going to die. So is the woman. How you both die will depend on your cooperation." He rocked back on his heels a little, one finger to his lips, as if in contemplation. "I'm afraid I have witnessed some of the most horrible atrocities that can be committed to another human being. Some of them, I'm sure, could easily be en-

acted by these men.'' He gestured to Ernie and Frank, but
Sully never took his gaze off the one with the real power.
The one who would order Ellie's death with no more emotion than if he were ordering a meal. ''Perhaps you are
really so courageous that you do not care about that for
yourself. But you do, I think, care about the woman. And
I promise you, she would be the first to die. And you will
watch everything these men do to make her suffer.''

The silence stretched as Sully's mind circled frantically
with ways to protect Ellie. But those plans would have to
wait. First he had to convince these men that he was de-
feated. He let his body slump dejectedly. ''All right. You
win.''

''I always do,'' Vargas murmured. He motioned toward
the desk. ''In those folders you will find maps of various
locations in Europe, with a chart of available runways. You
will turn all your ingenuity toward developing plans for
smuggling our product into the countries I have targeted.''
He gave a small smile. ''I have reason to believe you have
intimate knowledge with those countries, having worked in
them before. It would be a shame to let you take that
knowledge to your grave with you, especially when it can
be so useful to me.''

''Anything else?''

He pursed his lips and then shook his head. ''Frank will
contact me when you've finished. I will examine what you
have come up with, and your fate will be decided by how
well you've pleased me. Thomas.'' Conrad started at his
name, and swallowed visibly when Vargas turned to look
at him. ''Come,'' he said, almost gently. ''You and I have
much to discuss.''

The look on Conrad's face was pure terror, and the two
men left the room. Frank shoved Ellie into a chair and said,
''Show time, cop.''

Sully raised his brows. ''Are you going to have your

friend let go of me? I haven't learned to write with my teeth yet.''

Frank gave a short nod, and Ernie released him, pushing him toward the desk. He pretended to stumble close to Ellie's chair, muttering under his breath, ''Be ready.'' He couldn't afford to look to see if she'd understood.

He sat down behind the desk and took his time pulling out the maps and charts Vargas had left for him, pretending to study them carefully and making notations on a legal pad. It wasn't long before the two men in the room grew restless.

''You know what, cop?'' Ernie taunted him. ''I'm gonna ask Vargas if I can be the one to do the woman while you watch. Matter of fact—'' he grinned, revealing a broken incisor ''—maybe he'll let us have a little party with her beforehand.''

Sully leveled a cold, lethal gaze at him. It only served to encourage him.

''Yeah, maybe we'll start the party right now, huh, Frank?'' The other man shrugged indifferently. His gaze, and his gun, never left Sully.

Bolstered by his partner's lack of protest, Ernie sidled close to Ellie's chair. ''What about it, sweet thing? Want a real man before you die?'' He ran a dirty hand down Ellie's bruised cheek. She looked at Sully and he stared hard at her, hoping she'd follow his lead.

''Sorry.'' His pen dropped from his fingers and rolled to the edge of the desk. Sully made a wild grab for it before it dropped to the floor beside him. ''She objects to being touched by scum.''

Ernie stepped in front of Ellie and put his hand down her blouse. Frank was watching him with amusement. ''You mean like this?''

She exploded with a suddenness that surprised even Sully. Her legs came up between Ernie's with a force that drove a strangled scream from him. Sully ducked beneath the desk and lifted it, using it as a shield as he rushed at Frank, knocking the man off balance. The gun went flying, and Frank lunged over the desk, his hands outstretched. Sully stepped aside and with one smooth movement, pulled the knife from the sheath inside his boot, spinning back to meet the man head-on. With a quick, vicious slice across the man's throat, he disposed of him, and turned to Ernie, before stopping, freezing in place.

The man was in back of Ellie, with his arm cocked around her neck threateningly. "I'll break her neck," he screamed shrilly. "I swear I will."

"Okay, calm down," Sully said, his voice soothing. He sent a quick gaze to Ellie to reassure himself. Her eyes were wide, frightened, but focused on him intently. She was ready for a sign from him. He shifted his attention back to Ernie.

"Kick that gun over here. And drop the knife. Do it!" Ernie shrieked suddenly, sounding more than a little crazed. "Right now. Or she's dead."

"Do what?" Sully asked reasonably, moving slightly closer to the couple. "What do you want me to do first?" His gaze slitted as Ernie jerked Ellie's head back farther, his arm around her throat tightening.

"The gun. No, the knife. Drop the knife. Now!"

"Okay." Sully made a show of laying the knife gently on the floor by his side.

"Now the gun." Ernie licked his lips frantically. "Gently. Kick the gun over right in front of me." Sully did as he was told. Ernie bent awkwardly, pulling Ellie with him, and reached for the gun.

Ellie suddenly went limp, falling forward, pulling Ernie off balance. Sully grabbed the knife and waited a split second for the man to let go of Ellie and lunge for the gun.

He released the knife in a swift, unerringly accurate arc at the same time the gun went off.

The pain ripped into Sully's shoulder just as Ernie's eyes went round with disbelief. He clutched at the knife embedded in his chest for a moment, then, as if in slow motion, fell forward.

Sully dropped to his knees. "Ellie," he rasped. He shook his head to clear it. There was an alarming fog rushing into his brain, graying his vision and dulling the senses...all but the nasty fingers of pain radiating through his shoulder. He heard her voice dimly asking him how badly he was hurt. Rather than fashioning an answer, he'd meant to ask her the same, but his voice wasn't working. He tried to rise, and the next thing he knew the cool tile floor was beneath his cheek, and Ellie's frantic voice was in his ear.

"Don't you die, Sullivan. Don't you dare die on me, you hear? I swear if you do, I'll shoot you myself."

Her hospital door began to open, and Elizabeth whirled around guiltily, pulling the ruined shirt over her head with haste. She was prepared to do verbal battle with the newest nurse sent in to talk her into staying another day, but the argument died in her throat when she was confronted, instead, by Sully.

"What are you doing out of bed?" She barely checked her instinctive movement toward him. He was bare chested, except for the white bandages wrapped around his chest and over one shoulder. She'd never understand how he'd managed to pull on his filthy jeans, but the attempt must have exhausted him. They were only half-zipped, and unfastened.

"What are you doing out of yours?" he countered. He stood in the doorway, swaying just enough to have her springing to his assistance.

Muttering disparaging remarks about his lack of intelligence, she slipped her arm around his waist and led him to the chair beside the bed. When he was finally seated, his face was white with pain and his breathing labored.

"What were you trying to prove, Sullivan? That nothing can stop the great undercover agent, not even a speeding bullet?"

His attempt at a grin was lopsided and marred by the twist of pain on his face. "What, this?" He gestured to the bandage. "Hell, I've hurt myself worse shaving."

Because she wanted so badly to touch him, she propped her hands on her hips. "Is that how you got that charming scar beneath your chin? I've often wondered."

His laugh quickly turned into a groan. "Don't be funny, Ellie, not right now. I'm still recovering from putting my jeans on. Took me damn near thirty minutes."

She fought and won a battle with rising sympathy. "Am I supposed to feel sorry for you? You should be resting, not wrestling with your clothes. Besides, if you needed help, you should have called a nurse."

He snorted. "Yeah, right. They're a lot more interested in keeping me out of my clothes than in them." He bit off the end of the sentence as if he'd said more than he'd meant to.

She watched the quick flash of color in his face with interest. "Is that so?" she murmured. She glanced down at his hand pointedly. "They probably aren't going to be too understanding about you pulling out your IV, either."

His gaze never wavered. "I heard them discussing you. They said that you refused to stay another day. I had to talk to you, Ellie."

Her palms were damp with nerves, and she wiped them on her skirt. Swallowing around a baseball-sized lump in her throat, she asked, "What did you—?"

She was interrupted by the door opening. Collin O'Shea poked his head in. Spying Sully, he came all the way in and shut the door behind him. "When I didn't find you in your room, I figured I'd find you here." His gaze went to Elizabeth. "Good morning, Miss Bennett."

"I escaped," Sully said.

"So I see." The man pulled up another chair, and Elizabeth leaned against the bed. "I'm glad I've got the two of you together," he said. His eyes cut to Sully. "How much of last night do you remember? I mean, after you were shot."

Sully scratched his unshaved chin. "Bits and pieces," he said. Then, noticing Ellie's reaction, he amended, "Most of it. I remember giving Ellie your phone number."

"You gave her more than that," O'Shea said. "She was able to tell us where you thought Conrad and Vargas were headed. They were picked up at the Key Largo estate. I understand Conrad was almost grateful to see the agents. Seems he wasn't too certain of his fate at that point."

"So you got them both?"

He nodded, then added, "We also picked up the man responsible for selling you out and kidnapping Ellie. Baker was arrested today boarding a cruise ship heading to the Bahamas."

Sully stared hard at the man. "Baker? It wasn't Baker who burned me, it was Lowrey."

Elizabeth shook her head, drawing his attention. "The man who came after me was Ted Baker," she said firmly. "I saw his credentials. He said you'd been shot...." A quick shudder racked her. The agent's words now seemed prophetic. "He told me he was taking me to you. When I was walking into the warehouse, I was hit from behind. I don't remember anything more until right before I saw you again."

She recognized the cold, steely rage in Sully's eyes, and instant worry reared. "Maybe we ought to do this later."

"Not a chance," he retorted. His gaze went to O'Shea.

"How the hell did Baker get my badge and shield? He gave my credentials to Vargas to prove I was an agent."

"Kale said Baker asked him for them a couple of weeks ago. Claimed you told him you didn't trust Lowrey enough to let him keep them. He'd already relayed your... interest...in Miss Bennett. Baker used both to his advantage. He also used his technical knowledge to jam the receiver for the tracking device." A muscle jumped in O'Shea's jaw. "When Lowrey missed you at the meeting and raised the alarm, all we could do was spread out and cover the areas where you'd met with Conrad before. We already had agents on their way to the warehouse when Elizabeth's call came in."

"I still don't understand why, though," she put in. Both men looked at her. "Was it for money? Baker sold out the investigation and Sully for money?" It seemed inconceivable to her. That a man's life was worth so little—not just Sully's, but all those touched by the drugs that would continue to flow into the country when the investigation failed.

"Five years ago it became apparent that there was a major leak in the DEA," O'Shea told her. "Major busts were falling through—undercovers were being made as agents. When the arrests came, the big dealers were slipping through the most careful of investigations. I figured it was someone with a fairly high level of clearance, but I couldn't be sure who until you gave us his name." His tone turned bleak. "I have to admit, I never suspected my own assistant as being the source of the leak. He took a huge risk. This was a high-level investigation receiving a lot of scrutiny."

"I'm betting that it was the implication of the cartel that tipped the scales for Baker," Sully guessed.

O'Shea nodded. "Rumors are there's a race among the biggest Colombian manufacturers to establish the widest market bases in Europe and the Far East. You had experience over there, and that made you an even more attractive prize to turn over to Vargas.'' His voice hardened. ''Baker was holding out for another payment from the man. He admitted that he was going to turn over the names of DEA agents working overseas, along with the agency bases. With those facts and the how-to information Vargas was hoping to get from you, he'd have the inside track on overseas operations. It would be enough to get him established as a real power there, as well.''

Elizabeth looked away, sickened. They talked so matter-of-factly of betrayal, of men trading lives for money and power. The lives they were discussing could have been Sully's and hers. For the first time she began to recognize that Sully's guardedness had served him well in some instances. A certain level of distrust had been necessary to keep him alive. She wrapped her arms around her middle, shaken. She tried to imagine doing a job every day where you not only had to worry about the crooks but also your peers doing you in. She didn't like to contemplate it.

And she hated to think of Sully living that way.

Misinterpreting her silence, O'Shea reassured her, ''You can bet that there will be an airtight case built around Baker. And with the additional charge of your kidnapping against him, he's got no hope of ever getting out of prison.''

He got to his feet. ''Well, I'll head out. I suggest you get yourself back to bed, Sully. I've heard the nurses here are vicious when they're crossed.'' He chuckled at Sully's muttered oath. ''You've got vacation time coming after you've recuperated. Check with me when you get back to work. I've got a couple cases that might interest you.'' He missed the sudden indrawn breath from Elizabeth and went on, ''We'd have to establish a new cover for you, but that shouldn't be a problem.''

There seemed to be a stranglehold on her lungs. Another case. Another cover. She sprang from her chair, turning away when both men looked at her quizzically. "It's a little early to be talking about the next case, isn't it? I mean, I'd think you'd at least let Sully get used to the fact that he managed to live through the last one."

O'Shea hesitated, seeming to choose his words carefully. "I'm not sure how much you understand about the work of a DEA agent...."

"Oh, I think I understand enough." She turned and met his gaze squarely. "An agent's kind of like the child they use for alligator bait, isn't he? They tie him to the end of the rope, and he walks into the swamp. All the kid can do is hope they jerk the rope back in time."

There was an awkward silence, then, after a few more words to Sully, O'Shea left. Elizabeth busied herself pouring a glass of ice water she didn't want from the pitcher. "I thought I'd go visit my mom for a few days," she said, watching the ice cubes dance and bob in the cup. "Mr. Milway has agreed to give me some time off."

His response was slow in coming. "You're...going away, then?"

She nodded jerkily. "For a little while, anyway."

"That's too bad. I was hoping you could help me."

Slowly she turned her head and looked at him over her shoulder. "Help you? With what?"

He lifted his unbandaged shoulder. "Look for my brothers. You were the one who was so convinced I needed to find them. Now you're going to run off and leave me to search by myself. And I don't have the slightest idea how to go about it."

She turned completely around, stepped toward him, stopped. She tried, and failed, to keep the joy contained. "You...you're going to try to find your brothers?"

"I guess...yeah. I've been wondering what happened to them." He cleared his throat. "Maybe I owe it to my mother to find out."

Emotion clogged in her chest. "That sounds like a good idea."

"I'm going to need your help, though."

The word slashed through her with red-hot nails. "Need again," she murmured shakily. "You know, Sully, there was a time not too long ago when I might have settled for need. But I'm stronger now and I want more. I won't settle for less than everything a man has to give. And I can't live with the pain of being locked out of the most important parts of your life. I can't…" Her throat worked for a few moments. "You had ten years." The words seemed torn from somewhere deep inside her, and they were edged with pain. "Ten years, Sully. Your work is dangerous, I know that. But other agents manage to do your job with wives and families. They don't use it as an excuse to keep the rest of the world at bay."

"I realize that." His voice was stark. "But I had an excuse. At least I thought I did." He looked away and took a breath. "I was in Mexico." The words were low and strained. "It was my first job out of the country. We were stationed in a town at the foot of the mountains. The dealers were the law down there—our operation was a joke. The names of the agents, our building, the cars we drove, they were all common knowledge. Our job was to find out as much information as we could about the cocaine growers' operation, and turn it over to the Mexican and American governments.

"It was an impossible situation, but some of the people living there hoped we'd be successful. They actually wanted to end the dealers' reign of power over the town. One of those men was Alberto Ramon." His eyes met hers and they were filled with bitter self-recrimination. "He offered to help collect information. I was leery about using a civilian, but my partners and I decided it was the only way we could do our job. He'd pass us information he'd picked up at work, or at parties.'' She watched his hand go absently to his chest in search of a cigarette.

The emotionless delivery continued, an eerie contrast to the ghosts in his eyes. ''He turned up missing one day. His wife and children were frantic. Two days later pieces of him began to be delivered to the building we were using for our headquarters. The dealers were taunting us, flexing their muscle. It didn't matter to them that he was one of their own countrymen. He'd betrayed their cause, and because of that he'd been butchered. The mission was aborted and the dealers won that time. An innocent man died for nothing.''

Her gaze fell away and she drew a ragged breath. Perhaps she could understand a little better now what he was telling her, because she'd experienced firsthand the kind of evil he was talking about.

''I swore I'd never risk another innocent that way. And there was no way in hell I wanted to risk you. The further I kept you from my job, the safer I could keep you. Or so I thought.''

His gaze was steady, and his jaw squared. ''I'm not going to lie you, Ellie. Part of the reason I kept so much of my life from you was because of what happened to Alberto. The other part was because I just didn't trust worth a damn.'' He lifted a shoulder. ''Didn't know how, I guess.''

She closed her eyes, wishing she could deny that his words had scored a direct hit. ''And now?''

''And now...'' There was a pause, and the next words were spoken in her ear. Her eyes flew open to find him leaning over her. ''I figure you can teach me.'' He trailed a finger down the line of her throat and paused at the pulse point, which scrambled beneath his touch.

''You said I needed to let someone in,'' he reminded her. ''I figure I'm ready to take that risk if you're there beside me. I love you, Ellie.''

She reached behind her and grasped the rail of the bed, to avoid doing a slow, boneless slide to the floor. "You…you love me?" Hope was doing a crazy tap dance in her chest, and she waited half-dazedly for his answer.

There was a glint in his eyes, a smoky heat. "And I think you love me. But I still want to hear you say it."

She cupped his jaw in her hand, watched the impatience flicker across his face, and smiled, slowly and tenderly. "I love you, John Sullivan."

His mouth descended and caught hers in a brief, hard kiss. "We're going to do this right," he murmured against her mouth. He drew away a fraction and looked down at her. "I can make changes in my job. I don't have to work deep cover. Hell, I don't have to be an agent."

Touched, she stroked his rough jaw with her palm. "You can't make changes for someone else, Sully. I wouldn't ask that of you. It has to be what you want."

"I won't risk you again." She saw the terrible guilt in his eyes and knew that some ghosts would take time to banish. "We're going to do the whole thing—a wedding, a honeymoon and then a real home."

Her hand reached up and tangled in his hair. "And then—" her lips teased his again, brushed over his mouth lightly, and then away "—we can start the search for your brothers."

He went silent as he rested his forehead against hers. "Yeah," he said finally. "I have to try. But I don't want you to get your hopes up, Ellie." The warning seemed as much for himself as for her. "There's no guarantee that we'll ever find them."

"Life doesn't come with guarantees."

"Except for one." He pushed her hair back over her shoulders. "No matter what else happens…I'll always love you. That won't ever change."

Her arms twined around his neck. "Promise?"

His head descended so his mouth brushed hers when he spoke. "I promise."

* * * * *

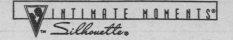

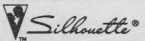

COMING NEXT MONTH

#883 BRIDES OF THE NIGHT *Two outstanding stories in one irresistible volume

"TWILIGHT VOWS"—Maggie Shayne

Wings in the Night

Donovan O'Roark would do anything to keep another Sullivan woman from betraying the vampires of Dunkinny Castle. But when Rachel Sullivan filled the void in Donovan's soul, would he grant the beguiling virgin's request for eternal life—and love?

"MARRIED BY DAWN"—Marilyn Tracy

Vampire Gavin Deveroux *had* intended to eliminate vengeful Tara Michaels to safeguard his people. Then Gavin and Tara found themselves racing against time to be married by dawn. Were they destined to discover the greatest love of all?

#884 HARVARD'S EDUCATION—Suzanne Brockmann

Tall, Dark and Dangerous

Navy SEAL Harvard Becker was aghast when he was forced to work alongside alluring *female* agent PJ Rogers. To Harvard's amazement, his no-nonsense partner taught him a thing or two—on and off the field. Could it be that Harvard had finally met his match?

#885 HER COUNTERFEIT HUSBAND—Carla Cassidy

Mustang, Montana

Even before her heartless husband disappeared, Elena Richards knew their marriage was over. But now a decidedly different "Travis" was back—with amnesia!—and Elena was carrying his child. Could this marriage be saved?

#886 FOR THE CHILDREN—Margaret Watson

Cameron, Utah

FBI agent Damien Kane had pledged to protect Abby Markham and her twin nieces. But could he risk heartbreak again? Even if it meant offering the woman he loved a family of her very own?

#887 HIDING OUT AT THE CIRCLE C—Jill Shalvis

Way Out West

Frightened for her life, Haley Whitfield sought refuge on Cameron Reeves's ranch. Despite her tight-lipped secrecy, the laid-back, warmhearted cowboy offered her solace in his tender embrace. Could Cam convince Haley to trust him with her uncertain future?

#888 MOTIVE, MEANS...AND MARRIAGE?—Hilary Byrnes

Women To Watch

When Helen Stewart was assigned to prosecute her former lover for murder, she vowed not to succumb to her smouldering attraction for the sexy Irish cop. Yet when Patrick Monaghan swore his innocence, Helen knew she couldn't turn her back on the man she still desperately wanted.